Honor and Redemption

M.A. Nichols

Books by M.A. Nichols

Generations of Love Series

The Kingsleys

Flame and Ember
Hearts Entwined
A Stolen Kiss

The Ashbrooks

A True Gentleman
The Shameless Flirt
A Twist of Fate
The Honorable Choice

The Finches

The Jack of All Trades
Tempest and Sunshine
The Christmas Wish

Standalone Romances

Honor and Redemption
A Tender Soul

To Have and to Hold
A Passing Fancy
A Holiday Engagement

Fantasy Novels

The Villainy Consultant Series

Geoffrey P. Ward's Guide to Villainy
Geoffrey P. Ward's Guide to Questing
Magic Slippers: A Novella

The Shadow Army Trilogy

Smoke and Shadow
Blood Magic
A Dark Destiny

Table of Contents

Prologue

Oxford
Fall 1820

C limbing up top, Patrick Lennox took his seat behind the coachman, sliding over to make room for his brother on the passengers' bench. He cast his eyes upwards and felt a swell of gratitude for the clear skies and unseasonably warm temperature. Patrick hoped the weather would hold for the entirety of the journey home; the last time, they'd passed through a deluge that had frozen him to the bones, and he did not fancy repeating that miserable affair.

"It's a fine day for a drive," said Kelly, taking his seat beside Patrick. "Far better atop than stuffed into the coach with the rest."

"It bodes well for the state of the roads. I would hate to be waylaid because of a muddy mess."

Kelly's eyes glinted, and Patrick awaited the teasing words that accompanied such looks. "I would hate for you to be separated from your sweet Miss Eloise a moment longer than necessary."

Patrick gave no reply, for there was none to give. Denying it only encouraged Kelly; they both knew where his heart lay, and the anticipation of the reunion had it thumping a rapid beat.

Finished with their preparations, the coach took off from the inn's courtyard, and Patrick found himself quite pleased with their situation. Though the wind bit, theirs was the best vantage point from which to witness the glorious fields and golden landscape. And most importantly, it allowed for more entertaining possibilities than were to be found inside the vehicle.

As their family coachman had decreed Patrick and Kelly needed far more practice with the simpler curricles and gigs before he would allow them to work with a four-in-hand team, their journey to and from university provided the only opportunity to do so. All the fellows at Oxford had stories of their heroic adventures along the rough and tumble roadways, and the Lennox boys yearned to be given charge of a coach as well.

The driver set the horses on a merry pace, and from the man's demeanor, Patrick thought this journey a lost cause. He had traveled enough to recognize which coachmen took their positions seriously, and this one had all the makings of such a one; there was no stench of spirits about him, and he kept the horses at a hurried but prudent speed.

However, Patrick's grim assessment proved flawed, for after only an hour of travel, the coachman glanced over his shoulder at the pair. "You two look like a fine pair of gentlemen with a good head about you. Would either of you like to take the reins for a few miles?"

While he kept one hand firmly on the ribbons, the other he offered up in clear invitation, and the lads were quick to drop a guinea into the outstretched palm. Pocketing the coins, the coachman motioned for Kelly to climb onto the front seat, and Patrick watched with an envious gaze as his brother was handed the reins and given a few curt instructions.

The horses slowed, and Kelly gave a great "gee-up," flicking the reins at the beasts, but the foursome continued to lag, their pace dropping to a walk. He shook the bits of leather, but the team had no intention of following Kelly's commands.

"What is going on up there?" cried a passenger from inside the coach. "Why have we slowed?"

"A bit of muddy road is all, sir!" called the coachman with a smile at the young men. "We'll be along shortly."

"I must arrive in Harrington by nightfall!" came the reply, and they heard the coach window shut once more.

"You're making a muck of it," said Patrick, leaning over Kelly's shoulder for the reins.

His brother pulled away. "I am not. They are simply stubborn."

"Give them a bit of the whip," said the coachman as he slouched in his seat. "That'll straighten them out."

With a nod, Kelly did as told, but the end knotted up in the harness, rendering the whip useless.

"You're tangling the reins," said Patrick, pointing to the ribbons all twisted together in Kelly's hands. "The team can tell you're a novice."

Shifting his grip, Kelly straightened the bits of leather, but the horses would not budge from their sluggish pace, and the coachman appeared utterly unconcerned.

"You're a natural," mumbled the driver with a lazy smile. "As good as any novice I've seen."

"May I have a go?" asked Patrick, leaning forward until he was hanging over into the driver's seat.

Kelly leaned away, causing the horses to list to one side. "It's only been a couple of miles. You'll have time enough later."

"We've got an inn coming up presently," said the coachman, jabbing a thumb into the distance. "We can change drivers then."

"But I want to try now," said Patrick with a groan. "I'll give you extra time after the stop."

Kelly's eyebrows rose. "Five miles?"

"Two."

Narrowing his eyes at the horses, Kelly pursed his lips as he contemplated the offer before handing the reins over. Patrick did not bother shifting seats. As it was, he was hanging over the railing between his bench and the driver's seat, which gave him space enough to manage, and he could not wait another moment.

Taking the straps in his hands, he mimicked the coachman's grip, carefully positioning the ribbons between his fingers. When comfortable, Patrick gave the reins a nudge, calling out for the horses to get a move on. And they did. Though nowhere near the pace the coachman had set, Patrick was quite pleased with the fact that it was not much slower.

"How did you get them to do that?" asked Kelly, and Patrick pointed out a few techniques he'd gleaned from watching coachmen. With another flick, he increased the speed once more, and it was thrilling and terrifying at the same time.

"Faster!" Kelly shouted, and Patrick grinned at his brother while pushing the horses to greater speeds.

The coachman tapped Patrick's arm, motioning to the right lead horse, whose ears were pricked and at attention. The foursome tugged at their leads, but Patrick kept a firm hand on them.

"Give the reins over," said the coachman.

"I have it."

The coachman reached for the ribbons, but Patrick held fast as one of the horses shied away from the road. Connected to the other three, it tugged the others along, causing the coach to lurch. The horses wrenched away from each other, fighting to get free of their harnesses, and Patrick pulled on the reins, struggling to keep the creatures in hand.

The coachman shouted at Patrick, but the ribbons tangled in his fingers as the horses jumped and danced along the roadway. Grabbing Patrick's hands and the reins all in one, the coachman yanked, but two snapped clean off, leaving limp bits of leather to tangle in the harnesses and hooves.

Horses and passengers screamed, and Patrick fought to free himself while balanced on his belly across the back of the coachman's seat. The coach shuddered and tipped side to side, and Kelly grabbed Patrick, holding him in place as they wobbled. Patrick's hands came free of the reins as the coach lurched, listing into the ditch. Leaning the opposite direction, they tried to right it, but there was nothing to be done. Gravity's pull was too strong, and the coach toppled onto its side.

Patrick leapt free and landed with a painful twist of his knee. He screamed but forced himself to stay upright and get clear of the vehicle as it slid across the ground.

"Kelly!" Patrick shouted when it came to a halt, but the groans from inside the coach drew his attention.

Limping to the bottom side, he found the coachman already there, bruised and bloodied and trying to get the frantic horses under control; the beasts reared and kicked as they fought their harnesses, each other, and the driver. The other passengers were climbing free, but Patrick didn't see his brother.

"Kelly?" Leaning against the coach, Patrick hobbled around it, shouting for his brother.

Sticking out from under the front end of the coach was a misshapen pair of legs. Ignoring the throbbing pain in his knee, Patrick ran to where his brother lay pinned beneath the edge of the carriage. He shoved against the coach, but it was no use. Patrick could not lift the hulking thing, and the horses were in no fit state to help. Shouting for the gentlemen of the party, he gathered them around, but even their combined strength could not budge it.

"Move!" he screamed at the wreckage, pushing until his muscles shook. Even after the others quit, Patrick kept shoving, not relenting until the last of his energy was spent, and he collapsed onto the ground beside Kelly.

Patrick's heart pounded in his chest as he searched for anything he could do, but someone had already gone for help. He listened to Kelly's agonized whimpers, unable to give him any comfort, for his brother's body was so mangled that Patrick dared not touch him.

"Don't fret, Kelly. Help is coming, and we'll have you right in no time."

His brother's eyes fluttered open, but they were filled with mindless agony. Blood dripped from his lips, falling onto the grass, and Patrick hovered over him, wishing for anything to relieve Kelly's suffering; his chest tightened at the wheezing, gurgling sound of his brother's breath.

"All will be well, Kelly," whispered Patrick, kneeling beside his brother while the rest of the party kept their distance from the dark tableau.

"Help is coming," he repeated as the minutes stretched on.

Lying there beneath the carnage, Kelly moaned as his blood seeped into the ground. Patrick clung to that uneven, halting sound and the flutter of his eyelids. But the breaths came slower. The twitches grew weaker. And Patrick could do nothing but watch.

It was not a peaceful passing, and Patrick felt every painful moment as his brother's soul passed from this world and into the next.

...

The sun beat down on Patrick's back. The last vestiges of summer were out in full glory, painting the world in a wash of golden light that mocked the solemn day. Standing beside the freshly turned earth, he stared at his brother's grave. The others had left after the vicar's final words, but Patrick was in no mood to face the mournful gathering at home.

Tipping the bottle up, Patrick took a deep swig, reveling in the burn of the spirits as it coursed down his throat. The pain brought with it a blessed numbness that wrapped his mind and heart in a downy cushion. Staring at the stone slab that marked his brother's final resting place, Patrick's muddled thoughts dredged up a convoluted mess of memories. The good and bad all mixed together to fill his mind with thoughts of Kelly.

But the drink helped.

"Patrick?"

Even in his inebriated state, Patrick recognized her voice, and just the sound of it filled his heart with warmth and peace. Eloise Andrews always had a gift for calming his soul, but he did not deserve such happy sentiments.

"Leave me be," mumbled Patrick, taking another pull from the bottle.

Her hand brushed his arm, giving a sympathetic squeeze, which only made his heart twist in his chest. He did not deserve the sympathy. The sorrowful looks. The kind words. His was not some shared grief. Patrick had killed his brother, and everyone was behaving as though a bit of empathy would erase that fact.

Through the drunken haze, Patrick heard his brother's final breaths and saw the mangled twist of Kelly's body. Ignoring the fierce pain the liquid brought, he downed another gulp. If he could not erase the memories, he could only hope to make himself so pickled that it didn't matter.

"Patrick, please stop," said Eloise. "I'm worried about you."

"Nothing to worry about," he mumbled, fighting to get the words out. He turned to look at her but stumbled. "I'm just honoring my mother's heritage with a proper Irish wake."

"Patrick—"

"Leave me be."

"Patrick, please!" Through the fog, Eloise's face came into view; her cheeks were pale though her light eyes were red, and tears clung to her lashes. She reached for the bottle, but Patrick yanked it away.

"Leave me be!" He shoved her with more force than intended, and Eloise stumbled, barely keeping her feet. The last rational vestiges of his mind screamed at him for his behavior, but with a few more drinks, he silenced them.

"Please, Patrick." Eloise's words were broken as she fought against a new bout of tears, but Patrick refused to listen.

"Leave, Eloise. I don't want you." The words came out stilted and slurred, but they came out, and some part of Patrick's mind recognized the pain they inspired, but he could not make sense of the world around him any longer.

The better son had died. There was no fighting that fact. Even in his drunken stupor, Patrick saw the truth for what it was. His family's grief was still fresh from the loss of his father and little sister, and he had wounded them all over again with his thoughtless actions. His mother's sobs echoed through the house late into the night. Because of him.

Patrick fought to keep his balance, but his drunken limbs couldn't keep him upright, and he fell onto the fresh grave. Broken, he lay there, watching the precious liquid leak from the bottle into the ground, and with a wobbly hand he grabbed it by the neck, clutched it to his chest, and closed his eyes to the world.

Chapter 1

London
Six Years Later

B atting her fan, Eloise Andrews fought to disperse the perspiration beading at her neck and temples; the ballroom was roasting. For all her girlish dreams of the fancy balls in London, Eloise had never thought that they would be quite so pungent, but the conflagration of candles around her filled the air with the scent of melting wax and tallow and mixed with the natural aroma of the overheated dancers.

Eloise wished the Felthams would be more circumspect with their guest list, for such an overabundance was bound to detract from the evening. Though the dancers had space, it was a tight fit. Each step and turn was done carefully to keep from colliding on the dance floor. To say nothing of the onlookers who were crushed to the sides.

"Isn't that the loveliest lace you've ever seen?" asked Susie, tapping Eloise's arm to draw her attention to a gown. "I must get an introduction and discover where the lady purchased it."

"I wonder if it is French," said Maria. "There is something in the pattern that makes me think it is. What is your opinion, Eloise?"

Staring at the bits adorning the lady's décolletage and sleeves, Eloise had not the slightest inkling as to its origin or why it mattered.

"I am certain you are right, Maria," said Susie with a smile. "You have such a good eye for lace and fabrics."

Eloise had nothing to add, so she smiled as well, allowing the others to make of it what they would.

"And look at the drape of that skirt," said Maria, pointing to another lady in a green gown. "I am positively envious! I must see if Madame Toulouse will fashion one for me."

Shaking her head, Eloise scanned the crowd. "You have a Season's worth of new gowns. Do you need another?"

Maria gaped with mock effrontery. "You are beyond the pale, Miss Eloise Andrews! There is always a need for more. Besides, it is my job to spend frivolously so that my parents are quite happy to be rid of me when I marry."

Eloise fought back the smile those words elicited, though she could not keep it from her tone as she asked, "Is that so?"

Maria gave her most winning smile. "Of course. I would hate for them to be devastated when I leave their household."

"Then your motives are purely charitable?" asked Eloise with a raised eyebrow.

Clasping her hands behind her, Maria gave a demure shrug.

"That is most kind of you," said Susie, her expression the picture of earnestness.

Both Eloise and Maria broke into laughter.

"Dear Susie, she was speaking in jest," said Eloise.

The girl blinked at her friends, her eyes fluttering rapidly as her mind worked through that revelation. Then, breaking into a grin, she laughed alongside the others.

"And what have you found to occupy yourself of late?" asked Eloise.

Susie wrinkled her nose. "I swear, Mama has been running me ragged with visits, but it is rarely anyone of interest. Her set never has any decent gossip."

"Then what do they talk about?" asked Maria with a furrowed brow.

Susie gave a vague wave of her hand. "Nothing of consequence."

"It must be of consequence to them," said Eloise as she batted her fan with such fury that her dark ringlets bobbed.

"I know I should not complain," said Susie, reaching over to pat Eloise's arm with a look of genuine dismay. "My mama may have little access to gossip, but at least she does not despise it. Whatever do you do during morning visits when yours will not abide such diverting conversation?"

The utter horror in Susie's tone made Eloise grin, though she hid it behind her fan. "Mother is adept at discussing the weather for hours on end."

"Take a look at Mrs. Croft's hair," said Maria, pointing her fan at the lady in question as she strode by the trio. "I am not a fan of turbans, but it looks lovely on her."

"You are quite right," said Susie with a decisive nod. "But I've always thought that such accessories favor a lady with a shorter coiffure."

Eloise struggled for something she might say, but if there was a subject she detested more than the origins of lace, it was the proper drape and styling of turbans. She adored a beautiful gown and all the accompanying accoutrements and had no qualms about spending great lengths of time on such things, but she did not share Susie and Maria's zeal for every minute detail. But feigning interest during the occasional lengthy fashion discourse was the least she could do for her friends.

Allowing the conversation to continue without her, Eloise's eyes drifted from her companions. Beating her fan, she wished she might have a bit of fresh air, but there was nothing to be done about it. With her mother standing guard mere steps away, there was no opportunity to sneak into the courtyard.

"Miss Andrews."

With a smile, Eloise turned to greet the gentleman. "How good to see you, Mr. Godwin."

"I had hoped you would honor me with a dance," he said with a bow. "I am told the next shall be *The Spirit of the Dance*, which, if memory serves, is one of your favorites."

Susie tittered behind her fan, and Maria gave a conspicuous smile. Eloise refrained from rolling her eyes at the young ladies and took his arm with a word of thanks.

"Are they quite all right?" asked Mr. Godwin, nodding back at the pair as he led her onto the dance floor. He looked so genuinely concerned that Eloise's heart warmed towards the fellow. However, his cherubic face gave him such an air of youth that she also felt the urge to pat him on the cheek, give him a biscuit, and send him to bed with a promise that he need not worry his little head about such things. Not exactly what Eloise hoped to feel towards the gentleman vying for her heart.

"They are simply laughing at my expense," she replied, taking her place in the line.

Mr. Godwin's head cocked to the side. "Why would they do that?"

Again, his sweet concern inspired a smile but no fluttering in Eloise's chest. "Because they are my friends, and like all the best ones, they tease me mercilessly when necessary."

His dark brow crinkled. "I should think not. It is better to surround yourself with those who are kind and uplifting."

Eloise merely smiled and gave a vague nod in response as the dancers took their places. There was no point explaining herself. As kind and good a gentleman as Mr. Godwin was, the fellow did not appreciate witticisms even when Eloise did her best to bait him. More's the pity.

The musicians struck their opening notes. Eloise took the first turn, throwing herself into the joyful steps, and nearly knocked into another lady. With a hurried apology, she continued through her part, keeping a weather eye on those around her. The floor was so filled that she struggled to get through the dancers and make the proper movements without colliding. Eloise held back the scowl threatening to form; she adored a good country dance, but it was difficult to lose herself in the frivolity when the dance floor was more packed than Hyde Park at the height of the Season.

"I am sorry to have missed our drive this afternoon," said Mr. Godwin as they passed each other.

"Yes," said Eloise, for it was all she could manage while navigating the swell. Luckily, he did not speak again until they reached a pause in the dance.

"Would you join me tomorrow?"

"If you wish me to."

"Then I shall be at your townhouse at our usual time," he said with a smile that did little to help the situation. He was by no means chubby, but when Mr. Godwin smiled, his cheeks had a roundness to them that made Eloise wish to pinch rather than kiss them. "Might I inquire after your mother?"

Fighting back another scowl, she remained composed, though her eyes flicked over to where her mother stood. Eloise would be surprised if the lady had ever been ill in her life; Mother would not stand for such an affront. "She is always in good health, sir."

"Very good," he said, clasping his hands behind him as he glanced at the others while they awaited their turn.

But the rest of the world faded from Eloise's notice at the sight of the phantom standing in the ballroom entrance. Her hands drew around her middle, as though she could melt the block of ice that settled there, but its cold tendrils snaked through her veins. His grey-blue eyes met hers, and though Eloise wished to look away, she was trapped.

Patrick Lennox was here.

Chapter 2

E loise had never felt so discomposed. Her breaths matched the rapid pace of her heartbeat, her limbs quivered like those of some soppy Gothic heroine, and she felt decidedly faint, though she had never fainted in all her twenty-two years. How she wished to flee from that place and hide until that specter disappeared once more.

The adjacent lady nudged Eloise, and she belatedly noticed that Mr. Godwin had turned once more, and she had missed the first steps of their round. Eloise's feet moved on instinct, but her head whipped back to the gentleman standing on the edge of the dancers, watching her with an intensity that both chilled and warmed her.

Biting her lips, Eloise forced herself not to cry. She would not shed another tear over that man. She had promised herself to never think of him again, but her mind could not rip itself away from that taboo subject.

If only her legs would work properly! They were so weak and shaky that she struggled through the skipping steps. Just as she placed her hand in Mr. Godwin's, Eloise tripped. Though there was a titter from the few who had noticed, his quick assistance kept her from tumbling to the floor and making an even greater fool of herself.

"Are you quite all right?" whispered Mr. Godwin as the pair made it through the last steps and paused once more to await their next pass.

"I fear I am not myself at the moment," she said, dabbing at her forehead. Her eyes shot to Patrick and then back to Mr. Godwin with equal speed.

"Allow me take you to your mother."

Eloise shook her head. She could not stomach a lecture on decorum at present, and there was no doubt that she would receive one if she appeared at her mother's side in such a state. "Please, no. I would like to return to my friends. I just need a bit of a rest."

"Of course," he said, taking her by the elbow as he cut a path through the crowd.

Maria and Susie wore clear signs of confusion as Mr. Godwin led Eloise back, but they showed restraint and said not a word, though their eyes begged an explanation.

"Might I fetch you something to drink?" he asked.

Eloise mumbled some reply, though she could not attest to what it was, for her mind was consumed with thoughts of Patrick. She had lost sight of him but felt his gaze on her still. Mr. Godwin asked another question, and Eloise reflexively nodded, her eyes scouring the crowd. The gentleman smiled, bowed, and departed, leaving Maria and Susie free to pounce.

"What is the matter, Eloise?" asked Maria.

"You look as though you've seen a ghost," added Susie.

That was a very apt description, for though she knew Patrick Lennox was a living, breathing man, his sudden reappearance was akin to the supernatural. Perhaps her mind had conjured a vision of him; that seemed more likely. However, Maria quickly dispelled that hope.

"Who is that gentleman?" she asked with unabashed admiration.

Eloise cast her eyes on the subject of Maria's inquiry. Patrick had been captured by Mr. Fortescue, who seemed eager to spend the evening conversing. She felt a brief moment of relief until Patrick's longing gaze turned to her once more.

"You think him handsome?" asked Susie.

"Don't you think he looks wonderfully roguish?" asked Marie.

Eloise gave a quick huff. He was far too lanky and fair-haired to be considered such a thing. "Roguish? Patrick Lennox?"

Both girls swung their gazes to Eloise with equal measures of curiosity and eagerness.

"As in Mrs. Lennox's son?" Maria asked while Susie asked, "You know him?"

"Their family is our nearest neighbor, and our mothers are quite close," said Eloise. "We knew each other as children."

Maria's eyes sparkled with the same excitement she displayed when chasing down a piece of juicy gossip. "Were you two close?"

Eloise struggled to swallow. "We were friends of a sort at one time, though I haven't seen him in years."

"He looks dashing," said Susie with a longing that surprised Eloise.

Her eyebrows rose. "Dashing?"

Maria nodded. "Most certainly. His scars make him look like a villain from a Gothic novel."

Susie sighed, her gaze softening as she stared at Patrick.

Eloise fought back a scowl. "You two are ridiculous. No Gothic villain has Venetian curls like Patrick."

"What curls?" asked Susie.

But Maria latched on to a more pertinent detail. "Patrick?"

"I mean Mr. Lennox, of course," said Eloise, blushing at her silly slip of the tongue. "But the point of the matter is that he is not some dark, dashing figure."

"I hate to disagree, but your Mr. Lennox is quite dashing," said Susie with that same love-struck tone.

Turning her gaze to their subject, Eloise tried to reconcile the Patrick she knew with the figure they described. She had long thought him handsome, but dashing was a stretch, for the fellow was tall and lanky with light coloring that gave him an impish air.

Eloise fought to keep her breath steady at the sight of his awaiting eyes. Mr. Fortescue still held Patrick captive, but she knew he would be coming for her when he freed himself.

"You were only friends?" asked Maria.

Her tone broke Patrick's hold once more, and Eloise turned to her friends, who looked at her as though they knew the un-spoken truth of the matter. Though she did not wish to dredge up that past, she knew they needed some explanation.

"At one point, perhaps," she whispered, hoping that the throng around them would keep any possible eavesdroppers at bay. "I had certainly thought... hoped..." Eloise struggled for the words. "Nothing was spoken, but I had thought we would marry."

Susie's eyes widened, and she took Eloise by the hand, holding it fast in wordless support.

"Why have you never said anything about him before?" asked Maria, nearly gaping at Eloise's confession.

Eloise nibbled on her lip. "Things did not end well between us, and I have neither seen nor heard from him in six years. I did not wish to relive the pain of our parting."

"Certainly," said Susie, her expression crumpling with sym-pathy.

Maria's lips pursed at the scant details, but she gave a half-hearted nod. "Of course, you need not speak of it if you do not wish to. But we are always here to listen if you do."

Eloise shook her head. There was no need to dredge up that history again. Her heart was rid of Patrick. This discomposure was due to the shock of seeing him after his self-imposed exile. A sudden fright. Nothing more.

"With the way he is looking at you, I would hazard to say he is interested in renewing your acquaintance," said Maria, glanc-ing between the pair.

But Eloise gave another, more vehement shake of her head.

"I assure you, he made his feelings clear, and even if he's had a change of heart, I no longer welcome his attentions."

"It is a shame, for he is terribly dashing," said Susie with another sigh.

Eloise allowed herself a moment to examine Patrick, and she tried to see what the others saw but was greeted with the face she'd known for many years. However, his riotous curls had been shorn, giving a more mature air to his features. Of course, he was four and twenty now, so that would have something to do with it.

His face turned fully towards her, and Eloise sucked in her breath. She avoided his eyes, refusing to trap herself in them once more, but that was when she finally noticed what Susie and Maria had meant when they'd dubbed him roguish. Along the right side of his face, a nasty scar spiraled out from his cheekbone like a crack in a windowpane.

Scouring her memory, Eloise tried to think how it had happened. Surely, it wasn't from the accident. Though she had seen him only once after that unspeakable event, Eloise was certain his face had been whole; the scene at Kelly's graveside had been burned into her memory, and she would have noticed.

Though Susie and Maria obviously felt it enhanced his appearance, it made Eloise want to cry at the sight of it. The angry lines must have hurt him dearly, and she felt the pain of them in her own cheek. For one brief moment, she wanted to rush over and embrace him as she had done so many times when he'd needed comfort.

With a deep breath, Eloise forced away the sympathy the scars garnered. Forced herself to remain calm and collected. Forced herself to pull her eyes from him. Patrick had made his feelings clear. He did not welcome her in his life, and she would not force her company on him. Six years of silence testified to how little he regarded her.

Yet when Susie warned that he was approaching, Eloise knew she had not the strength to face him. Not yet. She was too overwrought, and she would not give him the satisfaction of seeing her so agitated.

"Mother is calling for me. I must go see what she wants." Her friends stared after her as Eloise scampered away, hunting for a place to hide.

Chapter 3

Columns stood sentry around the edges of the ballroom, and the Felthams had hung long swaths of fabric between them like massive curtains; one particular pair had an alcove secreted behind them. That would do nicely, for it was hidden enough to be overlooked while allowing her a decent vantage point.

Eloise ducked between guests, carefully dodging around them, and glanced over her shoulder to see if Patrick was following. His attention was occupied by a demanding gaggle of girls, all fluttering their fans and eyelashes at him, and Eloise used the opportunity to slip into the obscured corner.

A young lady grunted as Eloise collided with her.

"My apologies!" Eloise leapt backward, nearly tripping over her hem as she untangled herself from the stranger.

The young lady smoothed her skirts, her cheeks flaming as red as her hair. A great pinkish stain soaked her bodice, and it was Eloise's turn to blush.

"Please tell me I am not the cause of that mess," said Eloise, pointing to the young lady's dress.

With another furious blush, the lady shook her head. "Oh, no. I was being so careful not to bump into anyone lest I spill my drink, yet I ended up tripping over my own feet not long after I arrived." Sticking her toes out from under the hem, the mystery girl displayed a gorgeous set of blue slippers with vines and flowers embroidered across the top. "My new dancing slippers have a most awkward heel, but I love them so much that I just had to wear them."

"Those are worth the risk," said Eloise with an appreciative smile.

"Yes, my hubris was my downfall." The girl gave a miserable laugh as she glanced down at the sopping stain. "I shouldn't care one whit what anyone thinks; it is not as though I am the only lady in attendance to have ruined her gown with a misplaced cup of punch, but I cannot bring myself to venture forth; navigating a crowd of strangers is difficult enough without having my foolishness on display..." The lady finally paused to take a breath and gave Eloise a chagrined smile. "I apologize. My mouth has a tendency to run away with itself when I am anxious."

The young lady was equal parts disarming and acutely uncomfortable, and in a strange way, it made her all the more endearing. As there was no one around to fuss about improper etiquette, Eloise gave a curtsy and introduced herself.

"I am Miss Eloise Andrews, and there is no need for you to be anxious. I was hoping to hide for a bit as well."

"Miss Kitty Hennessey. Please, do join me. You looked in need of an escape."

"You witnessed that?"

"Watching the crowd is far more enjoyable than navigating it on my own," said Miss Hennessey. She paused and added, "Of course, I have my parents, but clinging to them and their friends isn't particularly entertaining. I would much rather stand here and watch the party than to stand there awkwardly listening to their conversations. And I rather enjoy spying on everyone. It is quite entertaining to see them all in their element. But I am babbling again."

Miss Hennessey sighed and shrugged as though there was

nothing to be done about the matter, and Eloise grinned. Though she could not describe what endeared her to Miss Hennessy, she embraced the sentiment and said, "You are welcome to join my friends and me. Though I am not keen on returning to them at present."

Tugging at the tops of her gloves, Miss Hennessey smoothed out the wrinkles. "Whyever not?" But then her eyes widened, her cheeks growing red again. "That was far too bold a question, but I cannot seem to stop myself. It's a trait I inherited from my father. I despair of approaching people, but once someone engages me in conversation I cannot reign in my tongue. You needn't answer, of course. I was merely curious."

"To be honest, I find it rather refreshing," said Eloise with a smile she hoped would calm her companion. "At least your questions come from curiosity and not an obsession with secrets and gossip. Which is why I am happy to be free of my friends at present, for they know that there is potential tittle-tattle afoot, and they won't rest until they've unearthed it."

Miss Hennessey peered through the curtains at the scene around them, and her eyes fell on Patrick. The eager energy that filled the air around her faded as the young lady watched him. "Would it have anything to do with the gentleman who was stalking you across the ballroom?"

The tone was so quiet and somber that Eloise was startled into a reply. "Unfortunately, yes. He was a dear friend at one point, but we have not spoken in years, and his sudden appearance has me a bit shaken. It is bad enough that my friends wish to know our history, but they have it in their heads that he looks like some romantic Gothic villain."

Straightening, Miss Hennessey turned away, glancing out the darkened window behind them. "Villains are not romantic."

The mercurial lady kept her eyes fixed on the glass, though there was nothing to be seen in the darkness, and Eloise wished she could say something that would lighten the poor girl's saddened expression. "Is this your first Season?"

Miss Hennessey's eyes darted to Eloise. "In London, yes.

I've been out for four years, but I spent those Seasons in Bath. My parents thought a change of scenery would be good for us."

Emboldened by Miss Hennessey's open nature, Eloise felt free to share a bit of her own honesty. "Well, I am glad they did, for I am very pleased to have made your acquaintance."

Eyes wide, Miss Hennessey beamed, but before another word could be said on the matter, Eloise heard a familiar and unwelcome voice.

"Eloise, there you are." Her mother pushed past the curtains and stepped into the alcove.

Though she knew Emmeline Andrews as well as anyone could claim to know the creature, Eloise had no way of discerning the thoughts going through her head. Her mother's face was as expressive as a statue. Less, in fact, for statuary had some emotion etched into their frozen faces.

"Good evening, Mother," said Eloise with the required curtsy. "I needed a rest from the dancing, and Miss Hennessey was kind enough to share her sanctuary."

With a few words, Eloise introduced Miss Hennessey to her mother, and all the proper salutations and niceties were exchanged before Mother put an end to Eloise's respite.

"We must return to the party. It is rude to hide."

"Of course, Mother." She dutifully followed the lady out, but before they left, Eloise reiterated her previous invitation to Miss Hennessey. "Please, do come and join my friends. I would love to introduce you to them."

Miss Hennessey smiled and nodded, but Mother cleared her throat, drawing Eloise's attention away from the alcove.

"You really must behave with more decorum, Eloise," whispered Mother as she led her daughter through the throng. "I was worried you'd gone missing."

"I needed a moment away from the crowds, and it was better than sneaking off into the garden unaccompanied," said Eloise, garnering a glare from her mother.

"Do not jest about such a thing. Behaving recklessly will ruin your reputation in a trice."

Eloise merely nodded, turning her attention to the crowd. Though she scoured the faces, she did not see Patrick among them. She told herself she was grateful for it, but her heart sank as she realized he'd disappeared once more.

Chapter 4

Glancing back at the alcove, Eloise wished she were still hiding with Miss Hennessey, but there was nothing to be done about it now. Mother would not be so easily thrown over again.

"You must be more circumspect about the people with whom you associate," said Mother, speaking that oft-repeated refrain as she led her daughter through the ballroom. Though Eloise wanted to simply accept the lecture with her usual meekness, she could not let such a condemnation go unchallenged.

"Miss Hennessey is a sweetheart," said Eloise as her mother pulled her to the side of the ballroom. "I hope to count her as a friend."

"That is because you are unaware of her reputation. Whether or not Miss Hennessey is a sweetheart is immaterial, for her sullied name will taint your own."

"That is ridiculous, Mother!"

"Emmeline is often ridiculous, but we adore her all the same for it," said Mrs. Lennox as she joined the pair.

"Now, you are being ridiculous, Deirdre," said Mother with pursed lips.

"And you adore me all the same for it, Emmeline," said Mrs.

Lennox with a cheeky smile. Mother merely blinked in response.

Mrs. Lennox ignored that and grabbed Eloise up in a hug. "It is good to see you, dearheart. It seems an age since we last spoke. Are you enjoying London thus far?"

Eloise sighed. "Not when my mother is insisting my association with Miss Kitty Hennessey will bring about the ruination of the family."

"You are being overly dramatic," said Mother. Though her expression was stoic, her tone held just a touch of exasperation, which was as much of a rise as Eloise ever got from her mother. At times, she felt the strongest urge to shake her mother just to see if it garnered any genuine emotion from her stony facade.

"The Hennesseys are good people," said Mrs. Lennox. "Though I've only just become acquainted with them, I will vouch for their character."

"They may be lovely people, Deidre, but there are rumors running rampant about Miss Hennessey."

Mrs. Lennox gave her friend a saucy arch of her eyebrow. "Since when do you countenance rumors?"

If her mother were ever base enough to scowl, Eloise thought she might do so now, but Mother kept her expression schooled.

"I do not participate in such things, but my distaste for gossip is immaterial. As long as others bandy such things about, I cannot risk my daughter or family being tainted by association."

"That is ridiculous, Emmeline. From what I've heard, Miss Hennessey is the victim," said Mrs. Lennox.

"What happened?" asked Eloise, but Mother shook her head.

"It is not appropriate to speak of such things. All we need know is that her name has been sullied, making her an unfit acquaintance," said her mother.

Eloise scoffed. "So you do not listen to gossip, but you would judge her by it nonetheless? You cannot be serious, Mother."

The lady's lips pinched together for the briefest of moments. "It may seem unreasonable to you, Eloise, but regardless of your own feelings on the matter, others judge Miss Hennessey and you by association. I will not allow anything to jeopardize your reputation."

Before Eloise could say another word, her mother held up a staying hand, and Eloise fell silent as another lady approached.

"Mrs. Andrews, you must come and talk some sense into Mrs. Laury," said Mrs. Greenburg. "She is quite set on having our next charity event be a poetry reading, even though we already decided it should be a musical soirée."

Mother gave a nod befitting nobility and asked Mrs. Lennox to look after Eloise before following Mrs. Greenburg.

"She is impossible," grumbled Eloise with a huff. Mrs. Lennox took her by the arm, squeezing it with a sad smile.

"Dearheart, I know she can be trying at times, but your mother is a good woman who loves you deeply."

"I don't think she is capable of loving."

Coming around to stand before Eloise, Mrs. Lennox gave her a stern look. "That is ridiculous."

"But true," Eloise replied. "She is unfeeling! I don't understand how you can be friends with her. If she weren't my mother, I would want nothing to do with her."

Crossing her arms, Mrs. Lennox frowned. "I've known your mother a long time. My marriage to Mr. Lennox was rather scandalous, and few in the neighborhood deigned to acknowledge his Irish bride when he brought me home. Yet your mother readily accepted me and became my dearest friend. She wasn't always stern and distant, and that warm and loving heart still beats in her bosom. You are quite fortunate to have her as your mother."

Thankfully, the lady in question was not near to hear the undignified snort Eloise gave or the words that followed it. "Fortunate? I can't tell you how many times I have wished that you were my mother, or Aunt Mina or Aunt Betsy or just about anyone else for that matter—"

Mrs. Lennox's eyes hardened, her features growing frostier with each of Eloise's words. "You mother has her faults—heaven knows, I am well acquainted with how infuriating she can be—but Emmeline Andrews is a good woman and far better than she was raised to be."

"Uncle Simon grew up in the same household, and he is a good, kind man who dotes on his wife and children!"

"Your uncle had the same parents but not the same experiences, and I will not listen to you castigate my dear friend. Your mother is difficult, but only because you do not understand the demons with which she wrestles."

Eloise gaped. "But—"

"But nothing. Though she may not show it in the manner that you wish her to, she loves you dearly."

There was no point in arguing. Mrs. Lennox could be intractable when she wanted to be, and Eloise had long ago learned that the stronger her Irish brogue became, the more intractable she was going to be. Though there was little hint of it left during a normal conversation, the full sound of her motherland grew in her tone as she spoke to Eloise.

"She is right," came a voice from behind Eloise, making her jump. "But then, my mother usually is."

Eloise tried to school her features. Tried to keep her pulse from racing. Tried to control the sudden shaking of her hands. But she felt Patrick at her back, and having him so close brought back so many memories and emotions that she could not control the tempest consuming her. Closing her eyes, Eloise took a breath and called upon her mother's many lessons; it was the only time in her life in which Eloise wished to mimic that lady, but at that moment, she was grateful for that stony example.

"Mr. Lennox," said Eloise. Their positions forced her to turn to face him, but she did not meet his gaze. "I hadn't heard you were in London."

"Miss Andrews," he said with a tone that was more question than statement. "I am very glad to see you."

As her mind could not formulate a response to that non-sense, Eloise nodded while still refusing to meet his eyes.

"I had hoped to speak with you," he said in a quiet tone.

Her gaze snapped to his. "I have no idea why you would wish to when you were content to be silent for the past six years."

Growling internally, Eloise wished she had better self-control, for Patrick Lennox did not warrant any more of her attention. Nor did he deserve to know how her heart had broken or the anguish she'd suffered over the years: those memories belonged to her alone. Yet she feared that if she kept talking, there would be no controlling her wayward tongue.

"May I call upon you tomorrow?" he asked.

"I see no point. You've made it perfectly clear you do not wish to be acquainted with me," said Eloise. From the corner of her eye, she saw her salvation striding towards her. "Mr. Godwin, how good to see you!"

"And you, Miss Andrews," he said, offering up his arm to her.

"I was about to ask the lady to dance," said Patrick, and Eloise's hand itched to slap the bounder.

"But she has already promised me the supper dance," replied Mr. Godwin.

Eloise perked at that. With all that had happened, she had not realized the evening had grown late, but this was her deliverance from further conversation with the dratted Patrick Lennox.

"You've already had your dance with Miss Andrews," said Patrick.

"Only the first of the evening," said Eloise before striding away with her preferred partner.

Chapter 5

Patrick's heart fractured as he watched his love depart on the arm of another. Gritting his teeth against the nausea seizing him, he fought through the familiar tickle at the back of his throat. His mouth grew dry, begging for a sip of something refreshing. That desire grew in him, picking at his hard-earned control like a pickaxe. With a slow inhale, he took a calming breath, though the air was too warm and malodorous to be soothing.

"I hadn't realized they were courting," he murmured.

His mother took his arm and pulled him close. "They are, and they aren't, love. Eloise has not wanted for admirers since her entrance into society, but Mr. Godwin is the only one who seems determined not to retreat—even if they are ill-suited for each other."

"This was a mistake," said Patrick, stretching his neck as though that might loosen the cravat choking him.

Patrick cursed the cowardice that had convinced him to-night was the proper time to approach Eloise. Meeting in such a public space had saved him from the tongue-lashing he right-fully deserved. Of course, his decision hadn't been helped by the hefty dose of eagerness he'd felt to see her again; the thought of waiting yet another day had been unbearable.

"I hurt her," he said, not bothering to hide the distress he felt at having witnessed the truth of the matter.

Patrick was no fool. He'd known his final words and the subsequent silence had wounded her gravely, but some nonsensical part of him had hoped the pain was minor or fleeting. Seeing it blazing in her eyes was an agony no man should endure, though Patrick knew he deserved it.

"Be honest and she will forgive you. It will take time and effort, but she loves you still," said his mother.

"She ran away."

"And she will continue to do so until you can convince her you won't break her heart again," she replied. Ignoring the crush of people around them, she took his hand in one of hers and patted his cheek with the other. "You have much to atone for, but you are a good man, Patrick. I know you can make it right. Until Eloise tells you that she does not and will not love you, you must keep trying."

"And hound her into submission?" he scoffed.

"Of course not," replied his mother with a frustrated huff. Leveling a look at her son, she said, "But do not assume you know her heart, and do not make the decision for her by simply disappearing from her life once more. Your father learned that lesson the hard way, and I'm hoping you are not as stubbornly blind as he once was."

Patrick opened his mouth to reply, but his mother hushed him.

"Don't cry retreat so soon. Make amends, show her your heart, and then let her decide if she will accept it."

...

Noise choked the air like a malodorous vapor, and the crowd jostled Eloise until she was certain she'd discover a few bruises tomorrow. Yet still she jumped at every bray of laughter and touch, thinking Patrick had come to plague her once more. Luckily, the group around her required only the occasional smile and nod, for Eloise was not capable of carrying a conversation at present. Her chin trembled, but she gritted her teeth.

For six years, they'd had nothing but rumors and speculation to tell them if Patrick were alive or dead, and she couldn't believe his mother so readily forgave him that torture. Eloise didn't feel capable of such charity. Especially, when he appeared without warning and claimed he was "very glad" to see her as though his absence had been nothing out of the ordinary.

The group around her laughed, and she forced a smile.

And he wanted to dance with her! Eloise would rather kick him in the shins, but her slippers were too soft to be decent bludgeoners. And her fan would break under such an assault. A reticule would do wonders, but she did not have one on hand at present.

"Miss Andrews?" His voice startled her so thoroughly that Eloise stumbled to the side, but then Patrick's hands were there to steady her.

"Mr. Lennox," she said through clenched teeth, wrenching her elbow free. "You should not sneak up on a lady."

Beside Eloise, Miss Merriweather tittered with laughter and batted her eyelashes at Patrick. "He was standing there for several moments, Miss Andrews, and you did not notice him."

"I apologize for any distress I may have caused," he said with a bow of his head. "I had hoped to claim a dance. Mr. Godwin cannot occupy this one as well."

Eloise looked at Mr. Godwin, wishing she could enlist him for a third set, but Mama would have a fit over that breach of etiquette. Casting her eyes to the rest of her circle, she discovered (much to her dismay) that Mr. Kirkpatrick was the only other gentleman, and he was such an appalling dancer that his partner always sustained some injury after a set.

Thinking through the possibilities, Eloise weighed whether being crippled was preferable to standing up with Patrick, ignoring the traitorous flutter in her heart that wanted nothing more than to put her hand in his and be led onto the dance floor. Now was not the time for sentimentality. Giving in to hope had hurt her far too many times, and Eloise had learned her lesson.

But regardless of her own internal debate, Mr. Kirkpatrick was so thoroughly oblivious to the drama unfolding that he wandered off in search of refreshment, leaving Eloise with no escape.

"If Miss Andrews is otherwise engaged, I would love to stand up with you," offered Miss Merriweather, and Eloise gaped at her audacity. She did not care if another lady set her cap at Patrick. That had nothing to do with it. Nothing whatsoever. But Miss Merriweather was all but throwing herself into his arms. Her eyelashes were fluttering so much that Eloise could feel the breeze of it.

Patrick cleared his throat. "I do appreciate your offer, Miss..."

"Dianna Merriweather." With a fluid dip, she gave a deep curtsy more appropriate for royalty, and Eloise suspected Miss Merriweather had done so to enhance the already low cut of her décolletage. Mr. Godwin's eyebrows shot upward, and Patrick's cheeks grew rosy, and he kept his eyes fixed on Miss Merriweather's face.

Patrick mumbled a halting reply, and Eloise sighed, unable to suffer this awkwardness a moment longer. Taking him by the arm, she dragged him towards the dancers.

"Thank you for rescuing me from your friend," he muttered, glancing at her with a bewildered expression that was so terribly Patrick-like, Eloise's breath caught at the sight of it.

"Miss Merriweather is not a friend. She's hardly an acquaintance," she said, taking her place among the dancers. "And it was nothing. I simply do not like to see anyone so uncomfortable, and she was terribly forward. It was shameful."

Patrick took his place as well and nodded. Standing opposite each other, Eloise was forced to face him, unable to escape.

"But it was understandable," he said.

The musicians struck their notes, and Eloise held back a

wince, for the dance was *Cupid in Armour*. More than the unseemly name, it was far too sedate. Now was the perfect time for a rousing country dance that would leave them out of breath and focused on the steps. Instead, Eloise would get little respite from her partner.

"How is Miss Merriweather's brazen behavior understandable?" she asked.

"When one is terrified of the future, one often resorts to extreme tactics."

"Ridiculous," said Eloise with a shake of her head. "Miss Merriweather is a bold, fearless lady."

"You don't see it?" Patrick asked, cocking his head to the side. "She is frightened of spinsterhood, and in her desperation, she employs bold measures to secure a husband."

She glanced past Patrick to look at the lady in question, but Eloise could not see a single ounce of trepidation in Miss Merriweather's expression.

They followed the promenade, moving down the row, and Eloise glanced at their joined hands. Though separated by gloves, her memory supplied the feel of Patrick's fingers. He'd held her hand so many times that his touch was indelibly marked on her heart. She felt his eyes on her, and it set her cheeks ablaze. Her throat tightened, and Eloise blinked rapidly, surprised at the delicate sheen of tears that had gathered. Turning her eyes away, she focused on the dancers. That was safer.

"I've wanted to speak with you for a long while," whispered Patrick.

"I cannot imagine why," she replied, refusing to match his tone.

"We both know there is much to say after what has passed."

"It was nothing," she replied with a forced smile. Eloise would not meet his eyes once more, so she could not see his expression, but she felt the discontent radiating off him.

"It was not 'nothing,' Eloise."

They reached their destination, and she ripped her hand

from his. "I am Miss Andrews, Mr. Lennox, and it meant nothing."

Though she faced him, Eloise forced her eyes not to linger on the gentleman. But Patrick remained silent for so long that curiosity got the better of her. His eyes bored into her, and with his new scars, it gave him quite the brooding air. For a brief moment, Eloise mourned the sight of it, for this was not the boy she'd known. Again, she wondered what had happened to him during those silent years, but she refused to allow herself to go down that path. Patrick's past, present, and future were not her concern any longer.

"We were good friends—" he began.

"Yes, we were, but that was in the past, Mr. Lennox. A long time ago. Six years, in fact."

Patrick's gaze fell, his shoulders drooping, but Eloise would not allow his dejected state to soften her heart. He had brought this upon himself.

"Tell me you are happy with Mr. Godwin and want nothing more to do with me, and I will leave you alone," he murmured. "I give you my word I will never bother you again."

Straightening her spine, Eloise raised her chin. "I am very happy with Mr. Godwin."

But her lips would not form the other words. Her mind filled with all the accusations she wished to unleash, but even in that monsoon of emotion, Eloise could not give voice to the broken part of her heart that wanted nothing to do with him. Patrick's eyes rose to hers, a curious spark in them.

Another promenade brought them together, and Eloise forced her feet not to trip over themselves. Generally, she was not a clumsy girl, yet she was straining to keep upright tonight.

"Are you truly happy with him?" he whispered to her.

"Of course," she whispered back, her puzzled eyes meeting his. "Why would I not be? He is a good man."

The corner of Patrick's mouth twitched, and there was a hint of a smile in his eyes. "You always bite your lips when you lie, Eloise. You haven't changed."

Eloise wrenched her hand free of his. "And how would you know if I've changed? You haven't been here, Patrick! Mr. Lennox..."

Flustered at her slip of the tongue, Eloise broke from the dance, not caring that it wasn't finished. Weaving through the crowds, she honed in on Mr. Godwin and came up beside him. Sliding her arm through his, she clung to it, giving him a bright smile. He blinked at her for several seconds before giving her a warm grin in return and placing his hand atop hers.

Chapter 6

Fidgeting was unacceptable, and Emmeline Andrews had long ago cured herself of such low-born behavior, but there were moments when her fingers itched to fiddle with her necklace. It was a silly habit, but there was something about the motion that brought her a bit of peace. However, it put her nerves on display, and Emmeline would not allow herself to become a spectacle.

The coach rolled down the cobbled streets, and Emmeline hazarded a glance at her daughter. Though sitting with her hands and feet in the right position and maintaining the proper posture, Eloise looked deflated. Her dim eyes tracked the passing scenery with a lethargy that broke her mother's heart, and Emmeline longed to buoy the girl's spirits.

"Did you enjoy the Felthams' ball last night?" asked Emmeline, though she immediately wished she had not. She'd meant it as a simple nicety to spark a conversation, but the previous evening was not a happy subject for Eloise.

"It was too crowded," was the only response she received. Eloise's features tightened, and Emmeline thought it prudent to let the matter drop. However, curiosity was rarely prudent, and there was too much unraveling in her daughter's life to let the conversation lie.

"It was a pleasure to see Mr. Godwin," said Emmeline.

Eloise's eyes finally turned to meet her mother's, and Emmeline was met with cold irritation. "There is no point in being circumspect, Mother. If you wish to know something, simply ask."

"You two looked quite cozy."

Eloise turned back to the window. "Mr. Godwin is nice enough."

"You were clinging to his arm half the night."

Giving that put-upon sigh that Emmeline had heard many a time from her daughter, Eloise said, "That is an overstatement, Mother. We are courting, after all. It would be strange if I did not spend the evening with him."

Emmeline thought through the scene she'd witnessed the night before, and Eloise's resultant behavior was anything but usual.

"It was good to see Patrick..." began Emmeline, but her words halted when Eloise leveled a hard look at her.

"I do not wish to speak about Mr. Lennox." Eloise put extra emphasis on the formal address, but there was a brittleness to her tone that spoke of more than the anger she conveyed.

The urge to scoop her daughter up into a hug overwhelmed Emmeline. Her sweet little girl was hurting, and her arms cried out to hold her, to comfort her.

"Don't be so crass, Emmeline." Mother Andrews' voice came into Emmeline's mind as forcefully as if her mother-in-law were sitting beside her. Emmeline felt the stern disapproval, and she restrained herself, forcing those ill-bred feelings to the background. Then Emmeline heard another echo of her mother-in-law's voice. *"Good girl."*

That memory brought a prickle of tears to her eyes, though Emmeline beat it back. It had been over a year since that dear lady had entered her eternal rest, and Emmeline still felt the loss keenly—especially at times like this, when she was so desperate for guidance.

Reaching forward, Emmeline patted Eloise on the knee as Mother Andrews had done many a time with her, but Eloise tensed and shifted farther away, turning her gaze back to the window with a rigidity that had nothing to do with proper posture.

Holding in the sigh that desperately wanted out, Emmeline watched her daughter, wishing she knew the words to heal the breach between them.

"I thought we might visit Madame Collette's this afternoon," said Emmeline.

"I don't need another gown," came the quick response.

Emmeline's hand twitched, but she caught herself before it moved to her necklace.

Eloise may not need another gown, but Emmeline had seen a new style that would be perfect for her daughter. However, there was nothing more to say, for the coach came to a stop in front of Acton Court. In short order, the ladies were inside, divested of their cloaks and bonnets, and awaiting their hostess in the parlor.

Clutching her hands in her lap kept Emmeline from bouncing out of her seat. She could not wait to see her new daughter-in-law. As they had been married only a few short months, Emmeline knew that it was likely too soon for Kenneth and Angela to have any joyous announcements to share, but Emmeline could not keep herself from longing for another grandchild.

"Eloise, how good to see you!" Angela said, greeting her sister-in-law with an embrace.

Emmeline gave her daughter a small shake of the head at the display, and a quick scowl flashed across Eloise's face, but the girl calmed her overexcited energy and greeted her sister-in-law with a far more decorous curtsy. Angela stiffened, giving Emmeline a responding bob.

The trio sat on the sofas as a maid arranged tea and cakes, but none of the ladies deigned to speak. Angela and Eloise shared a grim look, which Emmeline ignored as she stirred her tea.

"How is Kenneth?" Emmeline asked, latching on to the first topic that came to mind. "Though I understand newlyweds need some space, I do wish you would stay with us at Caswell House."

"He is at his club," said Angela before lapsing back into silence.

Taking a sip of tea to cover her discomfort, Emmeline searched for a topic to broach. With all the training she'd received from Mother Andrews, Emmeline still had never developed a skill for creating conversation where there was none. When faced with such a situation, her mind seized and emptied, leaving her at a loss.

"The weather..." Mother Andrews' words fought through the awkward daze, and Emmeline felt like the foolish, green young lady she had once been.

"We've been enjoying very fine weather," said Emmeline.

Angela set her teacup down, the china rattling, and Eloise gave another of her sighs.

"Very fine, indeed," responded Eloise in a lifeless tone.

"Mrs. Kingsley paid us a visit last week," said Angela, turning her attention to her sister-in-law. "She brought me a gorgeous necklace and bracelet set to welcome me into the family. I believe she said they were an heirloom or something of that sort, and they are lovely. The most brilliant sapphire ringed with diamonds."

It was Emmeline's turn to rattle her dishes, but she recovered quickly. "Yes, I am quite familiar with those jewels. They are not old enough to be considered an heirloom, but I had thought them quite beautiful."

Eloise smiled, stirring her tea. "I had not realized that Aunt Mina and Uncle Simon were in London. I shall be glad to see them."

Emmeline's jaw clenched, and she fought to keep her fingers from crushing the delicate cake she held. Placing it back on her saucer, she picked up her spoon to stir her tea, though it needed no such attention. The metal banged against the china in an unruly fashion, drawing the attention of the others. With a quick clink, she set the cup down with far more force than intended. The girls stared at her, and Emmeline forced her lips and jaw to loosen, affecting the calm demeanor Mother Andrews had insisted every lady needed.

After a silent moment, Angela turned back to Eloise. "Not Aunt Mina. I meant Grandmother Kingsley. She is in Town and wished to pay a visit as she was unable to attend the wedding. No one sent her an announcement or invitation."

There was a hint of accusation in Angela's tone, but it did not bother Emmeline in the least. The slight against Amelia Kingsley had been intentional, and Emmeline would not feel guilty for protecting her children from that woman.

"My grandmother?" asked Eloise, placing her own teacup down and leaning forward. "What is she like?"

"A very amiable lady and quite generous," said Angela.

"Do you know where she is staying? I would love to meet her," said Eloise, glancing between the others.

"You've met her before, but it was so long ago you likely do not recall it," said Emmeline, "and it is best not to renew the acquaintance."

"Renew the acquaintance?" Eloise gaped at that. "But she is your mother."

"I have neither seen nor spoken to her in years, and for good reason," said Emmeline, smoothing the napkin draped across her lap. She channeled Mother Andrews as she spoke, adopting the tone her mother-in-law had used when making definitive statements that welcomed no further discussion.

The girls looked discontented, but neither spoke another word on the subject. Running her hands over her knees, Eloise fidgeted for a brief moment before a look from Emmeline stopped her.

"Angela, I hear you and Kenneth are throwing your first dinner party next month," said Eloise.

Emmeline looked at her daughter-in-law, though she forced away the excitement, for she did not wish to appear too eager; this was a moment she had anticipated since her son had first announced his engagement. There was a clear strain between Angela and herself that Emmeline could not seem to rectify, and this was the perfect solution to build a better foundation with her son's new bride. It was just such an occasion that had forever altered her relationship with Mother Andrews, and this was Emmeline's chance to take her own daughter-in-law under her wing.

"How wonderful for you," said Emmeline, clasping her hands in her lap.

Angela's lips pursed at that, and Emmeline was at a loss to understand how that innocuous statement had upset the girl. Eloise gave her mother a pleading look, as though begging her to be civil, but the words had been nothing but civil.

Changing tack, Emmeline asked, "Who is to be in attendance? The proper guest list is imperative to a successful party and must be approached with much forethought. And have you begun work on the menu? Such things can be quite tricky to coordinate properly, and I would gladly offer up my assistance. I do have much experience in planning such gatherings."

"I assure you that my mother taught me well, and I am more than capable of handling such things," said Angela, straightening with a near scowl. Before Emmeline could say a word in response, Angela stood and said, "Thank you for your visit, but I'm afraid I have another engagement and must be on my way."

Finding herself summarily dismissed and back in her carriage, Emmeline tried to comprehend what had happened. Her mind told her not to dwell on it, but her heart felt differently. With it brought remembrances of all that Mother Andrews had done for her, and Emmeline realized how much she'd hoped to mend things with Angela.

And to her horror, Emmeline's chin trembled. Focusing on keeping her breaths steady and face impassable, she watched the passing city. The rows of buildings, the trotting horses, the people weaving between them. But her thoughts ignored the sights before her and called up images and memories best left undisturbed.

"Mother, are you unwell?" asked Eloise.

Calling on her emotional reserves, Emmeline turned a peaceful face towards her daughter. "There is a park not far from here that your father and I used to frequent with Joanna and Lucinda when they were small."

Eloise looked puzzled at her words and shook her head. "I cannot imagine you in a park."

For one moment, Emmeline allowed a smile to form on her lips as she recalled those happy days they'd shared. "The girls adored feeding the ducks. We'd take a picnic and spend the afternoon stuffing those fowl until they were fit to burst."

Eyebrows raised, Eloise stared at her.

"Joanna was especially fond of scaring the poor things," said Emmeline, recalling the memories of her little girl's brown braids bobbing behind her as she chased the birds, forcing them to scatter and take flight. "Until one of the ducks relieved itself as it was flying over her."

The memories came in a wave, filling her mind with all those precious moments. When Emmeline finally came back to herself, she found Eloise watching her as though she were some alien creature.

"You never speak of Joanna," said Eloise. "Or Patience."

Hands twisting in her lap, Emmeline murmured, "Some things are best left alone."

The coach rolled to a stop, and Emmeline straightened, recalling herself. This was not the time nor the place to be having such maudlin conversations.

"A dress," said Emmeline.

Eloise cocked her head with a question in her expression

"We must get you a dress," said Emmeline. "There is a new style that will look perfect on you."

"Mother—" But before Eloise could protest, the door opened and Emmeline alighted, leaving her daughter to trail after her.

...

With a tug of the ribbons, Eloise removed her bonnet and handed it to Isaacs as their butler collected their things. Casting another look at her mother, Eloise wondered what was occupying the lady's thoughts. She'd hardly said more than cursory words during their shopping excursion and appeared content to continue in that vein.

Her mother seemed the same as always. Calm and implacable. Her delicate features conveyed not a shred of emotion. Not a hair was out of place nor a wrinkle to be found on her gown. But Eloise felt uneasy as her mother divested herself of her spencer, gloves, and bonnet.

"Are you unwell?" asked Eloise.

The lady glanced at her daughter with an arched brow. "What a foolish question to ask. I am perfectly well."

Eloise's mouth snapped shut before she could speak another foolish word, and her mother turned, taking the stairs. "I am spending the afternoon on my correspondence and am not at home to visitors, Isaacs. I do not wish to be disturbed."

With a sigh and shake of her head, Eloise left the foyer and wandered through the halls in search of a diversion. But none came to mind, for her thoughts would not stray from her mother's extraordinary behavior. The visit with Angela had been an unmitigated disaster but nothing out of the ordinary. Her mother had a knack for finding fault at every opportunity, so her rudeness was not surprising. Though Eloise still felt a rush of embarrassment at the cold manner in which Mother had questioned Angela's ability to play hostess.

And then that carriage ride. She struggled to believe that she had, in fact, heard her mother correctly. Though the lady occasionally subjected herself to a drive through Hyde Park, Eloise could not think of a single time in which her mother had actually traversed one on foot. But then, it had also been nearly two years since Eloise had heard her mother speak Joanna's name.

Eloise wandered the house, her feet carrying her from room to room, though her thoughts were too preoccupied to recognize where she traveled.

"Some things are best left alone."

Mother's words sprang to mind, and Eloise's spirits withered beneath that stark declaration. It had been two years since Joanna died bringing sweet Katherine into the world, and Mother carried on as though nothing were amiss. Eloise had been too young to recall much about Patience's passing, but Mother didn't seem distraught then, either. The detachment she displayed chilled Eloise's heart, making her wonder if the woman had any heart at all. Mothers were supposed to love their children.

A shiver ran down her neck, and Eloise decided it was time to stop thinking about such things. There was no understanding Emmeline Andrews, and it was pointless to try. Clearing her thoughts, Eloise knew precisely what she wished to do for the rest of the afternoon.

Chapter 7

Emmeline
Age Seven

Fingers brushed Emmeline's skirts, and she squealed, dodging out of Nurse Bliss's grasp. Emmeline fought to breathe, her sides twisting in delicious pain. With a great giggle, she paused, taunting her dear nursemaid.

"I will get you!" said Nurse Bliss, lunging yet again. This time the little girl was not quick enough. Scooping the lass into her arms, Nurse Bliss dug into Emmeline's sides, pulling peals of laughter from her charge.

There was a squeaky shout, and Nurse Bliss stumbled as Simon leapt onto her back with a mighty roar. But the pair were no match for their nursemaid, who had played such games many a time before. She had both of them at her mercy, and little Priscilla scooted across the floor to assist in the torture of her elder brother and sister; with a drooling grin, the babe flopped down on Emmeline's chest, smacking her sister's cheeks with her tiny hands.

Emmeline sputtered, but she could not free herself of the onslaught. Just when she could not breathe for laughing, Nurse Bliss released her prisoners, and Emmeline went limp, allowing the remnant giggles to fade into heaving breaths. On her hands and knees, Nurse Bliss loomed over the children with a grin.

"Come now, my darlings," she said, getting to her feet. "It is nearly luncheon, and we must tidy up the nursery before we eat."

"I don't want to clean," whined Emmeline as Simon groaned.

Staring down at the children, Nurse Bliss put her hands on her hips and tapped her toe. "Only because you know Simon can clean faster than you."

Emmeline bolted upright, eyes wide. "No, he cannot!"

"Yes, I can!" Simon shot to his feet and scrambled to the nearest toy.

Gasping, Emmeline hurried after him, scooping up blocks, soldiers, and dolls. Casting a glance at her brother, she put on a burst of speed as she outpaced little Simon. With a snap of the lid, their toy chest closed.

"I did it!" she shouted, throwing up her arms. "Did you see how fast I went, Nurse Bliss? Did you?"

"You were positively flying, sweetheart," she replied with a warm smile that made Emmeline's heart even lighter than before. Throwing her arms around Nurse Bliss's legs, Emmeline squeezed her tight, and then Simon's little arms came around them both with a giggle.

The crunch of carriage wheels against the gravel drive drew their attention, and the children hurried to the window to see who had arrived.

"Careful, Emmeline," said Nurse as she helped her and Simon climb atop the window seat to stare out at the visitor.

Emmeline pushed her face against the window, watching the carriage roll to a stop at the front door. "Who is it?"

But the question was answered when Simon let out a squeal, bouncing on his toes. "Mama!"

After so many prayers and pleadings, there she was, stepping out of the coach in all her finery, looking like the fairy princesses in Nurse Bliss's stories. Emmeline echoed Simon's shout, and the pair of them hopped from the seat, bolting out of the nursery with their nursemaid trailing behind them.

"Children!" Nurse Bliss called, but the pair would not listen, and the nursemaid was hindered by the babe in her arms.

Grabbing Simon's hand, she ran with all possible speed. Emmeline could hardly breathe at the thought of getting to see her. To embrace her. Perhaps they could play with her new dolls. Or she could show her mother that bit of field that had the loveliest wildflowers. That would make Mama so very happy.

Mama stood at the other end of the hall, and Emmeline put on another burst of speed, her little feet tearing towards her. Simon pulled free of Emmeline's grip to run faster, and the pair of them launched themselves at their mother.

But with a firm hand, Mama pulled free of the children's hold.

"Mama?" Emmeline grabbed at her mother's skirts, but the lady's face looked wrong. A great grimace pulled at her features, and Emmeline could not understand what the matter was, for she had been very good whilst Mama was away. There was no reason for her mother to scowl so. Nurse Bliss and Papa would tell Mama that she had been a good girl.

"Not now!" Mama barked, pushing past them and stomping down the hall.

Simon stared after her with tear-filled eyes, and Emmeline grabbed his hand, though her own lip quivered as their mother burst into their father's study.

"Amelia," their father greeted her, getting to his feet, but before he could say another word, their mother flew across the room, letting her hand fly with all her strength. It cracked against their father's cheek, making Emmeline and Simon flinch.

"Are you happy, you spineless cad?" she shrieked, bringing her hand back once more, but Papa's own shot forward, gripping hers and pulling Mama flush to him.

"Do not push me, Amelia," he growled with a sneer. "I have

tolerated too much from you already, and I shan't be pushed any further."

"From me?" Mama gaped, her eyes narrowing to slits as she pulled free of his grasp.

"You have made me a laughing stock!" he shouted. "You have forced me to take in another's by-blow, and then you go gallivanting off into the arms of your next lover!"

"Priscilla is your daughter—"

Papa scoffed. "Anyone with eyes can see she is the spitting image of the footman."

Mama screamed and grabbed a vase from a sideboard and launched it across the study in a flurry of flowers. The porcelain crashed against the wall, and Emmeline jumped, squeezing Simon's hand.

"Do not act so sanctimonious!" she shouted. "You pox-ridden letch—"

A hand came down over Emmeline's ear, pulling the child close and muffling the other in skirts that held hints of roses and almonds. Her complexion was her one vanity, Nurse Bliss liked to say, and though it cost her a pretty penny, she could not do without her Milk of Roses; the scent of it filled Emmeline's nose, bringing with it a peace that wrapped around her little soul. Her Nurse was here.

With a nudge, the nursemaid herded them back to her domain. But try as she might, Nurse Bliss could not protect both children while holding the babe in her arms, and though Emmeline could not understand all that was said, her parents' angry words burrowed into her ears. Even after the nursery door was shut, Emmeline still heard the sounds echoing through the halls.

"Emmeline?" Nurse Bliss knelt before her. With a delicate touch, she wiped at the tears streaming down Emmeline's cheeks. Bringing her arms around her nurse's neck, Emmeline clung to the woman, breathing in that heavenly scent.

"I know you are scared, but you must be brave," whispered Nurse Bliss. "You've got little Simon and Priscilla looking up to you. Can you be a good sister and help them?"

Nestled into the woman's neck, Emmeline gave a tiny nod. Allowing herself just one more moment in Nurse Bliss's arms, Emmeline took a deep breath. She was a brave girl. Pulling out of Nurse's hold, Emmeline went over to Simon and curled up next to him with an arm around his shoulders.

Bringing Priscilla over, Nurse Bliss sat cross-legged before the pair and smiled. "Have I ever told you the story of the Raven King?"

Simon's brows pinched together, his head cocking to the side. Though his words were broken with tears, he asked, "Who lived in the Great Forest at the edge of the world?"

"And had the seven golden balls?" added Emmeline.

"It appears it is time for new stories," said Nurse Bliss with a smile, bouncing Priscilla in her arms. "Have I told you about the princess who spins clouds?"

"I love that one," said Emmeline with a smile.

"I want the dragon story," he said while wiping at his cheeks.

"The dragon, eh?" said Nurse Bliss, her brows drawing closer together as she tapped a finger to her chin. "I don't recall that one."

"A long time ago..." said Simon, straightening.

"...in a land beyond the sea," added Emmeline with a smile.

"...in the highest reaches of the highest mountains," he continued.

"There lived a fearsome—" but Emmeline's words were cut short when the nursery door opened. Nurse Bliss shot to her feet and the children followed suit, but Emmeline kept her arm firmly around Simon's shoulders as their mother entered.

"Ah, my lovely, there you are," Mama cooed, striding over to snatch Priscilla from Nurse Bliss. The infant's lips puckered, her brows scrunching together a brief moment before letting out a sad wail as she twisted in her mother's hold and reached for Nurse Bliss. Emmeline and Simon drew closer to Mama, though they remained hidden behind the nurse's skirts.

"It is past her nap, mistress," said the nursemaid as she reached for Priscilla. "Perhaps I should take her."

"You will stay where you are, Nurse. They are my children, and it has been months since I've seen them," said Mama, motioning for Emmeline and Simon.

Stepping forward, Emmeline wrapped her arms around her mother's legs, but the lady's eyes remained on the squalling Priscilla. Mama patted Emmeline on the head and stepped away to look at Simon.

"Come here," Mama prompted, but Simon tucked himself deeper behind Nurse Bliss's skirts. Eyes narrowed, she ordered him again and Nurse prompted him to obey, but the child would have none of it. Clinging to his nursemaid, Simon refused to look at his mother.

Squatting down, Nurse Bliss faced the small boy. "Your mother has come an awfully long way to see you. It would make her very happy if you were to greet her properly."

Simon shook his head, but Nurse Bliss chucked him under the chin. "If you do so, we may finish our story."

"Promise?"

"Promise."

Simon dashed forward and squeezed Mama's legs, but he returned to Nurse Bliss's side immediately. There was something so dark and angry in Mama's eyes as she watched their nursemaid, though Emmeline could not understand why that should be; Simon had done as told.

"Mistress, please," said Nurse Bliss, motioning for Priscilla, who shrieked and arched. With a scowl, Mama dropped the babe into Nurse Bliss's arms and stormed out of the nursery. Emmeline jumped as the door slammed shut, and she drew her arm around Simon's shoulders once more as they stared after her.

...

Holding Simon's hand, Emmeline led him through the dance steps. She hummed a meandering melody and approximated the movements she'd seen the ladies and gentlemen use. It had been a long time since there had been a ball at Avebury Park, but Emmeline still remembered sneaking away from the nursery to spy on the guests in their finery as they twirled about the ballroom. Simon spun and lost his balance, landing on his rump with a scowl, and Emmeline hid a chuckle behind her hand.

"Quiet!" barked Nurse Jones, and Simon flinched.

"We were only dancing," said Emmeline, facing the crone camped in an armchair off to one side of the room.

"You were making a racket," she said before closing her milky eyes once again.

Priscilla fussed, squalling from the adjoining room, and Emmeline moved to the doorway.

"Leave the babe alone," said Nurse Jones, not bothering to open her eyes.

"But—"

"She's been spoiled rotten and has to learn that people aren't going to pick her up the moment she cries." And that was the end of the conversation, for she let out a rattling rumble of a breath as her muscles slackened.

Simon sniffled, and Emmeline crept to his hiding spot beside the toy chest.

"I miss Nurse Bliss," he said, his words broken by hitched breaths.

Emmeline put a finger to her lips and whispered, "I do, too."

The words pulled at her heart, and Emmeline felt tears rising in her eyes, but she blinked them away. She was a good elder sister and a brave girl. Simon needed her to be strong, and she would do that. She would make Nurse Bliss proud.

"Do you think she will come back?" asked Simon.

Emmeline wondered that herself. Nurse had never been

gone for so long. A few hours here or there was not an uncommon occurrence. A day was rarer but not unheard of. However, a week was another matter, and Nurse Bliss had been gone two.

With the added frustration Nurse Jones brought to their lives, time stretched to impossible lengths. Emmeline had taken to singing lullabies for Simon and Priscilla, but there were no such songs for her. No hugs and kisses or tucks into bed. Humming another tune, Emmeline rocked her brother, hoping for a bit of comfort herself, but she found none.

"The fluff!" Simon straightened, turning wide eyes on his sister.

Emmeline shushed him, and the pair cast wary eyes on their nurse, but her snores continued.

"The fluff," he repeated in a whisper. "The fairy queen sent a message through it. We could send one to Nurse."

"But we aren't fairies."

Simon's expression fell, his whole soul drooping under that realization, and it broke Emmeline's heart, so she added, "But maybe the fairies would help us if we bring them a treat."

Jumping to his feet, Simon yanked open the toy chest, pulling out his favorite soldier. "Would they like this?"

Emmeline grinned and took Simon by the hand. Creeping across the nursery, the pair snuck out the door and through the hallways. It took effort to keep hidden from the maids and footmen, but Emmeline knew all the best hiding places in Avebury Park. Within minutes, they were out a side door and running through the garden, straight to the field that was just over the hill. They were certain to find dandelions there.

Beaming as brightly as the sun above, Emmeline ran hand-in-hand with Simon. She reveled in the breeze brushing her cheeks, the sounds of birds and insects filling the air, and the bliss of being free from the dark clouds stifling the nursery. She could breathe again.

"There!" shrieked Simon, pulling her towards a thick patch of dandelions that had greyed and shifted into their fluffy form. Falling to his knees, he grabbed at the stems, but Emmeline stopped him.

"Wait, we must give our offerings first."

Simon nodded, and Emmeline motioned him to a group of toadstools. They were bright red, starkly contrasting against the deep green grass around them. They didn't form a proper fairy ring, but Emmeline hoped the little creatures might still be there. Pulling her favorite ribbon from her hair, she looped it around the base of the largest one. Simon crouched beside her and placed his soldier in front of it.

"Please get this message to Nurse Bliss," said Emmeline.

"We miss her," added Simon.

With a nod, the pair plucked the fuzziest dandelions, and Emmeline thought of her dear nurse and all the things she wished to say to her. Taking in a great breath of air, Emmeline blew the fluff into the air, watching the breezes catch the wisps and carry them out into the world.

"Did it work?" asked Simon as the last of his dandelion disappeared.

Emmeline stared at the bare stem left in her hand and shrugged. "Perhaps we should do more to be safe."

And they did, picking the field clean in the hopes that somehow their message would reach Nurse Bliss, and she would return to save them from Nurse Jones. How Emmeline longed to see her warm smile and twinkling eyes again. She needed her lullabies and soft, loving words, and those dear arms wrapping around her.

But Nurse Bliss never came.

Chapter 8

Sneaking across the library, Eloise reached under the arm-chair cushion and retrieved her novel. With Mother occupied, it was the perfect time to delve into the tale of Vincentio di Vivaldi. She said the name aloud, reveling in the Italian lilt, before opening the cover and escaping into a world of villainous monks, kidnappings, and all sorts of deliciously vile things—all of which were preferable to reality at present.

The door opened, and Eloise leapt from her armchair, tucking the novel behind her back. But she relaxed when the footman merely offered up a salver with a calling card from Miss Katherine Hennessey.

A spark of joy brightened her mood but was quickly doused again. Eloise had no doubt as to Mother's feelings about Miss Hennessey. But Mother had given orders not to be bothered and was unlikely to notice Eloise entertaining a visitor. Biting on her lip, she stared at the calling card, her fingers running along the edges.

"Please let her in," said Eloise before she thought better of it.

Moments later, the young lady entered with a broad smile. "Good afternoon, Miss Andrews. I hope I am not intruding, but

I was dreadfully bored at home and thought you might join me for a turn about the park."

The young lady fairly buzzed with excitement, as though the prospect were the greatest thing in the world. Eloise grinned in response but paused. She wanted nothing more than to give an easy acceptance, but she knew her mother too well to do so.

The light in Miss Hennessey's eyes dimmed, and she nodded, her shoulders stiffening. "I apologize for being so forward, Miss Andrews. I had thought you would welcome the invitation—"

"I would love to join you, but my mother is sequestered with her correspondence this afternoon and cannot accompany us.

Miss Hennessey shook her coppery curls and waved away Eloise's objection. "My abigail and a footman are in the coach, and that is enough chaperoning for a simple stroll through the park. Even sticklers would not think that untoward."

Eloise huffed. Her mother was more than a mere stickler and would not appreciate her daughter being so reckless, though no one else would think it untoward for them to be out of doors with no less than two servants accompanying them.

However, Mother was locked away in her rooms at present, unlikely to notice Eloise's absence.

"I apologize. I don't mean to sway you if you think you ought not to go," said Miss Hennessey, moving towards the door.

"Of course not," said Eloise, her resolve firming as she spoke. "I would love to join you."

Before her nerves got the better of her, Eloise bundled Miss Hennessey to the front door and retrieved their things from the footmen. It was only then that she recalled the novel in her hand, and she scoured the entry for a hiding place. Isaacs appeared and gave a subtle cough, gesturing for her to hand it over.

Tucking the novel into his pocket with a wink, he stepped forward to help Eloise with her pelisse while whispering, "Is this wise, Miss Eloise?"

"We are simply going to a park to walk for a bit and shall return before Mother notices," she whispered back.

"At least take Daniel or Gregory with you."

"Miss Hennessey's footman and abigail are accompanying us. It will be fine and proper."

Worry wrinkled the butler's brow. "I am not worried about propriety, miss. I am worried about your safety. London is dangerous."

"Not in this part of the city."

But his furrowed brow did not ease, and when the girls hurried off to the waiting coach, an Andrews footman trailed behind them and climbed onto the boot at the back. The promised abigail sat inside, her attention fixed on her needlepoint, and the Hennessy footman and coachman occupied the box seat, ensuring that the young ladies had quite the entourage.

Scouring her memory, Eloise tried to think of another time when she had been in the city without a relative accompanying her. Not that this was a solo outing, as her new friend and three servants were in attendance (four, if she counted the coachman), but still, Eloise felt euphoric. This was freedom.

"Are you a great reader?" asked Miss Hennessey. At Eloise's questioning glance, the young lady continued. "You were holding a book, and I thought you must enjoy reading."

Clutching her hands in her lap, Eloise replied, "Not a great one. Not as good as I should be, at any rate. I fear I cannot abide stodgy tomes meant to improve one's mind. I do have a fondness for novels, though my mother believes novels are a 'vulgar diversion and liable to do damage to my delicate mind.'"

"Do not say you are an avid reader of Gothic novels," said Miss Hennessey with a good-natured wrinkle of her nose.

Eloise laughed. "I am afraid to disappoint you, but I do enjoy a lurid tale. I find the works of Mrs. Radcliffe and Mrs. Shelley quite tantalizing. It is impossible not to get swept up by such stories, even if I find them ridiculous at the same time."

"And now I am afraid to disappoint you, but I find I would

much rather haunt the halls of an art gallery than read about the ridiculous haunts in those books," said Miss Hennessey.

With a dramatic sigh, Eloise shook her head. "Then I am afraid this friendship is doomed to fail, for I am not at all entertained by dusty old paintings."

Miss Hennessey laughed at that and tucked her arm into Eloise's. "We are a hopeless pair, but perhaps if I try one of your novels, I might entice you into looking at some dusty old paintings."

Eloise tried to remain stoic, though there was a spark of mirth in her eyes. "I suppose I might be willing to subject myself to such an abhorrent pastime. Perhaps."

The coach filled with laughter, and upon coming to a stop, the ladies spilled out into the afternoon air. Arm-in-arm and with a string of servants behind them, the pair walked along, their conversation skipping along with an ease that Eloise had rarely experienced. In fact, she could think of only two people with whom she'd shared such an easy friendship, and those brothers had both been absent from her life for a long time.

It was too early for the fashionable crowd to be present, which suited Eloise. The few times she'd come to Hyde Park were during that mob, and it did not allow for her to truly appreciate its beauty. If it weren't for the smell of soot hanging in the air, she could almost pretend she was in the country, enjoying a bright afternoon.

Miss Hennessey was so affable that they conversed about everything and nothing, their thoughts flitting from one topic to the next like energetic bumblebees as they strolled along the tree-lined lanes.

"Miss Andrews!" called a voice that made Eloise's steps falter.

"Isn't that the fellow who was bothering you last night?" Miss Hennessey asked as she cast a furtive glance at her companion, and Eloise's expression supplied the answer. The young lady's eyes widened, and Miss Hennessey turned them back towards the coach, though it was a fair way off.

"That scoundrel," she muttered, glancing at Patrick as he hurried to catch them. "I shan't allow him near you. Our footmen will send him on his way—"

But Eloise shook her head. "Unfortunately, he is no scoundrel. If he were, it would be far easier to be rid of him."

Miss Hennessey stopped Eloise with a determined gleam in her eye. "You needn't face him if you do not wish it. I will keep him occupied while you make your escape."

She turned to do just that, but Eloise held her in place. "I appreciate your offer, but it is unnecessary. Mr. Lennox is merely bothersome."

Miss Hennessy studied her, her brows drawing close together. "Do you care for him?"

The question shocked both of them; Miss Hennessey immediately apologized for being so forward while Eloise vehemently insisted she harbored no romantic notions for Patrick Lennox. He may not be a scoundrel, but he was no hero, either. He did not hold her heart and never would. Or rather, he never would again.

"Miss Andrews." Patrick's voice came from just behind them, and Eloise had enough forethought to school her expression before facing the gentleman. Miss Hennessey said nothing as they turned, but there were questions aplenty in her gaze. "I see you are enjoying a walk. Might I join you?"

But it was his question last night that stood center stage in Eloise's thoughts.

"Are you truly happy with him?"

Patrick had no right to question her about such a thing. Mr. Godwin was everything a lady hoped for in a husband. He would never abandon her and his family without a word when they needed him most. Though Eloise was uncertain whether Mr. Godwin would ever truly lay claim to her heart, she knew that he was infinitely preferable to Patrick, and she needed to convince him of that.

Eloise straightened her already straight shoulders. "We'd be delighted if you joined us, Mr. Lennox."

Miss Hennessey's brows drew even tighter together, though she said not a word as Eloise introduced them to one another. Though Patrick offered up his arm, Eloise ignored it and remained a polite distance apart as they continued down the lane. She kept her attention firmly on the nature around them and Miss Hennessey on her right side, but not the fellow at her left.

The trio walked silently until Miss Hennessey spoke. "I gather you two are old friends?" But that was quickly followed with, "My, we are having lovely weather today, don't you think?"

Eloise glanced at Miss Hennessey, and the manner in which the young lady's eyes widened in silent apology made Eloise want to laugh. Her new friend was a walking bumble-broth, but it was done with such artlessness that one couldn't help but like her.

"Our families are neighbors," said Patrick. "Miss Andrews and I spent our youth together. Where does your family hail from, Miss Hennessey?"

"A little village of no consequence in Surrey," she replied.

"I adore little villages," said Eloise. "I enjoy the city as well, but country life is so peaceful and beautiful."

Miss Hennessey nodded. "It's true. I am quite overcome by all that Town has to offer, but I missed seeing spring in all its glory."

Patrick smiled and added, "Like the haze of green that begins to show in the tree branches when the buds start to form."

Miss Hennessey straightened and glanced around Eloise to grin back at him. "Precisely."

Patrick's words sparked a stream of memories of all the springs they'd spent wandering the fields among the new blossoms. That smell of the snow melting away to reveal fresh soil, and the vitality floating through the air as the world awoke once more.

She felt Patrick's gaze on her, and Eloise focused on the false country setting that had been cultivated in the heart of the city. It had been so lovely just moments ago, but compared to the memories that sprung to her mind, the park paled in comparison.

"I am well acquainted with London," said Patrick in response to some question Eloise had not heard. "I lived here for several years, though I found it did not agree with me, and I returned to the country."

"What brought you back here once more?" asked Miss Hennessey.

The question stole Eloise's breath. She feigned great interest in the canopy overhead and the winding path before them, but her thoughts were fixed on Patrick's reply. His eyes turned to her once more, but Eloise would not meet them as they lingered on her face.

"My sister, Nora, is soon to be engaged to Mr. David Atwell, so I came for the inevitable celebrations."

But there was an unspoken sentiment lingering in the air, and Eloise sensed it as surely as if Patrick had spoken the whole truth aloud. That long-forgotten part of her heart had always been attuned to the man at her side, and Eloise knew he'd come to London for her.

Chapter 9

"Oh, there's a ballad seller," said Miss Hennessey, pointing to a group of vendors standing around the park entrance. Each cried out, announcing their wares, but a clear singing voice cut above the noise. "Would you mind if we stopped? I haven't heard this one, and I would love to purchase it."

"Certainly," said Eloise, and the trio turned that direction.

Several street vendors approached, hawking oranges, ribbons, pies, bootlaces, and the like, but Patrick cleared a path to the ballad seller. The girl was no more than sixteen or seventeen, and she beamed when Miss Hennessey offered a few farthings. Handing over a piece of rough paper that contained the lyrics, the singer proceeded to teach Miss Hennessey the accompanying melody.

Eloise watched as Miss Hennessey mimicked the various notes, but her thoughts were on Patrick. Her hand brushed against his, and it was only then that she realized how close she stood to him. Straightening, she stepped away.

"This reminds me of that traveling fair we snuck away to see." Patrick's voice was a low murmur, and though the noise should have swallowed it up, Eloise heard each word.

The memory of that day was as clear as the world around her. Though they'd been little more than twelve and fourteen at the time, Patrick had escorted her about like a grand lady. And when she'd mentioned how much she admired a particularly fine ribbon at one stall, he had insisted on buying it for her, though it had taken the last of his money to do so. Patrick had smiled as though he wanted nothing more in the world when he draped it across her palm.

Blinking, Eloise took a deep breath, for she was decidedly lightheaded. Her silly heart liked Patrick's nearness far too much for her good.

"I am sorry," Patrick murmured.

Those words brought her eyes straight to his, and Eloise swallowed the lump that formed at the sight of his sadness shining in his gaze.

"I hadn't meant to upset you last night, but the conversation got away from me," said Patrick. "I had intended to tell you that you have every right to be upset with me."

Her heart thumped against her chest, pounding her ribcage as though trying to break free, and Eloise couldn't decide if it was an unpleasant feeling. It was painful yet thrilling, crushing yet enlivening, and she didn't know what that fickle organ was trying to tell her.

"You have no reason to forgive me," said Patrick, taking a step closer and lowering his voice. "I have no right to ask it, but you need to know I regret my behavior—whether you accept my contrition or not."

In full sunlight, his eyes looked more blue than grey, and they sent a flush of warmth through her. Eloise had always struggled to keep her wits about her when held in his gaze; it was as though time would grind to a halt, making her a willing captive in that moment.

And then he'd left her.

"You refused to see me," she whispered back. "I tried to visit you, but you would not even *see* me. Then you disappeared without a word."

His fingers brushed hers, entwining in a feather-light touch. "When Kelly died, I was lost and broken, and it took me years to come back to myself."

"You weren't the only one to lose Kelly." Eloise's chin trembled, and she fought for her composure. "I lost my two closest friends that day."

"You were never just a friend, Eloise." His voice was low and rich, with an earnestness that nestled into her heart and brought tears to her eyes. Patrick reached for her face but caught himself, glancing at the crowd around them. "I know there is no way to undo the hurt I've caused, but please tell me how I might earn your forgiveness."

Her traitorous heart had the words ready on her lips, but sense gave way and held her firm. The thought of having her Patrick in her life once more was an enticement almost too strong to fight, but her eyes turned to the scraggly scar lining his cheek, reminding Eloise of all those dark, ugly years that she had mourned him. And she would never recover if it happened again.

"Patrick..." she began, but the words fled her. Eloise could not accept or reject him. The turn of events left her so befuddled that she could not make sense of her own desires. "I don't know if I can forgive you."

He stood firm before her, seeming so strong and self-possessed, but the light in his eyes dimmed for a brief moment, giving him the look of the tortured Gothic villain Maria and Susie thought him to be. But that dejection disintegrated as a new resolve entered his gaze, his muscles tightening as he nodded.

"Then I shall keep trying," he said, squeezing her hand. "You are worth fighting for, Eloise, and I shan't give up until I am certain there is no hope. I broke us, and I shall set us right again."

"Patrick..."

But it was in that moment that Miss Hennessey rejoined them, tucking her purchased lyrics into her reticule while humming the new melody, which made Eloise realize how close she was to Patrick. Her skirts were flirting with his toes, his body nearly touching hers. Jerking away, Eloise turned from him and went to Miss Hennessey, taking the young lady's arm.

"I am quite fatigued," said Eloise, turning her attention from Patrick. "Perhaps it is time to return to the coach."

Miss Hennessey's eyes widened. "Of course. I do apologize for keeping you so long. I had not meant to take so much time."

"It was a sudden turn," said Eloise, patting her friend's arm. "You must promise to sing your new song for me."

The pair began the trek back to the carriage with Patrick striding beside them. Eloise clung to Miss Hennessey, for she did not trust herself around him. Distance was best. Miss Hennessey glanced between the pair, her brows pinched together. Eloise knew she had questions aplenty, but the lady showed admirable restraint and said not a word as they hurried back to their equipage.

Patrick remained equally tight-lipped as he handed the pair into the carriage, though his grip lingered on Eloise. With a tip of his hat, he bade them farewell, and Eloise saw another flash of steely resolve in his expression as they departed.

"Are you quite all right?" asked Miss Hennessey, turning a worried look to Eloise. "I didn't intend to leave you alone with Mr. Lennox for such a long period, but the song was far more difficult to learn than I had anticipated."

"Do not fret."

"If Mr. Lennox upset you, I shall give him a piece of my mind," said Miss Hennessey with a fierce scowl that would do a puppy proud.

That declaration brought a smile to Eloise's lips, and she squeezed her friend's arm. "I assure you all is well. Mr. Lennox was a perfect gentleman. We simply have a complicated history."

There was silence in the coach for a few brief moments, though Eloise swore she heard Miss Hennessey's thoughts churning. When her words finally emerged, they came in a hurried jumble.

"I know we are newly acquainted, and you have no reason to confide in me, but if you are in need of a listening ear, I offer up my own. I find that speaking about one's troubles can help."

Most ladies had female friends who filled the role of confidant, but Eloise had never been blessed with that sort of friendship. Her mother was certainly not one to empathize with plights, and Eloise did not share that sort of relationship with her sisters, either. Though she had friends aplenty, they were good for passing an evening together and not the type to entrust with secrets.

Patrick had once filled that role, but as he'd surrendered that position, Eloise found herself in dire need of counsel.

Looking at Miss Hennessey, Eloise felt a desire to share all—not simply because she needed it, but because instinct told her that Miss Hennessey was a kindred soul and a loyal friend. But with the abigail sitting opposite them, Eloise knew it was best to hold her tongue.

"Do not worry about Hill," said Miss Hennessey with a wave. The lady's maid glanced from her sewing to her young charge with a saucy twinkle in her eye, and Miss Hennessey smiled at the aging retainer. "She is good with secrets, and I give you my word she will not repeat anything she overhears."

With no more prompting, Eloise told all, sparing no detail as she unraveled her story and heartbreak. The coachman was ordered to continue on, and the carriage wove through the streets as the story unfolded. In the private confines of the vehicle, Eloise was able to unburden herself. Miss Hennessey—Kitty—offered up no judgment, no critique or commentary. She merely listened as Eloise spoke of all that had passed between the pair.

It wasn't until she finished that Kitty finally spoke. "Did he give no excuse for his behavior?"

"None, but there was no time to go into such detail."

"Perhaps you should wait to decide until you know the whole story," said Kitty, her expression downcast. "I know he hurt you, Eloise, but tragedy can cause even good people to act contrary to their nature."

Eloise straightened. "Are you saying you think I ought to forgive him so easily?"

"Certainly not, but do not allow your heart to harden past the point where you cannot accept an earnest attempt to redeem himself." Kitty paused, and then asked, "Do you think his intentions sincere?"

Eloise reflected on that, battling through her confusion to discover the truth beneath it. "I believe him to be sincere at present, but I do not know if I can trust him to remain true to his word."

Kitty smiled and squeezed Eloise's arm. "Luckily, you need not decide yet. Do not lose your head nor harden your heart. Give him time to prove whether he is worthy. And in the meantime, I have two listening ears whenever you have need of them."

"Thank you, Kitty..." But her next thoughts vanished when she caught sight of a familiar face in the crowd outside.

The coach moved slowly along the roads, navigating through the thick afternoon traffic and giving Eloise ample time to see her brother-in-law walking along the street.

Eloise raised her hand to wave at him, but paused as he knocked on one of the townhouse doors and was greeted by a buxom woman with arms held wide. She gaped as her sister's husband took the woman into his embrace with a kiss that was fiery and wanton. Cheeks flushed, Eloise dropped her gaze, though not fast enough to miss James nudging the door shut behind him.

"Are you unwell?" asked Kitty, glancing in the direction of Eloise's gaze. "Did you see something upsetting?"

Eloise couldn't countenance that her eyes had seen the truth, and she shook her head, making some half-hearted excuse about feeling lightheaded. Thoughts of Patrick fled at what she had witnessed, and she struggled to make sense of it.

But it had been James. Eloise knew it.

Chapter 10

Emmeline
Age Eleven

Working the needle through the linen, Emmeline made another stitch. And another. She had already put dozens in, yet it was only the beginning of this interminable sampler. This was not the first of its kind she'd rendered, and Emmeline could still not see the use in expending so much effort for such a useless thing.

"No, no, no," said her governess, leaning over Emmeline's shoulder to point out her flaw. Without looking up from her work, Emmeline moved on to the next stitch, which she took great pains to make even more askew than the others.

"You shall never excel if you do not take greater effort with your needlework," said Miss Hardy with a sigh and a shake of her head, which set her ringlets bouncing. "How will you ever find a proper beau if you produce such shoddy work?"

Emmeline held back a scoff, keeping her face composed as she asked with perfectly feigned sincerity, "At what stage of courtship does one reveal one's needlework?"

"Every proper lady has her thread and needle nearby to show her industrious nature, and you must be found working on it when visitors call," said Miss Hardy. "Neat stitches and intricate designs show determination and can serve as a mark of superiority."

Eying her drooping flower, Emmeline knew it was a lost cause. Whether she had the skill or not was immaterial, for she had no interest in mastering it. Needlework was so rigid and lifeless, and though Emmeline appreciated the talent it took to produce the intricate detail, she had no desire to do so herself. Not that what she desired mattered to her governess.

If only she could join Priscilla in the nursery; Emmeline would love an hour or two to play with her little sister. The lass would soon be consigned to Emmeline's dreaded fate, but she still had a few scant months before she moved from nursery to classroom.

Though Simon's rare letters home described school as an unending torture, Emmeline wondered what it would be like to join him in his lessons. She had no interest in science or Latin, which were his subjects *du jour*, but even such staid lectures must be preferable to Miss Hardy's endless nattering. At least Simon had other lads in his classes; only she and Miss Hardy occupied that tiny room in a forgotten corner of the house.

Making the next stitch, Emmeline found herself struggling to keep hold of the needle. Her shoulders slumped as she listened to Miss Hardy's ramblings without hearing a word. The governess was an endless deluge of words but had the unfortunate habit of saying little of value and rarely acknowledging that anyone else might wish to speak. Casting her thoughts to the previous week, Emmeline realized Miss Hardy hadn't allowed her to speak of anything significant in all that time. Other than the occasional response to Miss Hardy's instructions, Emmeline's life was mute.

Glancing to the window, she shifted in her seat, wishing she were free of the classroom. Free of Miss Hardy. Free to explore the gardens and fields. To breathe fresh air. To feel the sun on her skin. The more Emmeline thought of what lay outside, the closer the walls pressed in on her.

A knock sounded at the door, and Emmeline shot to her feet before it opened, her needlework cast to the side.

"Papa!" She greeted him with a wide grin as he crossed the threshold. Going over to him, Emmeline reached for a hug and received a cursory pat on the shoulder.

"How are you faring with your lessons today?" he asked. Though his question was directed to Emmeline, his eyes sought Miss Hardy.

"We are practicing my needlepoint, Papa," said Emmeline.

"I hope you are working hard. It is the mark of a well-bred lady," he said, without looking at his daughter.

Emmeline fought back a blush, afraid he might discover where her thoughts had been mere moments before. "Of course."

"I need to speak with Miss Hardy."

"Certainly, sir," said the governess, giving him a curtsy. "Continue working on your sampler, Emmeline, and I will check your progress when I return."

With a sigh, Emmeline returned to her seat, retrieving her dreaded needlework as Papa led Miss Hardy from the room with his hand at the small of her back. Their footsteps retreated some distance, fading into silence.

There was not a sound to be heard. No tick of the clock. No ambient movement. Not a word or breath. It was as though she were trapped in the silence. Emmeline tapped her toe against the floor just to give some life to the room as she worked, but it was not enough. As much as she disliked Miss Hardy's chattering, the oppressive silence was worse.

Emmeline moved to the window, staring out at the beautiful summer day. Her fingers traced the pane of glass, and she wished she could leave. Even a few minutes in the garden would be a blessed relief.

Without a clock, Emmeline couldn't know how much time had passed, but it had been a fair bit. Going to the door, Emmeline peeked out, looking and listening for any sign of her governess.

A few minutes. That was all she needed.

Emmeline hurried down the hall, slipping silently through the corridors until she was free of the suffocating walls. Abandoning her slippers and stockings beside the doorstep, Emmeline sprinted into the garden, her fingers brushing the flowers and leaves as she passed. She stopped at a patch of grass, sinking her toes into the blades as she sucked in a great lungful of warm summer air heavy with the scent of blossoms.

The world was awash with the fragrances and colors of the garden. The delphiniums, sweet peas, nigella, stocks, allium, and foxglove were in fine form, and Emmeline admired each one. Mr. George had added a few new friends to the beds, and she needed to ask him their names the next time she saw him.

The thick blossoms begged to be plucked and woven into a crown, but there was no time at present. Emmeline ought to return, but she couldn't bear to lock herself inside once more. However, neither could she bear to face Miss Hardy's wrath should she be caught wandering about in such a fashion.

With each step back to the house, her shoulders slumped, and that pressing feeling returned. Back to the solitude and silence. Plucking one blossom, Emmeline held it close to her nose, allowing the scent to chase away some of the darkness that crept into her heart. She would be back to spend time with all her lovely flowers.

Emmeline stepped into her slippers but did not bother with her stockings; instead, she wrapped them around her hand as she wandered back to the classroom.

Then she heard her father's voice and Miss Hardy's tittering laugh.

Ducking back, Emmeline jumped into an open doorway, hiding behind the frame. Peeking out, she saw the door to her father's bedchamber open, and Miss Hardy stepped out, straightening her skirts with a giggle. Papa grabbed the chit by the hand and pulled Miss Hardy flush to him.

"John, stop," said Miss Hardy, though her tone contradicted her words. "I must return to your daughter."

"Balderdash. Her lessons aren't important," he mumbled, and Emmeline covered her ears against the ardent sounds coming from the pair as their conversation lapsed into fevered kissing.

Long moments later, Miss Hardy whispered, "I must return."

"Stay with me, my love," said Papa.

Miss Hardy sighed, sending a shiver of disgust down Emmeline's spine. It was naught but a load of tripe, yet the silly governess was eating heaping spoonfuls of it as though it were a chocolate gateau. Miss Hardy was a fool if she believed the words Papa tossed out with little care or meaning. Their tryst would end as they all did. The only question was whether or not Miss Hardy would be in the family way when she was dismissed.

The bedchamber door shut, and Emmeline couldn't wait another moment. With silent steps, she sped past, ignoring the sickening moans coming from the pair inside. This was a scene she had stumbled on one too many times, and the memories came roaring back into her mind like demons sent to torture her.

There was only one solution.

Sneaking past her classroom, Emmeline crept into the nursery to find Nurse Jones in her usual chair while Priscilla played silently in the corner with her dolls. Motioning for her sister, Emmeline took the child into the empty schoolroom and sat on the window seat. Priscilla climbed onto her elder sister's lap and wrapped her arms around Emmeline's neck.

"I missed you, sweetling," said Emmeline, rubbing Priscilla's back.

"Me, too." Priscilla burrowed into Emmeline's neck, a happy sigh on her lips. "I hate Nurse Jones."

"Don't say that," she said, but Priscilla tightened her grip, and Emmeline knew that they both needed a distraction. "Have I ever told you the story of the Raven King who lived in the Great Forest at the edge of the world?"

Priscilla released her hold on Emmeline and leaned back to

give her a smile. "With his six golden balls."

Beaming, Emmeline brushed a strand of hair behind Priscilla's ear. "A long time ago in a place so very far from here, there was a kingdom on the edge of an enchanted forest..."

Chapter 11

A woman of fifty years should have more control, but Emmeline was incapable of maintaining her composure. Heedless of the damage to her gown, she curled up on her bed and stared through her tears at the portrait clutched in her hand. Though Joanna was only sixteen when she'd sat for it, it was a good likeness and one of the only images she had of her dear, sweet daughter. She had no such remembrances for Patience.

Thumbs brushing against the metal frame, Emmeline's vision blurred.

The fresher grief of Joanna's loss fed into that older pain, opening the wounds Patience's sudden departure had left all those years ago. Together, they mingled into overwhelming agony.

Without a portrait of Patience, the child's features had grown foggy in her memory, though Emmeline still recalled the sweet, timid smile she'd inherited from her father. They'd had only six years with her, and the memories were too few. Emmeline longed for her journals tucked away in their country estate; she ached to remember those little details that were fading into obscurity.

But Emmeline's memories of her eldest daughter were still fresh. All the hours they'd spent in the garden teaching Joanna the names of the flowers, and afternoons filled with needle-point; Emmeline never found a liking for that odious pastime, but Joanna had adored it. The years flew through Emmeline's mind, and she watched anew as Joanna threw herself in the whirl of parties and balls. Falling in love. The wedding. Her first child followed soon by a second.

The feel of her daughter's hand as Joanna fought through that ordeal. The blessed moment of Katherine's first cries followed by the ragged sound of Joanna's final breaths. Wracked with sobs, Emmeline buried her face in the pillow, as though that might block the recollection of the panic that followed as they fought to save her life. But none of it kept Joanna from quietly drifting from this world while her mother watched.

Surely, she should be stronger. It had been nearly two years since that awful day, and Emmeline had thought her heart healed enough not to be undone by such a simple moment. But the mere sight of a park from a passing carriage was enough to remind her of Joanna and rip open the wound she'd thought had healed.

The doorknob twisted, and Emmeline covered her mouth to mute her tears.

Hand on the doorknob, Norman paused. He'd stood thusly many a time, but rarely did he give in to the urge to open it. There was little reason to hope that his wife would welcome this intrusion; however, the sounds of Emmeline's pain were too demanding to be ignored. They called to him from his bedchamber, begging him to comfort her, and his arms longed to hold his wife once more.

"I wish to be alone," she said as the door opened. Her voice was fairly even, but Emmeline excelled at hiding her true self.

Norman moved to the bedside, and Emmeline bolted upright, rubbing at her face—but there was no hiding the evidence of her tears. Silently, he waited for a stroke of brilliance to guide his actions, but nothing came. Emmeline fidgeted with her gown, her eyes fixed on her hands as she smoothed the wrinkled fabric.

Joanna's portrait sat on the bed beside her.

Picking it up, Norman took its place on the bed beside his wife and stared at the image of his daughter.

"I had forgotten you had this," he murmured. It was not as fine as the accompanying painting hanging at home in Pendleton Hall, but it captured his daughter's innocent beauty, and he treasured the opportunity to see her again.

"Might I borrow this and have it copied?" he asked, glancing at Emmeline.

Her eyes were wide, her chin trembling as she watched him. She held herself with her usual rigid posture, but there was a brittleness to it that made Norman think she would shatter with the slightest touch. Setting the miniature aside, he reached for Emmeline's hands, which were twisted in her lap. Her eyes followed his movements as he rested his hand atop hers, and they sat there for several long, silent moments.

Then a sob ripped from her throat, and Emmeline turned to him, burying her face in his neck. Without hesitation, Norman brought his arms around her, his own heart breaking to see her so pained. And yet, joy coursed through him—which brought an additional pang of guilt. He found no pleasure in seeing her so broken, but getting a glimpse past that cold façade was elating. His dear, loving Emmeline still existed.

"I miss her so," Emmeline whimpered through ragged breaths. "Whenever I feel at peace, something comes along to remind me she is gone."

"I know, dearheart," he crooned, holding her tight and giving the only comfort he could. His hand rubbed her back as he held her to his chest, her tears soaking his lapels and cravat.

Even when her cries lessened, Emmeline remained in his embrace, and Norman was afraid to speak lest it disturb this precious moment. He caught the scent of rosewater, and time stripped away, leaving him a besotted man holding his sweetheart. His darling Emmeline. The sensitive soul who had entranced him from the first moment.

"I feel as though I am losing all my children," she said, a few lingering sniffles cutting through her words.

Emmeline stared into the distance, and one of her hands moved to fiddle with the buttons on his waistcoat. It had been years since she had done so, and Norman longed to place a kiss on her head, but he did not want to draw attention to her unconscious movement.

"Marcus has all but disappeared after Joanna..." Her words trailed off as she could not speak the word. "He won't respond to my letters, and I fear I shan't see my grandchildren again. And Kenneth hardly speaks to me because his wife dislikes me so; I've tried to befriend her, but she rebuffs my every attempt."

She paused, her breath hitching. "Lucinda is disinterested at the best of times, and Noah never comes home. To say nothing of Eloise, who is forever belligerent and resentful. I've tried my best, but they're determined to cut me from their lives."

Pulling away, Emmeline gazed into Norman's eyes, her own filled with despair. "I love them all so much, and I've tried my best to give them a happy life, but I feel as though I have failed them as a mother. What have I done wrong?"

Norman's breath froze in his lungs, as though the slightest movement might disturb the beauty of this moment. He could not count the times he'd wished to discuss this very issue with Emmeline, but it's sudden appearance had him blinking as he struggled to form his thoughts into words. Knowing what he wished to say was easy enough, but Norman wasn't certain it was what he *should* say.

What would help Emmeline to see the truth? To change her ways? And what would cause her to retreat into old habits once more?

"Emmeline..."

But the bedchamber door opened, and Morris entered. The lady's maid paused before dropping into a quick curtsy. "Sorry, madam, but you told me to come when it was time to dress for dinner."

Emmeline stood, shoving her emotions away and locking them beneath that frosty exterior before the servant had finished speaking. "Yes, thank you, Morris. Is Miss Andrews dressing?"

"She hasn't returned from visiting Mrs. Strickland, madam."

The slight flare of Emmeline's nostrils was the only outward expression of emotion, but it was enough for Norman to know she was not pleased. "What do you mean?"

"She went out with Miss Hennessey this afternoon..."

Those nostrils flared even more.

"...and returned for a few minutes before setting off again to visit Mrs. Strickland."

"Thank you, Morris, but it appears I will not be needing your services at present," said Emmeline. "Let Cook know that dinner will be late and have the coach prepared."

"Forgive me, madam, but Miss Andrews took the coach."

Another flare. "Then have Isaacs call for a hackney. I need to fetch Miss Andrews home."

"Yes, madam." The lady's maid gave another curtsy and hurried out the door, shutting it behind her.

Emmeline's lips tightened, her hands clenching together, though she retained her usual aloofness. Standing, Norman moved to the door. There was no point in speaking with Emmeline now, not when she'd reverted to a replica of his mother. But he halted when Emmeline spoke.

"I thank you for your comfort, Norman," she said, her tone lacking any of the warmth or emotion that he knew lurked beneath the surface. "And I apologize for my outburst."

"You speak as though offering comfort to my wife is a terrible burden," he replied, crossing his arms. "We've lost two children, and it is natural for you to be overwrought at times."

"Emotion is the plaything of the lower class." Her tone was even and her words perfectly delivered, and it sent a shiver of revulsion through Norman.

"When you say such things, it's as if my mother has risen from the grave."

Emmeline smiled. Or rather, the corner of her lips twitched faintly in an approximation of a smile. "Mother Andrews was the best of ladies."

"She was a cold-hearted shrew." Though Norman had never spoken the words aloud, doing so released a bit of pressure from his heart as though the vice holding it had suddenly released.

That broke through Emmeline's calm reserves, and she gaped at him. "She was a good woman! She may not have been as demonstrative as you wished her to be, but she wasn't some common farmer's wife. She was a lady and comported herself as such."

"She was a cold-hearted shrew, Emmeline, and everyone knows that but you," he said with a shake of his head.

Emmeline's expression pinched, a blaze of fire burning in her eyes. "You have no idea how blessed you were to have a mother like her. She was kind to me in ways that my own never was."

"My mother was an unfeeling creature who turned my loving wife into a heartless copy of herself."

Norman watched that horrid self-reserve lock back into place as the anger drained from Emmeline. Standing before him was not the woman he adored but a lifeless approximation of her. And he hated his mother for it.

"I do apologize if you are unhappy with me, but I am doing what is necessary to better my children's life, though you clearly do not understand that," she said, gathering her hands in front of her with that classic lady of the manor stance his mother had been so fond of. "Speaking of which, I must attend to my daughter before she ruins her reputation."

Sweeping out of the bedchamber, Emmeline left Norman alone, and his shoulders sagged as he wondered if his true wife would ever return to him.

Chapter 12

This was silly.

An unwelcome intrusion.

It was none of her business, but Eloise couldn't rest while the question plagued her. Though she'd clearly seen her brother-in-law kissing a woman who was most certainly not his wife, there must have been some misunderstanding or mistake. The doubt was driving her mad, which was why she was standing in her sister's parlor.

Eloise paced the floor as she awaited Lucinda. She didn't know if the nerves were from the coming interview or the impending doom that awaited her if Mother discovered her missing, but that anxiety forced her to move. If only she knew how to broach the subject; there was no easy manner in which to ask if James was an immoral cur.

"You look quite undone, Eloise. Is something the matter?" asked Lucinda, striding into the parlor.

With a laugh, which was meant to be disarming but verged on frantic, Eloise waved away the concern and sat with her sister on the sofa. "I simply wished to see my sister. It's been too long."

"At this hour? I was about to dress for dinner when you arrived." Glancing at the otherwise empty room, Lucinda gave her sister a stern look. "And you are alone?"

"I brought a servant in the coach, and I am visiting family, so there is no impropriety."

Lucinda leveled an incredulous look at her. "Mother would not approve of such an outing, and we saw each other just four days ago. Now, what is the matter?"

Eloise gave what she hoped was an airy smile and grasped for the first excuse that came to mind. "Mother has been beastly of late, and I needed to escape her. I thought a visit with my sister and her family would do the trick. Are the children around?" Eloise paused before tacking on, "And James? Is he here, dressing for dinner, too?"

A single brow rose as her elder sister regarded her. "The children are in the nursery, and James has been at his club all afternoon. You and Mother are often at odds, but you've never come looking for refuge before."

"Then James is not at home, but is most certainly at his club?"

"He dines there when the mood strikes him." Lucinda's tone was staid, but she watched her sister with a confused gaze.

"Of course." Eloise nodded and smiled with a slight sigh as the tension eased from her. James was at his club, spending time with his chums and playing cards—not entangled in the arms of another woman. "I could've sworn I saw him on the street not an hour ago, but I must've been mistaken."

Lucinda's expression shifted into a derisive smile, and she scoffed. "You mean you saw him over on Barrington?"

Eloise bit her lip and shifted in her seat. "I don't know what street it was, but clearly, it wasn't him if he is at his club. And it is a mighty relief. For a bad moment, I thought the worst of him."

"Because you discovered him visiting his ladybird in the townhouse he keeps for her?" Lucinda asked with another arched eyebrow.

The blood in her veins frosted over, chilling her through as Eloise gaped at Lucinda. "How did you guess?"

Her sister laughed, though it was not a happy thing. "Do you really think gentlemen spend as much time at their clubs as they claim? What did you see?"

Eloise blinked, her mind struggling to comprehend this turn in the conversation. "He stopped at a townhouse where he was met by a woman..." Her cheeks blazed, and her words faltered as she recalled the wanton display.

"You need say no more, for your expression speaks volumes," said Lucinda with a shake of her head. "It appears James and I need to have a discussion about discretion."

"Discretion?" Eloise gaped, leaning onto the edge of her seat. "You are not upset about the..." She dropped her voice to a whisper. "...other lady?"

"Mademoiselle Justine is hardly a lady," replied Lucinda with a shake of her head. "*Mademoiselle Justine,*" she repeated with a mocking sneer. "As if anyone really believes that Manchester doxy is a French *émigré.*"

Eloise had no response to that, for her body was frozen through, stiff and unmoving as a statue.

Lucinda's expression softened, though it held more pity than concern. "Are you really that naive, Eloise? All men have mistresses. It is part of life. They have their needs, and I am grateful he has someone else to see to them. I've done my part in furthering the family line."

"But..." Eloise stuttered the word a few times before the rest of her words could form. "How can he carry on like that and claim to love you?"

Her sister's eyebrows shot upwards, and her voice took on a pitying tone. "Love? Marriage is a contract. It's about merging bloodlines, fortunes, and social positioning. Love has no part in it."

"That is absurd!"

Lucinda huffed, shaking her head. "I've seen enough of love and marriage to know they don't mix. Men play the lovelorn swain during courtship, but that disappears the moment they marry. What need have they of such romantic overtures when their lady is already snared? Those who claim to have loving marriages are merely putting on a good show."

Just as Eloise was formulating a valid argument, the parlor doors opened, and Mother strode into the room. Though she would never be so gauche as to cause a scene, there was a fire in her eyes that Eloise hadn't seen before. With clipped words, she thanked Lucinda for looking after Eloise, and they took their leave.

Once Eloise was deposited in the coach and they were on their way, her mother finally spoke. "What possessed you to do such a foolhardy thing?"

"Kitty Hennessey is allowed to travel with escorts, so why shouldn't I?"

Her mother clasped her arms and gave as much of a scowl as the lady was wont to do. "*Miss* Hennessey has little reputation to protect."

"*Kitty* is a good person and a dear friend," said Eloise, crossing her arms.

Mother's nostrils gave a slight flare before she spoke. "Whether or not she is good is immaterial. She is not appropriate company, and I will not have her reputation blackening yours. Nor will I allow you near her corrupting influence. Or did you think I wouldn't discover your outing with her?"

"We had two footmen and a maid. We were hardly without protection or chaperoning! Plenty of young ladies are allowed that privilege, so why can't I?" Eloise jutted out her chin, her muscles tensing.

"Because you are my daughter, and though you may not appreciate my efforts, I will do everything in my power to ensure your reputation is pristine. I will not allow anyone to ruin your future," said Mother, her tone so final that Eloise knew there was no use in arguing. Though that did not mean that she accepted the dictate.

In fact, she should invite the Hennesseys to tea: Mother

would never withdraw an invitation once extended. Eloise smiled to herself and vowed to write Kitty the moment they returned home.

"But you have not answered my question," the lady continued when Eloise gave no further protest. "Why could you not wait until tomorrow? I would've gladly taken you to visit Lucinda if you were so desperate to see her."

Eloise sat silent for a moment before replying. "It could not wait. I needed to speak with her immediately."

"About what?"

"I saw something unpleasant..." Though Eloise did not wish to recall the previous conversation, she found herself unable to move past Lucinda's stark declaration. It picked at her, worming itself through her thoughts until it was the only thing she could think about. As much as she wanted to ignore her mother and return home in silence, curiosity drove her to speak.

"Do all men have mistresses?" blurted Eloise in a grand imitation of Kitty Hennessey's awkward forthrightness.

Her mother's eyes widened for mere seconds before the shock disappeared as though it had never existed. "Where did you hear such a thing?"

"Lucinda," she replied, her hand rising to grip the pendant at her neck. Twisting it along the chain, Eloise explained, "She said all men are unfaithful to their wives."

Mother remained silent for several moments before asking, "You saw James doing something indiscreet, didn't you?"

Eloise did not meet her mother's eyes as she nodded.

"Yes," came Mother's reply. When Eloise met her mother's gaze, there was the barest hint of sadness there. It disappeared as quickly as the shock did before it, and Eloise was left to wonder if she was imagining these emotions as Mother continued, "All men are unfaithful. Though there are plenty of women who are just as guilty."

Sucking in a quick breath, Eloise's gaze fell to the floor of the carriage as a lead weight settled in her stomach. The scattered, dizzying thoughts that had filled her head fled, leaving her in a vast nothingness.

"All men?" Eloise finally whispered. "Even Father?"

There was a pause before the quiet answer came. "Yes."

Eloise longed for a cup of tea or cider or anything that might quench the barren desert in her mouth, and she bit down on her lips to keep the tears from coming. She did not have a weak constitution, but for the second time in less than a day, she felt faint. Reaching up, Eloise touched a hand to her head.

Though she'd never thought her parents' marriage a loving one, her father was a good, honest man. The type who honored his marriage vows and treated his wife with respect, if nothing else. Eloise could not reconcile the man she knew and loved with the type who spent afternoons in illicit townhouses.

"I cannot believe it," said Eloise, shaking her head. "I am not fool enough to believe all gentlemen are faithful to their marriage vows, but Father would never behave in such an underhanded manner."

Her mother's face turned to the window so Eloise could not see her expression. Not that it would have mattered, for there was little emotion to be found on her visage.

"Whether you believe it is immaterial as it has no bearing on the truth. It is the way of men," said Mother.

Her mother's words mixed with Lucinda's, and their combined weight pressed upon her thoughts, crushing her reality as readily as a flower beneath a boot. The coach was stifling, and Eloise longed to run to her bedchamber and lock herself away from all that had happened.

Mother spoke, but Eloise did not hear the words. She focused on the window, but her eyes did not see the passing buildings or people. The ride was interminable, intolerable, uncomfortable, and every other horrid descriptor available in the English language. Trapped in that stuffy box, Eloise could not think of anything other than a frantic desire to be free of it.

Her life was not filled with many surprises. It was quiet and rather simple—to her way of thinking, at any rate. Yet the past few days had seen an upending of those familiar things. Though she could not lay all the blame on Patrick's doorstep, he'd been a harbinger of the unrest.

Ignoring all else, Eloise hurried from the carriage the moment she was free to do so, scurrying up the stairs in a most undignified (but thoroughly necessary) manner, not sparing a backward glance as she hurried to her bedchamber and shut the door behind her. Throwing off her bonnet, she fell onto the bed and clutched a pillow. It was blessedly silent, and Eloise burrowed into her covers.

She wanted to cry. Perhaps that might release the pressure building in her head. But no tears came. They always appeared when she wished them gone, and now that she needed a good sob, they were being entirely uncooperative.

A timid knock at the door broke through the mountain of blankets, and Eloise shoved them aside to snap, "Leave me be!"

"Sorry, miss, but a message arrived for you," came the tremulous reply.

Wanting nothing more than to send the young maid away, Eloise fought to keep herself from lashing out; the poor girl didn't deserve such treatment. Shoving aside the pillow and blankets, Eloise forced herself upright and called for the maid to enter.

The girl wasn't much younger than Eloise, and the maid looked ready to shake apart as she approached. With a trembling curtsy, Lucy offered up the letter and a small linen bundle, and then hurried out the door the moment her task was completed. Eloise liked Lucy and felt a niggling of guilt for having been such a beast to her, but thoughts of the maid faded when Eloise saw her name scrawled across the envelope.

It was handwriting she knew all too well. Eloise had read dozens upon dozens of letters written in this hand, and though it had altered somewhat since the last time she had seen it, there was no mistaking Patrick's penmanship. Laying the letter on the nightstand, she turned her attention to the accompanying bundle.

Tugging at the twine that held the edges of the handkerchief together, Eloise opened the linen to find caramels resting inside. Lifting one to her nose, she breathed in the scent of butter and sugar, and though she had no appetite, Eloise dropped a piece onto her tongue. That heavenly taste made her smile, lightening her heavy heart as the flavor called forth glorious memories of her childhood.

Eloise ran her fingers over Patrick's monogram in the corner of the handkerchief, and though she had not thought to read the letter at present, curiosity got the better of her, and she reached for the envelope.

My Dearest Eloise,

I sit here, uncertain about how to begin such a letter. It is something I should have written long ago, but I fear I've been too cowardly to do so. Perhaps it would be better to speak to you directly, but I mustn't delay this any further. Especially as you seem determined to avoid me. You deserve an explanation.

I killed Kelly.

Eloise's eyes widened at those three words, and she shook her head at that lunacy. She'd surmised Patrick's guilt over the accident—it was only natural after surviving when his brother had not—but to make such an accusation against himself sickened her.

No doubt, you are thinking I am a fool for writing such a thing, listing all the reasons I am wrong, and planning the scolding you are going to give me when we see each other next.

Eloise scowled at those prophetic words.

But it is true. I was driving the coach when it overturned, and more than that, it was my pride that put us in such a dangerous position. If I had given up the reins when bidden by the coachman, the accident might not have happened. Kelly's death was unintentional, but it was a direct result of my arrogance.

Eloise touched the stain where Patrick's tears had smeared the ink, and her own eyes filled at the sight of it.

I cannot begin to describe what that did to me, Eloise. Every time I saw my mother's red eyes or heard her muffled cries, that guilt grew until the only peace I could find was buried at the bottom of a bottle. I spent five years hunting for that peace.

Tears trickled down Eloise's cheeks as she remembered him at the cemetery, clutching that horrid bottle as though his life depended on it. The memory of Patrick broken and collapsed atop Kelly's grave had haunted her.

I left you and my family because I could not face the sympathy and consolations. I thought I didn't deserve such forgiveness. I felt like a monster and wanted to wallow in the misery I felt. There were so many times when I wanted to find my way back to you, but I truly believed I did not deserve you. I was poisoned by my own self-loathing.

Eloise's tears dropped onto the paper, mingling with the remnants of Patrick's.

And then one day I woke to see how far I'd fallen, and I despised the man I'd become. At present, I cannot bring myself to tell you what brought about that change of heart, but know that for the first time since losing Kelly, I hoped to find redemption. However, it was not easy to pull myself free of the trap I had crawled into; the drink had too firm a grip on me.

I wanted to speak to you. See you. Write to you. Anything. But I knew I was still too broken. Only now do I feel as

though I have healed and am worthy of declaring myself
to you. I only hope it is not too late for me to make amends,
my dearest friend.

P.L.

With the taste of the confectionary on her tongue and his
heartfelt letter in her hands, Eloise stared at those final words.
    "...my dearest friend."
Perhaps some ladies preferred an ardent declaration of
love, but to Eloise, those three little words were as dear to her
as any flowery speeches. They sunk deep into her heart, dredg-
ing up memories of all the years they had spent together.

Standing, Eloise took the letter to her armoire and opened
the bottommost drawer. Hidden beneath a pile of gloves and
handkerchiefs was a bundle of letters. Kneeling, she untied the
ribbon. The color had not faded, and it was still as lovely as the
day Patrick had purchased it for her. She still loved the feel of
the silk wrapped around her fingers.

Taking the topmost letter from its envelope, she carefully
unfolded it. The creases were so worn that the letter was nearly
in pieces, and she knew its contents well enough that she did
not need to read it to remember what it said.

Patrick's last letter. He'd laughed about the foolishness of
sending such a thing right before he was about to board a coach
for home, but he knew how much she adored receiving post. It
spoke of simple things. A vast array of nothingness that meant
all the more to her, for it had arrived after Kelly's death.

And now that Patrick was returned to her, Eloise found herself thinking of things she hadn't allowed herself to ponder in a
good many years. Was there still a chance for them?

But Lucinda's warnings cut through her warm memories.
Men were unfaithful creatures. Fickle. They pursued until they
caught their prize, and then abandoned her to spend countless
hours "at their club." A pain stabbed at Eloise's temple, and she
winced, rubbing at the megrim that had been building for the
past few hours. Her thoughts were too muddled and her heart

too conflicted for there to be any rational decisions made to-night.

Tucking the newest letter in among the rest of Patrick's missives, Eloise returned to the bed and hid under the pillows. Life had been simpler yesterday.

Chapter 13

Emmeline
Age Sixteen

Raising a hand to shield her eyes, Emmeline stared across the glimmering waters of Bryer's Pond. A hint of gold edged the trees round about, and the air held the promise of autumn. Though part of her mourned summer's loss, Emmeline longed for the crisp winter days when the world was wrapped in a blanket of snow.

"Shouldn't we return?" asked Priscilla. "Miss Rowe will be wondering where we are."

"We have some time," said Emmeline. "The household is in an uproar over Papa's guests, and we shan't be missed for another hour or two."

"But Mama—"

"Is too occupied with her own affairs to care what we do."

Priscilla crumpled a bit of grass and tossed it into the water, while Emmeline sifted through the stones at her feet. Finding a perfectly flat one, she threw it with a flick of the wrist, skipping it along the pond's surface.

"Isn't that the Orbrooks?" asked Priscilla, shading her eyes with one hand and pointing to the right. Before Emmeline answered, the lass grabbed her by the hand and dragged her off in that direction.

"Sally! Rebecca!" Priscilla shouted, waving at the pair.

Hand-in-hand, the sisters moved to the tree where the Orbrooks and their governess had set up a picnic.

"How good to see you here," said Priscilla with a grin on her face, unaware of the frosty manner in which the governess glowered at the Kingsley girls. Emmeline's cheeks pinked as the woman pointedly took stock of their defects. Their bonnets had been abandoned long ago, and it had not even entered Emmeline's mind to bring gloves, a painful oversight at present. Bending a touch, Emmeline hoped her skirts hid her bare toes, but from the pinching of the woman's lips, Emmeline knew they hadn't.

"Are you and Emmeline coming to the harvest festival?" asked Sally as she twirled the end of her braid around her fingers.

"Yes!" said Priscilla, clapping her hands. "Shall we pair up for the races again? I just know we can beat Jonathan Bixby this year."

"No, you cannot. That's ridiculous," said Rebecca. Emmeline held back a burst of laughter at the girl's haughty manner. For being merely thirteen, she was certainly lording her extra three years over poor Sally and Priscilla.

"Come, girls," said the governess, rising to her feet.

"But we just arrived!" said Sally. "And we have enough to share with Priscilla and Emmeline. May we stay?"

"Absolutely not," came the reply.

"But Miss Dollie—"

"Hush, Sally!" Miss Dollie put everything in the picnic basket and had them marching away in short order. Though the governess placed some distance between her charges and the Kingsleys before explaining, it wasn't far enough for Emmeline to miss.

"It is entirely inappropriate for you to spend time with the likes of them," said Miss Dollie with a frown. "They may be from money, but they are not well-bred, which is no wonder when you consider their parents..."

Priscilla had already abandoned the tree and returned to the pond, so she was none the wiser, but Emmeline felt flushed with shame at the words. It was not the first time she'd heard such things, but it did not make it any easier to bear.

"Emmeline, is anything the matter?" called Priscilla.

Forcing a smile, she shook away the melancholy. "No, dearest. But we must return to the house."

And so they went, retrieving their cast-off articles along the way before Emmeline surrendered herself to the necessary preparations for dinner. Perhaps there was some joy to be found in dinner, but to Emmeline's thinking, they were naught but hours of awkward conversation. Though she would admit that readying herself for such an event was not wholly distasteful.

"You look lovely," said Priscilla when the last hairpin was placed and Emmeline was ready to face the evening.

Emmeline hardly recognized herself in the mirror's reflection. Her thick hair was arranged in an intricate series of hairpins, and though she preferred her hair down, the style lengthened her neck in a becoming manner. And the gown was gorgeous. Moss green and feather-light. So fine and soft that she kept brushing the bare bits of her arms against it just to feel it.

The Emmeline before her wasn't the girl she knew but some foreign creature. A lady. And the sight of it was both joyous and frightening as she turned and watched the skirts swirl around her.

"I would rather stay here with you," said Emmeline, smoothing her elbow gloves.

"And I would rather go with you," said Priscilla with a dreamy tone as she spun, holding her muslin skirts out wide.

"Perhaps we might trade places, then," said Emmeline.

Her heart thumped in her chest as her mind raced with the

possibilities the evening offered. A proper dinner. Such a thing was a rare occasion at Avebury Park, and Emmeline both anticipated and dreaded it. Would she know what to say? How to act? Her long line of governesses had attempted to teach her such things, but without sufficient experience, Emmeline felt terribly ill-prepared for the task at hand.

A knock at the door drew her attention away from her nerves.

Simon poked his head inside. "Father sent me to fetch you."

With hurried goodbyes and promises to tell all tomorrow, Emmeline left Priscilla and stepped into the hall to see Simon standing to one side, his hands tucked behind him as he stared off at nothing.

"You could offer me your arm, brother," said Emmeline.

Simon jerked out of his thoughts with a grimace. With as much gentlemanly decorum as could be expected of a thirteen-year-old boy, he threaded her hand through his arm and dragged her down the hall.

"Are you pleased to be home from school?" asked Emmeline, glancing at Simon from the corner of her eye.

He gave a grunt that told her as little as his scant letters had conveyed over the past school term.

Scouring her thoughts, Emmeline tried to think of any subject that might engage him, but she knew so little about the young man her brother had become. "Are you enjoying your subjects?"

"Some."

"Are you not going to elaborate?" she teased, squeezing his arm.

Simon shrugged. "There is nothing more to tell."

"That cannot be true," she said, but Simon remained silent, and as much as she longed to heal the growing divide between them, Emmeline did not know how to do so.

Silently, the pair descended the stairs and made their way to the parlor. The candles were out in force tonight, illuminating each corner of the room in a soft glow as the guests milled about, awaiting the call to dinner.

"Simon." Papa greeted his heir, giving Emmeline a cursory nod before ushering Simon towards a group of gentlemen.

And thus, she found herself standing alone. Her posture grew more rigid with the ensuing seconds as she debated what to do. Mama did not claim her as Papa had with Simon, but as Emmeline could think of no better course of action, she took a place beside the lady. Introductions were made, but Emmeline forgot the names as soon as they were spoken. With a brittle smile, she pretended to understand the conversation that revolved around people and events she did not know.

"Now, Mrs. Kingsley, you must introduce me to this exquisite daughter of yours," came a low voice from behind Emmeline. Turning, she found a gentleman old enough to be her father. The man leered at her with a gaze that made her wish she had a fichu to cover her décolletage.

"Why, Mr. Parsons," purred Mama, which sent another sickening shiver down Emmeline's spine. Her mother's smile widened and her gaze caressed Mr. Parson as she slid her hand through his arm in a manner so intimate that no one in the company could miss the implication. From across the room, Papa's eyes narrowed on Mama, and Emmeline searched for something to break the growing tension.

"Mr. Parsons, I am pleased to make your acquaintance," said Emmeline with a curtsy. She despised the thought of drawing his attention back to her, but it broke the spell Mama had cast over the room. Mr. Parsons caught Emmeline's hand in his and placed a kiss on her knuckles, his eyes never leaving hers, and for once Emmeline was grateful for gloves as they provided a barrier to his touch.

"The pleasure is all mine, Miss Kingsley," said Mr. Parsons.

Emmeline blushed, which only made the gentleman's smile broaden. Mama's eyes flicked between the pair, but one of the other ladies drew Mama's attention; releasing her hold on Mr. Parsons, she returned to the previous conversation. But the gentleman still held Emmeline's hand, his thumb rubbing along the back of it. With a tug, she freed herself. The gentleman chuckled.

"Shy, are we?" he asked in a low murmur. "I see you inherited your mother's beauty but not her spirit."

Before Emmeline could think how to respond, the final guests arrived, and the party was ushered into the dining room. However, she found no reprieve. Though Mr. Parsons sat on the other side of the table, his gaze followed her throughout the meal. With each minute, Emmeline grew more flustered. She fumbled her fork and bumped her glass, spilling the drink. And Mr. Parsons grew more amused with each agitated movement, his attention never leaving her.

When the ladies finally left the gentlemen, Emmeline seized the opportunity to slip away from the dinner party. Her spirits were in such a state that there was only one place in which she would find solace.

Stepping through the side door, Emmeline sighed. The evening air was crisp against her flushed skin, and she raised her eyes to the full moon, basking in its white glow as she strolled among her beloved flowerbeds. Though many of the plants were dormant for the coming winter, the smells of the soil and grass mixed together and wove their way around her heart, calming it. Emmeline would not risk removing her gloves and stockings, but she toed off her slippers and took in another lungful of evening air, letting it wash through her.

"I thought I might find you here," said Mr. Parsons, making Emmeline jump. Though some faint instinct warned her to keep her distance, she remained rooted in place as the gentleman strode towards her.

"You are entrancing," he murmured, drawing so close that she felt his breath on her cheek. And still, her feet would not move. "So beautiful, like your mother. Though far more..." Mr. Parsons' voice lowered to a brief whisper that tickled her ear, "...coy. She was not much of a conquest, but you make a man work for your favors. I bet if I visited your bedchamber that frigidity would melt away."

Emmeline gaped at the insinuation, and she wanted nothing more than to run back to the safety of the house, but fear trapped her in place. Then his fingers grazed her neckline, his wet lip brushing her earlobe, and the shock broke her free. Stepping back, Emmeline put two firm hands between them.

"Keep your distance, sir," she said, wide-eyed, though he looked mildly amused.

"Are you going to continue playing the part of the prim miss?" Mr. Parsons smirked.

"I am not playing a part!"

"There is no point in playing the saint in public as your father does, for no one believes him, either," he said with a chuckle. Mr. Parsons stepped closer, and Emmeline stepped back, but he grabbed her extended hands and brought them to his lips with a wicked grin. "It is better to embrace your nature, like your mother. It is far more enjoyable, at any rate."

Yanking free, Emmeline stepped around him, but Mr. Parsons blocked her path with another lecherous laugh. She moved to the other side, but he grabbed her.

"I've got you now," he said with a chortle, as though it were nothing but a lark. Leaning in, Mr. Parsons brought his lips towards her, and Emmeline twisted away, arching her back and struggling against his hold, but his hands surrounded her—grasping, wrenching, squeezing. His mouth hit her neck, his tongue lathed her skin like a wet snake. Emmeline threw her weight against him, and they fell, knocking him atop her.

Mr. Parsons looked down with fevered eyes. "I see you are all passion and fire. And such utter perfection..." He shivered, and a wave of nausea rolled Emmeline's stomach, twisting it in knots as his hands pawed at her.

Sucking in a breath, Emmeline tried to scream, but his mouth covered hers, leaving only her terrified whimpers as his tongue invaded. Shifting her leg, Emmeline brought her knee up and used it as leverage, rolling the pair of them. Mr. Parsons laughed when his head hit the grass.

"Definitely your mother's daughter—" he began, but Emmeline did not wait. She launched herself to her feet and ran for the house. A hand snaked around her ankle, and Emmeline collapsed. Scrambling upright, she tried once again, but Mr. Parsons was there, holding her from behind.

"So feisty..." His voice was a purr. His sticky breath clung to her ear, and Emmeline fought his hold. His hands pawed at her, rubbing and pinching as tears coursed down her cheeks. One of his hands brushed her mouth, and she chomped down, biting into his fingers. With a sharp breath, he released her, and she spun, shoving against him with all her weight.

The rocks dug into her feet, ripping at her stockings and skin as Emmeline tore along the pathway. He gave chase, and her heart pounded in her ears, warning her to run faster. Move quicker. He was there behind her. The thought of what would happen should he catch her spurned her on to greater speeds. And still, she felt his panting breath on her neck and heard his giddy chuckle in her ear.

His fingers brushed her arm.

But Emmeline knew the way blindfolded, and he was stumbling in the dark. Reaching the side door, she flung it open and sprinted to her bedchamber, not halting until she had the door shut tight behind her and locked. Sliding to the floor, Emmeline gasped for breath.

The door handle twisted and soft fingers tapped at the wood as Mr. Parsons whispered her name.

"Emmeline, what is the meaning of this?" Another knock, and the knob twisted harder. "You have me right where you want me. Do not lock me out now, you tease."

Curling into herself, Emmeline hugged her knees, her tears wetting her silk skirts.

"You've been begging for this moment since you first laid eyes on me. Open the door, and I will give you everything you desire," he murmured, his voice thick with desire as he described the many things he wished to do to her.

Jumping to her feet, Emmeline hurried to the bed, diving

under the covers and wrapping a pillow around her head to block the foul words that no young lady should hear. Mr. Parsons waited only a few more minutes before giving up his quarry with a curse.

The silence that followed offered no peace, for every creak of the floorboards brought nightmarish visions of him breaking into her bedchamber. Never had she prayed or cried so hard as she did that night, huddled in her bed.

Please keep him away. Please keep her safe.

Chapter 14

"Don't fidget. You don't want people thinking you are distressed," whispered Mother, and Eloise let go of the pendant at her neck. With her gloves on, fiddling with her necklace did not have the same calming effect, so it was no great loss, but Eloise's hand still wished to twist it, for distressed was precisely how she felt.

"Is your head still paining you?" Mother asked, giving a few bats of her fan as she surveyed the crowd in the Gardiners' ballroom.

"No," she replied. In truth, her head had not pained her much for the past few days, but it had served as the perfect excuse to keep herself out of sight. Not that the solitude had done much good, for Eloise was no closer to unraveling the tangled mess her life had become. Just thinking about it made her feel a little faint, and Eloise opened her fan to cool the sudden flush she felt.

Gazing at the growing crowd, Eloise searched for anyone she might know, but the Gardiners had the most eccentric taste in guest lists, and she hardly recognized a face. Perhaps she might have a quiet evening after all. As much as she adored dancing, Eloise hoped to sequester herself in a quiet corner.

In normal circumstances, Eloise enjoyed the Gardiners' gatherings. Theirs were never too full nor too empty; the right amount of people to fill their house, yet without making it the unbearable crush so many preferred. Personally, she did not see the point in arranging a party in which your guests are decidedly uncomfortable, but far too many hosts and hostesses felt differently.

From across the room, Eloise saw Kitty and her parents enter the ballroom, and not caring one bit for decorum, she fairly leapt in the air and waved at her new friend.

"Eloise." That was all Mother said, her tone conveying all her expectations in that one little word. The Hennesseys started towards them, and Mother stiffened, closing her fan with a snap.

"Kitty is a dear—"

"*Miss Hennessey*," corrected Mother. But Eloise would not be daunted.

"*Kitty* is my friend," said Eloise, holding her smile in place as the trio crossed the room.

"I've told you she isn't a proper companion for you."

"What could she have possibly done to warrant such treatment? Though a tad eccentric at times, she is a dear."

"What happened is immaterial," said Mother, tapping her fan against her fingers.

Casting a glance at her mother from the corner of her eye, Eloise couldn't help but murmur, "Don't fidget, Mother. You don't want people thinking you are distressed."

The lady's eyes narrowed on her daughter, and she poked Eloise in the side with her fan as the Hennesseys approached. Greeting each other with a buss on the cheek, the girls made the proper introductions, though to Eloise's eye, Mother looked quite put-out. However, the lady showed the Hennesseys the same cold disinterest she displayed to everyone.

"Have you met Miss Maria Allder?" asked Eloise, pulling Kitty towards another group of ladies before any objection could be made; as she already anticipated a stern lecture from her mother about keeping company with Kitty, Eloise didn't mind adding to her list of offenses. Hooking their arms together, the pair made their way across the ballroom towards Maria.

"There is so much to tell you," said Eloise.

"But we only spoke three days ago," said Kitty with a laugh. "How can you possibly have more drama to share?"

"I can hardly believe it myself, but it has been a trying few days," said Eloise, glancing over her shoulder to see her mother still standing with the Hennesseys.

"Eloise!" said Maria, greeting her with a buss on the cheek. "I hadn't realized you were coming tonight. What a pleasant surprise, for I had despaired when I learned Susie had another engagement. I was quite certain I would be all alone and miserable."

Glancing at the growing group of young ladies and gentlemen surrounding Maria, Eloise thought that highly unlikely. Kitty stood behind Eloise with a false smile plastered on her lips and the look of a frightened rabbit in her gaze. Taking Kitty by the arm once more, Eloise made the proper introductions, though the others' eyes widened upon hearing Kitty's surname.

"Miss Hennessey," Maria said with a little curtsy. "How wonderful to meet you."

But the moment Kitty was engaged in conversation with one of the others, Maria whispered from behind her fan, "Kitty Hennessey, Eloise? I've heard she's quite scandalous. They say she was compromised by a gentleman and then patently refused to marry him."

"Nonsense!" Eloise hissed. "I adore her. We met at the Falthams' ball, and I already consider her a dear friend."

There were more questions in Maria's gaze, but she kept them to herself and dropped her fan. "Miss Hennessey, what a positively gorgeous gown. Gold is such a lovely color, but I fear it looks ghastly on me. However, it is quite striking with your Titian hair."

Kitty beamed, and the pair began dissecting the various

fashions on display. Though Eloise had little to add to the conversation, she was quite content to observe. Watching Kitty grow more comfortable in her surroundings filled Eloise with more pleasure than was usually found at such gatherings, and that feeling only grew when Mr. Hillard claimed Kitty's hand for a dance.

Couples paired off and took their places on the dance floor, and Eloise's eyes wandered the room, searching the crowd for familiar faces.

"Looking for your Mr. Godwin?" asked Miss Croome. The young lady grinned behind her fan, giggling at Eloise.

"He is not my Mr. Godwin. And he is otherwise engaged for the evening. A dinner party, I believe."

"But you are looking for someone, aren't you?" Miss Croome spoke with such a pointed tone that one would have to be a fool to miss the insinuation beneath it, though Eloise could not fathom what the young lady meant. Until she caught sight of Patrick.

Miss Croome tittered behind that silly fan again, but Eloise ignored her. Patrick's eyes met hers, and he wove his way through the crowd, ignoring the other guests as he came to her side.

"Miss Andrews," he said with a bow. "You look lovely tonight."

Eloise murmured a polite response and gave a curtsy that was far more sedate than she felt. Her heart and thoughts were thrown back into disarray, reminding her of every agonizing question and concern of the past few days, eradicating the peace she'd gained at aiding Kitty. Yet the rapidity of her heartbeat was not an altogether unpleasant sensation.

"You must be the mysterious Mr. Lennox," said Miss Croome, and Eloise's lips pinched at the young lady's smug smile. "I have heard much about you."

"Not all of it is true." Patrick's smile stiffened, and it pulled at the scars marring his cheek; an old instinct told Eloise to take hold of his hand, but she kept her composure and ignored it.

"Miss Croome, I think your mother is waving for you," said Eloise, pointing towards a group of matrons who were more focused on the punch and gossiping than their charges. But the diversion worked, and Miss Croome bade them farewell, which was enough to loosen some of the tightness in Eloise's chest.

"Did you receive my letter?" asked Patrick.

The tightness returned in force, but Eloise welcomed it, for this was a necessary conversation. This moment together would not last, and there was much to say, but still, Eloise struggled to get out the words.

"Yes," she said. "Thank you for the sweets."

Patrick nodded and cleared his throat, his eyes falling to the ground. "You are most welcome. I hoped you would enjoy them."

Her hand rose to her necklace, and Eloise nodded in return. "I did."

Silence followed those two words, stretching into a long, awkward pause as both she and Patrick fidgeted and avoided looking at one another.

And then Patrick huffed, shaking his head. "We never had trouble speaking when we were children."

"That was years ago."

Patrick sighed, his shoulders dropping as his eyes met hers. "I know. Can you forgive me for that?"

There were a myriad of questions plaguing Eloise at present, but that was not one of them. Just the memory of his letter brought sympathetic tears to her eyes. "Of course, Patrick."

And she meant it. She may not comprehend what had happened to her friend, but she could no longer hold his grief against him. The pain caused by his disappearance still lingered in the corners of her heart, but his explanation had granted her better understanding and empathy.

"Then will you dance with me?" he asked with a smile, holding out his arm to her. Glancing at the dancers already in motion, he grimaced. "Though I feel honor-bound to warn you I am abysmal at such lively country dances."

"You cannot be as bad as all that."

Patrick widened his eyes with another grimace. "Yes, I can. I am passable at slow or simple dances, but anything more is fraught with disaster."

"Well, I shan't complain if you tread on my toes."

He snorted. "You cannot expect me to believe you would overlook an opportunity to tease me, Eloise. You always found great sport in amusing yourself at my expense."

"Tally-ho, Patrick," she replied with a grin, and his own grew in response.

"Tally-ho, Eloise."

The pair made their way to the dancers and found an opening. Patrick had been entirely honest in his assessment—perhaps even a bit generous. He was a hopeless dancer. He turned the wrong directions and was rarely where he was supposed to be. When he had to apologize for the sixth time to his neighbor, Patrick's expression tightened, making his scars pull in angry ways.

When he passed in front of her to change places with the lady to her right, Eloise caught his eye. In those scant seconds, an old instinct took hold of her before she knew what she was doing. With a puff, she blew out her cheeks like a bullfrog. The silly expression was there and gone in a flash before anyone else saw it, but she knew Patrick had, for there was a definite gleam of humor in his eye. The irritation over his ineptitude faded, and soon he was embracing the ridiculousness of the situation.

With every turn, Eloise found a way to send him a private laugh; the thrill of doing so without being caught by the others only added to the fun of their game. Before long, they were making a fine spectacle of themselves. Eloise tried her best to stifle her laughter, but she could not keep it contained as Patrick spun her about the dance floor.

The music was lively, the conversation varying, and the

lighting plentiful. All in all, the evening was a success, but Emmeline struggled to find any enjoyment in it as she watched Eloise and Patrick trip their way through the dance. Though it did her good to see them so happy, too many guests watched them, whispering behind their fans as they stared at the pair.

"I cannot remember the last time I heard Patrick laugh," said Deirdre, coming up beside her.

"I am pleased to see him looking well," replied Emmeline.

Deirdre turned her eyes to her friend with a raised eyebrow. "Pleased? That is cold, even for you, Emmeline. It is a miracle to see my son in such good spirits. No matter how much I hoped and prayed for this, there were times when I doubted he'd right himself."

A smile slipped into place, though she felt a phantom rap of a fan on her wrist.

"Don't be so gauche, Emmeline." Mother Andrews' voice echoed in her mind, and Emmeline schooled her expression. *"Good girl..."*

The brightness in Deirdre's eyes dimmed as she watched the shift, and Emmeline struggled to know what to say.

"I am very happy for him," she said.

Deirdre sighed. "However...?"

"However?"

"Your tone implied more was forthcoming," said Deirdre, a glimmer of humor returning to her eyes as she turned her gaze back to her son.

"I hadn't meant to imply more," said Emmeline, which was true, though there were many thoughts passing through her mind.

Deirdre leveled a disbelieving look at her.

"I worry for them," said Emmeline. "Eloise seems taken with Mr. Godwin, and I'm certain she can expect a proposal any day now."

"You wish her to marry him?" asked Deirdre with a raised eyebrow. "Mr. Godwin is a fine gentleman, but theirs would not be a happy union."

Emmeline's eyes darted to a figure hidden in the far corner. Though Norman rarely spent the evening at her side anymore, she always seemed to know precisely where he was.

"Do you think so?" asked Emmeline. "I thought I detected a change in her opinion as of late."

"You mean you hoped she had changed her opinion rather than marry the scandalous Patrick Lennox."

Emmeline's eyes widened, her mouth dropping open for a brief moment before she caught herself. "I beg your pardon?"

"Do not act so innocent with me, Emmeline Andrews. You cannot be so sanguine about the prospect of him renewing his addresses."

Hands tightening around her fan, Emmeline watched the couple in question. "I adore Patrick, and I do think him a good match for Eloise, but I know what it is like to have your life tainted by gossip. I do not want that for my daughter."

"Your life wasn't tainted as much as your mother-in-law had you believing," said Deirdre with a frown.

But Emmeline's mind provided vivid evidence to the contrary. "I am merely worried about my daughter."

Deirdre sighed and shook her head. "And that is precisely the problem, Emmeline. You worry more than is necessary. Eloise is a good girl, and Patrick would make her a fine husband."

"Unfortunately, that is not always enough," replied Emmeline, slipping into silence as she watched the young pair.

Chapter 15

Pumping her fan, Eloise tried to cool herself, but after a few sets, such efforts were ineffective, and she was quite flushed from her exertions on the dance floor. Her eyes darted from her companions to the figure standing to the side of the ballroom, and she promised herself that Patrick had nothing to do with how warm she felt.

Propriety demanded he keep his distance for some of the evening; he could hardly follow her about for its entirety without raising eyebrows. Not that it made a bit of difference, as he watched her with an intensity that was quite improper—even if it brought a crimson glow to her cheeks.

Eloise sighed, wishing she understood her erratic heart better, but the world kept shifting, leaving her at odds with herself. Did she wish for Patrick to court her? Did she wish for any gentleman to court her? Marriage had been a priority before, but Lucinda's and Mother's words had soured that former dream.

"You are awfully quiet," whispered Kitty.

"I have much on my mind," replied Eloise, forcing her attention away from the confusing Patrick Lennox.

"Or rather, one thing on your mind," said Kitty with a smile as she gave a pointed glance at that gentleman. "Though he is imposing at first, I like your Mr. Lennox. He is quite an affable fellow."

"He is not my Mr. Lennox," said Eloise, though her traitorous cheeks grew even hotter. She flapped her fan harder to stave off the blush and sought out a change in topic. "You appear to be enjoying yourself."

Kitty beamed. "Very much so. My welcome to London was disheartening until you offered your assistance."

Eloise scrunched her face. "I didn't do anything."

"You did far more than you realize. I am positively envious of how easy it is for you to navigate such things."

Her fan paused as she realized it was all due to good training, but Eloise wasn't about to give her mother such credit. "Well, I am positively envious of your freedom to wander about on your own."

The girls glanced at Eloise's mother, who lurked some ten feet away. It was enough distance to give them the appearance of privacy, but not far enough that anyone would think the impeccable Emmeline Andrews was shirking her duty.

Kitty took up her own fan, staring at the backside as she batted it. "Yes, well, you have a reputation to protect, and I have none. There is no point in my mother going to such lengths when it will do no good."

Before Eloise could think of a reply, a buzz of conversation caught her attention.

With so many noises around them, a few more voices would hardly make a difference, but there was a shift in the air as more people cast furtive looks at the entrance and spoke in hasty whispers. Rising to her toes, Eloise tried to see above the crowd to glimpse the object of their conversation, but she had not the height to do any good. Tapping Maria on the arm with her fan, Eloise asked her friend if she knew what was happening.

"I believe Mrs. Gardiner wanted a bit of a scandal to highlight the evening," replied Maria with a mischievous grin.

"And what does that mean?" asked Eloise.

"She invited the Dowdings," said Maria with an arched eyebrow. When Eloise did not respond to that, she continued, "As your mother does not participate in gossip, you likely have not heard about Mrs. Dowding's *special acquaintance* with a certain old friend of yours."

Kitty gaped. "That is a terrible accusation. Mr. Lennox is far too stalwart a gentleman to do something so unseemly."

Maria fluttered her fan, one shoulder rising in a delicate shrug. "Many a gentleman is known to dally with married ladies, and I heard Mr. Dowding stumbled upon them in a compromising situation..."

But Eloise heard no more of their conversation, for her eyes shot towards Patrick. He stood in the same place, but his gaze was no longer on her. His face paled as he stared at the entrance like everyone else; even the dancers' attentions were not on their partners or steps as they moved through the motions.

"It looks as though Mrs. Dowding is alone tonight," said a nearby lady, though Eloise could not tell which it was. She wished she knew, for she wanted to give the lady a set-down for her insinuating tone.

Then through the crowd, Eloise caught sight of the lady in question. Though closer to Mother's age than Eloise's, Mrs. Dowding was gorgeous. Her gown was the height of fashion, and she walked with an elegant confidence that had the crowd parting for her. Mrs. Dowding's eyes held Patrick's, and though she made a show of giving passing salutations, she did not stop her trek across the ballroom to his side.

It could not be true. It couldn't be. Despite her doubts about the honor and morals of gentlemen, her heart still trusted in Patrick. For all his faults, she could not believe he would act in such a manner.

Mrs. Dowding greeted Patrick, and he comported himself precisely as a gentleman ought, but his expression showed no pleasure at seeing her. Though not a word of their conversation could be heard, it held everyone in rapt attention. Mrs. Dowding lifted a hand to touch the scars on his cheek, and Patrick stepped away, tucking his hands behind him as his eyes darted around as though searching for an escape.

"He would never do that," she said to those within hearing distance before hurrying to Patrick's side.

Patrick had expected their paths to cross at some time, but he'd hoped that inauspicious meeting would be at a more opportune moment. Certainly not when his courtship with Eloise was on such tentative footing, and certainly not at such a public gathering where they were meant to be the main event. The entire ballroom watched as Mrs. Dowding wove her way towards him.

The coward in him wanted to flee. It would be so much better to avoid this altogether, but Patrick was done hiding from his consequences.

"Patrick," Mrs. Dowding murmured. "I cannot tell you how good it is to see you. I had feared the worst."

"Mrs. Dowding, I beg you to remember yourself," he said through clenched teeth.

"Oh, 'Mrs. Dowding,' is it?" she asked with an arched brow.

Patrick sighed. "Yes. It is. And that is all it shall ever be."

The lady studied his face, her eyes softening as they tracked the scars. "I will never forgive my husband for what he did to you."

Her hand rose to brush his marred cheek, but Patrick pulled away, his skin flushing as he glanced at all the wide eyes staring at them.

"On the contrary, Mrs. Dowding. I thank him for it. It is a reminder of how far I fell and my determination never to do so again."

The lady's expression shifted, her features slackening for a moment as she watched him before they hardened once more, her eyes narrowing. "Does this have anything to do with that silly little maiden you are chasing?"

"That question is beneath both of us, madam," said Patrick.

"But I will tell you that my stance has nothing to do with anyone else. I have changed. I do not wish to return to that life again. I will not do it."

Patrick could not decide if it was opportune or ill-timed, but Eloise appeared just behind Mrs. Dowding with that fierce glint of battle in her eye that spoke of the warrior lurking in her heart. Mrs. Dowding followed his gaze and stared the girl down.

"Mr. Lennox!" said Eloise with a forced smile, her words falsely bright. "Where have you been? We were supposed to stand up together, and the set is nearly halfway over."

Oh, how those words made him want to kiss her. Of course, he felt that way quite often, but now, it was especially strong.

Mrs. Dowding watched Eloise with a tight expression. "And if he wishes to claim his dance, he will find you."

Eloise ignored the lady's dark eyes glaring at her and held on to her brittle smile as Patrick blinked at the pair of them. This was a monumental mess, but Eloise had provided him an escape.

"Yes," he said, straightening with a grateful smile. "Of course."

"Mr. Lennox," said Mrs. Dowding with an insinuating tone that made Patrick's hackle rise. "Won't you introduce your lovely young friend before you go?"

Patrick narrowed his eyes on the lady. He knew better than to believe her possessive posturing meant anything of significance, for he had no hold on her heart. Whatever hurt she had felt had long since faded, and this was nothing more than pettiness at having lost her plaything before she was finished with him.

"No, I will not," he said with a curt bow.

He offered his arm to Eloise, she took it, and the pair strode to the edge of the dancers. Thoughts of Mrs. Dowding held his attention as dancers took their places, and it was only then that Patrick realized the upcoming number was a waltz.

Glancing at Eloise's red cheeks, he guessed that she had not realized it either. Patrick's heart tapped a rapid beat that was contrary to the languid tempo of the dance. Though he was no grand dancer (a fact that had been proven many times over that evening), there were no elaborate steps for this. It was hardly a dance at all. Merely a chance to hold his love in a manner that was socially acceptable.

They found a place on the floor, and Patrick restrained himself from pulling her closer than was respectable. Moving with the music, they rotated in line with the other dancers, and this time it was Eloise who struggled to keep her steps. It took a few turns before she steadied and met his gaze.

"Dancing a second set is liable to raise speculation," he murmured.

"There is already plenty of that tonight. And you looked to be in need of rescue."

Patrick let out a halting chuckle. If anyone had needed rescuing tonight, it was certainly him. "Eloise Andrews, Defender of Gentlemen."

"You needn't laugh at me," she said with a scowl.

"I am not laughing, Eloise." Her name was a mere whisper on his lips. "I am entirely honored and humbled that you would put your reputation on the line for me."

He shifted their position, bringing her as close as he dared; his hand was at her shoulder blades, holding her scant inches from him. So close that for a brief moment, Patrick wished he could wrap his arms fully around her. Eloise held his gaze, and her eyes were filled with such a confusing mixture of emotions that Patrick hurt for her. Eloise had such a big heart, but she often felt too much, leaving her lost and struggling to comprehend it all. He'd been the one to help her sort through such things, but now, he was the cause of it.

Yet beneath it, he saw the longing in her eyes as her gaze dropped to his lips. Then, the tiny intake of breath as her cheeks reddened. Oh, how Patrick longed to close the distance between them and steal a kiss.

Eloise stumbled over her own feet, though his arms kept

her from collapsing. Her face was a bright crimson, and she nibbled on that lovely lip of hers.

"It…" she swallowed and tried again. "It wasn't my reputation I was worried about."

Patrick gave a silly, wide grin. "You were protecting my honor?"

Eloise huffed. "I am still not certain I like you, but I am certain you do not deserve such slander."

His heart dropped to his toes, and his conscience's frantic whispers had him wishing to flee for a second time tonight.

He had to tell her. He knew he must, but things were too tentative. Too fragile. Too early. To admit the truth might drive a final wedge between them. Patrick struggled for breath as the awareness of what he stood to lose spread through him, sparking each of his nerves.

Tonight had been pleasant. More than pleasant, in fact. They had shared moments that were unspoiled by the past, and it gave him a hard, honest hope that with time, they would have a future together. It was possible. He only needed more time.

He could wait until they were on better footing, and then tell her all.

But even as Patrick thought such things, his conscience twisted and writhed in his stomach, telling him what he knew: Eloise deserved the truth.

"And what if I said I deserved that slander?" he asked.

Chapter 16

Eloise's eyes snapped to Patrick's. "Do not start with that again. It was an accident, and you needn't take on every sin of the world because of it—"

"No, I am not speaking of Kelly." Patrick swallowed, his gaze falling to his toes. "What if I told you the rumors were true? Or at least some of them."

Silence. Despite his determination to speak, Patrick had not the courage to look her in the eyes. Not yet.

"Oh." The word was quiet but filled with shock and pain. Then Eloise gathered herself and spoke with more than a hint of relief. "Surely, you do not know the extent of the rumors, Patrick. They claim you and Mrs. Dowding were...intimately acquainted."

His shoulders sagged, his eyes closing for a moment as he tried to gather the strength to face her properly. His sad eyes rose slowly, reluctantly, but Patrick straightened his spine and met her gaze once more.

"I told you I fell far, Eloise, and I meant it. As much as I wish to keep such things hidden, I cannot bring myself to lie to you."

Eloise blinked rapidly, her breath coming in shaky pants.

"But... when you..." She paused and tried again. "I hadn't thought you meant such things."

"For the most part, I didn't," said Patrick. The couple behind them nearly collided with them, and he snapped back to attention, speeding up their lagging steps. "Do you remember when our families visited the seaside at Wexington?"

Eloise did not answer, and he did not press her, for they both knew she did.

"The three of us waded out into the water. At first, we were content to stay by the shore, like we were told to do, but we went out a little farther and farther." Though he stumbled through the dance, Patrick held her attention with a fevered determination, caring only to explain himself now that he had the opportunity. "One step here and one step there hadn't seemed like much."

"Until that wave struck me," Eloise whispered.

And the memory struck Patrick equally hard. Though many details had grown hazy over the years, he still remembered the abject horror he'd felt as the water pulled her under and swept her away. If he and Kelly hadn't acted quickly, she would've been lost.

"Exactly," he said, his eyes growing misty. "Those years were filled with little steps here and there. One bad choice led to another, each deadening me to the danger of my situation. I met Mrs. Dowding at my lowest moment. It started as a flirtation, but then inch by inch, I justified each line I crossed, thinking I was still within the safety of the shore."

They bumped into another pair, who grumbled loudly about the incident while Patrick apologized profusely. Seeing the other dancers lining up for the next set made him realize the waltz had ended, unnoticed by either of them. Eloise released him and stepped away, but he stayed her, leaning close to whisper.

"Please, give me another moment to explain." He was not above begging if that gained him a few more minutes. Taking her by the arm, Patrick led her to a corner, their progress tracked by quite a few of the company. Though there was no opportunity for true privacy, he continued his story once he had her as alone as they could be in a room full of people.

"It was innocent for the most part," said Patrick. "Not entirely honorable but mostly innocent."

The thought of having to outline his indiscretions brought a bitter taste to his tongue, but Patrick took a breath and calmed the churning in his stomach. Opening his mouth, he allowed the words to spill out, for there was no point in withholding anything.

"I cannot describe the logic with which I justified calling on her that night. It makes no sense in the present, but in the past, I thought it perfectly rational and harmless," he said. "I had turned down so many of her invitations, but this one caught me at the right time—or wrong time, rather. I arrived on her doorstep, telling myself it was merely a visit between friends. And I was in desperate need of one."

Patrick paused and let out a low sigh, closing his eyes with a wince. "Little steps here and little steps there. The night was a blur, but then Mr. Dowding burst in and saved me from losing the last shred of my honor."

Shaking his head, he gave another shaky sigh and met her gaze again. There were tears in his eyes, his jaw tightening as he stared at her for several silent moments. "It was the wave that brought me to my senses and made me realize how far I had strayed. As ashamed as I am of my behavior, I am grateful for that night because it forced me to see what I had become."

Straightening, Patrick sniffed and cleared his throat, tucking his hands behind him as though they were speaking of mundane topics. How could he ever explain the full extent of his madness when he could not understand it himself? His broken soul had twisted logic, good sense, and the values his parents had instilled in him until they were a foreign, misshapen thing that somehow made the distasteful acceptable.

"And what of the lady?" asked Eloise.

Patrick blinked at her before answering. "So you haven't

heard all the gossip? Though Mr. Dowding had every reason to run me through right then and there, he did the honorable thing and called me out instead. I took my punishment and have neither seen nor heard from the Dowdings until tonight."

Eloise stared at him with a furrowed brow. "'Took your punishment?'"

Wordlessly, Patrick turned his head to put his scar on full display. "Pistols at dawn, as they say. I had honor enough to face him without raising my firearm."

"You didn't protect yourself?" Eloise gaped at him, but Patrick leveled a hard look at her.

"Though my indiscretions were not as numerous nor as abominable as they say, I did wrong the gentleman. He had every right to demand satisfaction, and I had no right to lessen that."

"He could've killed you," Eloise murmured, blinking away fresh tears.

"He almost did, but I survived and made my way home—"

Eloise sucked in a quick breath, her muscles tightening. "Home? When?"

Patrick's brow furrowed. "A year ago."

Of all the things he'd confessed tonight, Patrick couldn't comprehend why this inconsequential detail mattered so much, but the intense manner in which Eloise gaped at him spoke of its importance to her. Her nostrils flared as they always did when she was in a temper, her chest heaving as she sucked in a breath. Patrick stared at her, dumbfounded as to what had her in such a dither.

"You were in Holbrook for a year and did not tell me?" she asked through gritted teeth.

"I was hardly fit company," he said with a huff. "I spent months recovering from my injury, and I had to sort myself out before I could see you."

"But you didn't send word? Not even a message to tell me you were alive?"

"And if I had, would you have simply sat at home and let

me be?" Patrick's brows drew together. "I wasn't myself, Eloise, and in no state to be around you or anyone. Our mothers thought it best to keep my presence in Holbrook secret until I was fit, and they were right—"

"My mother knew you were there?" Eloise's nostrils flared again as she filled her lungs to capacity.

Patrick stared at her, struggling to think of how to respond to this strange turn of the conversation. "I had been shot, which led to a serious infection and fever, and after that, I needed help to break free of my vice, and my mother could not nurse me alone."

Eloise actually laughed at that. "And she turned to my mother to care for a sick man? My mother, the frigid, unfeeling lady—"

"I hate that you speak of her so," said Patrick with a scowl. Much of those dark months were lost in the fog of fever and pain, but he remembered Mrs. Andrews at his bedside as much as his mother. Even now, he could hear her voice talking him through the worst of it, nursing him not only through his fevered moments but those when he thought he might die while his body cried out for a drink.

"You are defending her?" she hissed.

"Unequivocally," he replied, crossing his arms. "She is imperfect—like everyone is. She has her own cross to bear, and she helped me to bear mine when I needed it most."

"I could've done that for you!" Eloise's voice rose, but she checked herself and repeated the words in a calmer tone. "I could have helped you. I could have been there for you, but you turned to my mother instead?"

"That doesn't matter. You are focusing on the wrong things, Eloise."

"Yes, it does matter, Patrick. You turned your back on me and welcomed my mother into your life instead," she said, placing her hands on her hips while glaring at him.

Patrick frowned. "You are looking for reasons to be angry with me."

"Ridiculous!" Eloise turned away, but Patrick grabbed her hand.

"Please, Eloise, don't leave. I understand you are still upset—"

Tugging her hand free, she stormed away, and though Patrick wanted to follow, he knew better than to press the matter. For now.

Chapter 17

Emmeline
Age Eighteen

Y ears of training and months of planning were put into a young lady's debut into society, and Emmeline hardly believed tonight marked her entrance into adulthood. Standing just inside the ballroom doorway, Emmeline beamed as she watched the servants bustling like a teaming anthill as they prepared Trafford Place for the occasion. Massive vases of flowers dotted the edges of the room and hundreds of candles illuminated the chandeliers and sconces. Everything was primed to make her grand ball a spectacle.

Emmeline's hands trembled. Though her lonely heart yearned to be celebrated, she shuddered at the thought of all those eyes on her, watching her every movement. She was bound to make a mistake, and there would be no hiding it tonight.

Taking in a breath, she smelled the wax from the furniture, floor, and lights, but underlying it was the scent of the flower arrangements. If she closed her eyes, Emmeline could pretend she was standing in her garden once more. Perhaps that would be enough to calm her nerves.

"Emmeline, dear, what are you doing here?" cried Aunt Vivian, dabbing at her glistening forehead. Her round cheeks were red, and she radiated frantic energy. "You should be dressing, not gawking. Your father will expect you to look your best tonight."

"I wanted to see it before the guests arrive," said Emmeline.

"There will be time enough for such things after you dress," said Aunt Vivian, taking her niece by the arm and pulling her towards the door.

Emmeline nodded, desperately wishing her siblings were there. How she longed to speak with someone about the anxiety coursing through her, but neither Simon nor Priscilla had accompanied them to Town.

"My dear!"

At the sound of her mother's voice, Emmeline froze as if one of the fairies from her old nursemaid's tales had petrified her. Wide-eyed, she watched her mother stride through the hallway.

"Amelia." Aunt Vivian spoke the name as though it were a curse and scowled at her sister-in-law. "What are you doing here?"

Mother's eyes narrowed on Aunt Vivian, and she brushed past the lady to embrace Emmeline. "My dear girl, I would never miss your debut."

Despite the shock, she wrapped her arms around her mother, and as they embraced, a slow smile crept across Emmeline's face. Perhaps she should be upset at her late arrival, but the heart wasn't logical, and Emmeline reveled in her mother's affection. Mama had come, despite all worries to the contrary.

No young lady should face such a day without her mama.

"We were not expecting you," said Aunt Vivian through gritted teeth. "We thought you were too busy gallivanting about the Italian countryside."

Mama turned, keeping her arm firmly around Emmeline's shoulders, and gaped at Aunt Vivian. "You think I would miss such a momentous occasion in my daughter's life? Even if you and my husband tried your best to make certain I was not in attendance."

"They did?" asked Emmeline, her eyes darting between her mother and her aunt.

But Aunt Vivian ignored that, her eyelids lowering as she glared at Mama. "We assumed you would not wish to abandon your latest plaything."

"Who said I abandoned him?" Mama said with a sickly-sweet smile. "As my husband sees fit to keep a slew of light-skirts on hand, I think it fitting I do the same."

A sneer twisted Aunt Vivian's lip. "Harlot."

"Self-righteous prude," she retorted with a light tone and a taunting smile. "Now, if you'll excuse us. My daughter needs her mother's assistance to dress for tonight, and I am certain you have much to attend to." Mama paused, inspecting Aunt Vivian's plump physique. "Though I am certain you have the food well in hand."

The insult was veiled, but Emmeline blushed on her aunt's behalf. Aunt Vivian's face also reddened, though hers was due to anger rather than embarrassment. Without a further word, Mama took Emmeline by the arm and led her through the townhouse.

"Are you excited, dear?" she asked, beaming at her daughter.

"You came," said Emmeline.

"Of course I did," Mama replied with a chuckle. "Do you think I would miss this?"

Emmeline refrained from expounding on all the moments her mother had missed, for now was not the time to rehash old wounds. She squeezed Mama's arm, and the pair walked to Emmeline's bedchamber.

"I brought you a present," said her mother, throwing open the door to reveal several maids fluttering about the room.

Mama drew Emmeline's attention to a gorgeous gown draped over a maid's arm. Layers of white gauze wrapped around the bodice, swathing the sky-blue underskirt like a fine mist. Along the edges of the neckline and shoulders, the dressmaker had embroidered delicate periwinkles.

"It's perfect," whispered Emmeline, her fingers brushing the stitched flowers.

"She has a gown," said Aunt Vivian with a scowl as she appeared in the doorway. "She doesn't need your frippery. The dress I chose is perfect—"

With a few quick strides, Mama shoved Aunt Vivian back through the doorway and slammed it behind her. Then, snatching a jewelry box from a servant, she grinned at Emmeline. "And look what I have to pair with it."

Emmeline's breath caught at the sight of the sparkling gems in the box. The pendant was simply designed, but that was to showcase the beauty of the sapphire in the center. The gem was a good inch in diameter and ringed in tiny diamonds. The bracelet and earrings had much smaller gems but followed the same motif, and Emmeline could hardly believe she would be allowed to wear them for the evening.

"They are gorgeous," she whispered, her fingers brushing the smooth surface of the pendant.

"They are yours," replied Mama.

Gaping, Emmeline stared at her mother. "You cannot be serious."

Mama grinned, a gleeful twinkle in her eye. "Every lady needs fine jewelry, and I knew your father would be too stingy to provide them."

There was an edge to her tone that sent a shiver down Emmeline's neck; some niggling warning she couldn't comprehend. This was a present from her mother. That was not an uncommon occurrence for such an occasion, but Emmeline felt uneasy as Mama left her to the care of the maids.

They primped and polished, pinned and poked to get Emmeline into the ensemble her mother had chosen. Emmeline had never taken so long to dress before, but she could not argue with the results. Standing before her mirror for one final inspection, she was awed by the transformation. She looked gorgeous and far more grown-up than she felt.

However, there was a lingering fear in the back of her heart. Phantom memories came to mind of standing in a similar position not long ago—and the awful evening that followed it—but Emmeline refused to think about the past. Twisting her hands in front of her, she took a breath to calm her racing pulse.

Tonight would be different. Tonight was her night. Tonight she would be surrounded by people who were there to celebrate her. Both her father and her mother.

A knock came at the door, and Mama poked her head inside. "Ready, dear?"

Emmeline turned to show her mother the finished product, but she received only a vague smile before her mother led her from the room.

"The guests are set to arrive soon, and we must be ready to welcome them," said Mama as they walked down the hall towards the staircase.

"Of course," said Emmeline, glancing at her mother. There was an odd twist to her lips. That shiver of apprehension grew, making the natural nerves that accompanied such an evening grow until Emmeline half wished she could escape to her bedchamber.

Papa stood at the top of the stairs, his expression darkening as the pair drew closer. He spoke Mama's name in a growl, his eyes narrowing. "I thought you weren't coming tonight."

Mama clutched Emmeline's arm, patting it with a smug smile. "You think I would allow you to shunt me aside? To have my role usurped by that cow you call a sister? Introducing Emmeline into society is my responsibility, not Vivian's."

"Insufferable nonsense. You've never cared for your motherly responsibilities, and I see no reason for that to change now." Papa's nostrils flared, his jaw tightening as he glowered at his wife. "Emmeline deserves an appropriate chaperone.

Someone who knows how to comport themselves, and you are only fit for a brothel."

Emmeline gasped, but Mama laughed.

"You would know all about brothels," replied Mama.

"Keep a civil tongue—" But Papa's angry words were cut short when the butler appeared and announced that the first guests were arriving.

"We must go down and greet our guests, my love," said Mama with a vindictive grin and a demure flutter of her eyelashes at her husband.

Papa held out his arm for Emmeline, but Mama took it.

"I am your wife," she reminded him, a taunting gleam in her eye.

"Then behave like it," he retorted. But then his eyes turned to Emmeline and widened. His expression hardened, his muscles tensing. "What are you wearing?"

Emmeline opened her mouth, but Mama responded first. "It was a present. From me."

The lady squeezed her husband's arm, every inch of her expression crowing in triumph.

"I can change..." Emmeline whispered, her cheeks reddening and hands shaking from the fury burning in Papa's eyes.

"There isn't time," said Mama, pulling Papa down the stairs.

Emmeline stood in the hall, staring after her parents as they descended. All her former nerves were forgotten amidst the fresh fears that sprouted from that tense interlude. Her evening, indeed. Shoulders drooped, Emmeline followed them down and into the ballroom, arriving moments before the guests appeared.

"Mr. and Mrs. Garvey," said Mama with a brilliant smile. "How lovely to see you."

"Welcome," echoed Papa, his smile equally fervent. "We are pleased to have you here to celebrate our dear daughter."

Emmeline fought back her gape at the radical shift in her parents' moods. Though she had seen them play the doting couple in public before, she had never witnessed tension melt with such ease, for no one looking at the pair could think they had been so close to a shouting match mere moments before.

Struggling through the proper words and curtsies, Emmeline felt held together by a fraying thread. She smiled and danced, laughed and chatted, pretending all was well while a tempest raged in her heart. She longed for this terrible evening to end yet feared what would come when the last guest left. But all things must come to an end, as they say, and Emmeline watched the guests trickle home in the wee hours of the morning with growing apprehension.

The door was hardly shut before Papa stormed over to his daughter. "Take those blasted things off this minute!"

Emmeline's mouth opened, though she had no idea what to say. When she did not move fast enough, Papa snatched the pendant, yanking it clean off; the metal scratched and bruised her neck, and Emmeline cried out in fright, but he ignored it as he ripped the bracelet from Emmeline's wrist.

"How dare you, you brute!" shrieked Mama, but Papa flung the jewelry at her.

"I will not allow my daughter to be dressed in the profits of your whoring!" he bellowed.

Mama let her hand fly, striking Papa's cheek, and he snatched her arms before she could land another. Instead, she spat in his face. "At least my lovers give me something more than the pox!"

Ignoring the spittle on his cheeks, Papa leaned in close. "We both know it wasn't my lovers—"

But Emmeline placed her hands over her ears and fled the ballroom, not pausing until she escaped into her bedchamber. Once the door was shut tight, she flung off the rest of her mother's tainted presents. She should've known better. Her mother's pin money could never afford such things, and the thought of how her mother had acquired those "gifts" set her stomach churning.

Dressed in her chemise, Emmeline collapsed onto the bed, curling into herself and wishing she could erase the entire evening. It was supposed to be her night, and now it was her regret.

Chapter 18

Calm and demure.

Sitting on the sofa in their parlor, Eloise repeated those two words in her mind until she was their physical embodiment. A breath in. And a breath out. She allowed the air to fill her with serenity. To clear her mind of irritating things. Like gentlemen. Or more specifically one gentleman who left her so addled that Eloise hardly knew what she was feeling.

If only she had someone to speak to about such things. Kitty filled that role admirably, but Mother was decidedly against their friendship, leaving them with little opportunity to visit one another. Though they'd stolen moments here and there over the past sennight, Eloise needed more.

That brought Patrick to mind once again. And again, Eloise shoved the thought aside. He was the last person with whom she wished to speak, even though her convoluted, erratic heart longed for him.

"What is wrong, Eloise?" asked Mother, looking up from her needlepoint.

"Pardon?"

"You sighed in quite a tragic manner."

Eloise tugged at her neglected needle, adding a stitch to yet another ridiculous and utterly useless piece of embroidery. "It's nothing, Mother."

The lady's eyes flicked between her work and her daughter.

"Are you certain? You've seemed agitated of late." From anyone else, the words might sound like a genuine expression of concern, but her mother's lifeless tone drained any heart from them.

"You are sighing again," said Mother as she added another stitch.

That made Eloise want to sigh once more, but she held it in while feigning a singular interest in the work on her lap. Try as she might, she could not see a single reason why her mother had engendered such loyalty from Patrick. To think, he had actually defended the lady! Even after watching Eloise struggle under her mother's dictatorial regime throughout her childhood, Patrick spoke kindly of her. Warmly, even. It was clear from his tone and expression that he held the lady in high regard.

Pausing, Eloise took another breath to calm the mounting pressure in her chest and relaxed her aching jaw. Serenity. Peace.

It did no good to dwell on that subject. Patrick Lennox had brought nothing but upheaval into her life. She hadn't slept soundly in the week and a half since he'd reappeared, ushering in a slew of unanswerable questions and conflicting sentiments.

Patrick.

Eloise's needle paused, and she turned her attention to the window. Carriages rolled by, their wheels and hooves clattering on the cobblestones. There were not many people out and about as it was still too early for most in their neighborhood, but it was a day that begged to be enjoyed. Eloise longed to sit in the light filtering through the windows and lap up the sunshine. Perhaps that might clear her mind of the gentleman who haunted her every thought.

Patrick's words played through her mind, repeating that painful confession over and over. Then the heartbroken words in his letter joined the throng, bringing tears to Eloise's eyes for those dark years when Patrick had suffered alone. As much as she had wished to hold on to her anger, there'd been too much remorse and pain in his confession for her to condemn him. However, Lucinda and Mother's accusations against men picked at her, demanding she remember the inconstancy of men's hearts.

It was a confusing cacophony of questions and concerns that left Eloise hopelessly lost, and she was heartily sick of the feeling.

"Eloise?"

Looking to her mother, Eloise found the lady gazing at her with pinched lips.

"Are you unwell?"

Shaking her head, Eloise mumbled some reply.

Mother opened her mouth and closed it with a frown. Her brows drew ever so slightly together, and her eyes darted from her daughter to her needlepoint to the floor and back again. Eloise merely stared as her mother looked almost uncomfortable, though she had no thought as to why the lady would feel so.

The vague expression cleared from her face, and Mother turned her attention back to her work. "I would love to take you to Madame Leclaire's shop this afternoon. She has a lovely new style of bonnet that would be most flattering on you. However, if you feel undone, perhaps you should rest instead as it would be most disappointing if we were forced to cancel our dinner at the Kimballs'. We can visit Madame Leclaire tomorrow if you are up to it."

Before Eloise could respond, her mother added, "And you are sighing again."

Eloise was saved from responding when they heard a knock on the front door. She and her mother put away their needle-point and awaited Isaacs to open it. Two words were all it took for Eloise to recognize the voices of their callers, and she shot from her seat. Running to the foyer, Eloise launched herself at

Aunt Mina. The lady stumbled back a step and laughed as she squeezed her niece.

"I hadn't realized you were coming to London!" cried Eloise, moving to hug her uncle and cousins in turn.

Little Lily tugged at Eloise's skirts until she had her cousin's full attention. "We spent all day in the carriage, and we had a picnic with jam tartlets and Shrewsbury cakes!"

"That sounds delightful," said Eloise, crouching down to give the girl a kiss on her cheek. "I thought I told you that you were not allowed to grow any further, Lily Kingsley, but I see you've ignored me and grown into quite the young lady."

Tucking her hands behind her, Lily gave Eloise a gap-toothed grin.

"You didn't think we would miss such an auspicious Season?" asked Aunt Mina with a grin. "We heard rumor that a special young lady was soon to be engaged, and we could not stand missing the festivities."

Eloise's eyes widened, and she straightened. "I am not soon to be engaged."

"Mr. Godwin is a fine gentleman," said Mother, drawing the group's eyes to her as she stood in the parlor doorway. "He is speaking with Mr. Andrews at this very moment."

An icy hand latched on to Eloise's heart, squeezing it.

"Then we are just in time," said Uncle Simon, but his smile dimmed when he glanced at Eloise's stricken face.

"Please, do come in," said Mother with an expression that looked more sour than usual. "It is unseemly to be standing about the foyer like ragamuffins."

Uncle Simon stiffened, but Aunt Mina touched his arm and motioned for him to follow Mother into the room.

"Mr. Godwin is speaking to Father?" Eloise whispered to her mother as they took their seats on the sofa.

"Of course," said Mother, straightening her skirts. "I don't know why you should look so surprised at that. You've shown a marked attachment to him of late."

Lily climbed onto the sofa beside Eloise and snuggled into her cousin's side while Mina and Simon's eldest, Oliver, wandered over to the shelves and began examining the knick-knacks.

"Dearest, be careful," said Mina, calling the boy over to sit beside her and her husband on the other sofa.

"How kind of you all to come to Town to join in the celebration," said Mother.

Though Eloise wanted to shout that there was nothing to celebrate, she held her temper in check, choosing instead to take a few calming breaths.

"Perhaps we should have you to dinner," said Mother.

"That sounds delightful, though I would hate to burden you," said Aunt Mina. "With a wedding to plan, you shall have your hands full. Perhaps I might be allowed to host a family dinner, and then we might meet Eloise's young fellow."

The change was subtle, but Eloise swore her mother stiffened. Of course, she was always stiff, but there was a slight tightening of her muscles.

"Are you certain?" asked Mother. "There is much to do when planning such an event—"

"Mina is more than capable of throwing a dinner party, Emmeline," said Uncle Simon with a scowl, and once again, Aunt Mina placed a hand on his forearm and squeezed.

"It is no trouble at all, Emmeline," said Aunt Mina.

A surge of jealousy shot through Eloise; she had no idea how her aunt remained so affable when faced with the cold judgment of Emmeline Andrews, but Aunt Mina merely smiled before Lily and Oliver began regaling the group with the ever-important intricacies of their young lives.

"Perhaps we might invite the Hennesseys to the dinner," Eloise blurted as she narrowed her eyes on her mother. "They are not family, but Miss Hennessey is a dear friend of mine."

Mother's expression grew more brittle, but Aunt Mina's smile grew equally more joyful as she questioned Eloise about Kitty and her parents, which did not improve Mother's mood.

However, it was Eloise's mood that took significant damage when the parlor door opened and Mr. Godwin entered with Father at his side.

Eloise shot to her feet and regretted it immediately; her head spun until it felt as though the room had shifted around her.

"Miss Andrews?" asked Mr. Godwin, his hand at her elbow to steady her.

Pressing a hand to her temple, Eloise feigned a smile. "My apologies for startling you. I merely stood up too quickly."

"She was feeling poorly just before the visitors arrived," said Mother.

"I was not," said Eloise, shooting a look at her. "I am only a little tired, I assure you."

But Mr. Godwin's brows drew together, his gaze filled with concern. "I had hoped you might join me for a drive, but I would hate to aggravate your condition."

Eloise let out a startled huff. Everyone was aggravating her condition, and there was no cure in sight.

"Perhaps you might accompany her to the garden," said Mother, motioning towards the door. "Fresh air might do her some good."

Eloise's mouth hung open while her mind refused to produce any objection. In a trice, she was bundled off with Mr. Godwin, the door shutting tight behind them so that they were alone. Which only made Eloise's heart pound harder.

However, there was a slight breeze that kissed her cheeks. It held the scent of the city and horses, but the flowers and shrubbery were in full bloom, masking much of the stench with their floral bouquet. Though three sides were surrounded by the townhouse, the southern side had only a wall just high enough to block the sight of the stables but low enough to allow in the sunlight. Eloise closed her eyes and stepped into its warmth. The sounds of their visitors and the cityscape were muted, quieting enough to give Eloise some semblance of peace. The garden was not entirely hidden from the touches of the city, but it was enough of a haven that Eloise could finally breathe and think.

In that moment of clarity, Eloise knew what she wanted, and it was not a proposal.

Chapter 19

"Miss Andrews," said Mr. Godwin, motioning for her to take a seat on a stone bench in the center. Choosing the side that faced the sun, Eloise steeled herself for what she knew she must say.

"I am terribly sorry I was unable to attend the Gardiners' ball," he said, taking the seat beside her. "I would've liked to dance with you again."

"You are too kind, Mr. Godwin," said Eloise, her gaze focusing on a particularly lovely rose. Though the winter had been bitter, summer had come early and strong, causing many of the bushes to bloom early.

Eloise wished she understood the protocol for such a moment. Though her mother and governess had been thorough in their lessons, not a single one had covered this situation. Should she wait until Mr. Godwin declared himself? Or should she nip it in the bud? Her gaze darted to the flowers, and the absurdity of her predicament and unconscious pun nearly had her laughing, though she kept her wits about her.

And that was when she realized Mr. Godwin had been speaking for some time, and she hadn't heard a word of it until he took her hand in his.

"...I have come to greatly admire you," he said, his smile growing. "Though that does not do justice to the depth of my feelings. Miss Andrews, would you do me the honor of becoming my wife?"

Eloise dropped her head. Her mind sorted through all she might say and could not decide on any route that would lessen the pain she was to inflict. When she lifted her head once more, she found herself locked in Mr. Godwin's sweet and earnest gaze.

"I am most flattered," said Eloise, but clearly, it was the wrong thing to say because he fairly beamed at that pronouncement. "And I am honored to have earned the good opinion of a gentleman such as yourself."

"It is not only a good opinion," he said, squeezing her hand, and a lump formed in Eloise's throat.

"However, I fear I cannot accept your kind and generous offer."

There were a few silent seconds before the smile faded from his face. "Pardon?"

"I do admire you, Mr. Godwin," she said in a hurry, her heart squirming as he tried to cover his heartbreak. "But I do not love you, and I cannot fathom entering into matrimony without my heart engaged. In all honesty, I am not inclined towards matrimony at present. I am sorry to cause you any pain—"

Mr. Godwin shook his head and gave her a sad smile. "There is no need to continue, Miss Andrews. I may not seem the sentimental type, but I have no interest in marrying without love, either. Or marrying when my love is not returned."

Standing, Mr. Godwin adjusted his jacket and brushed a bit of lint from his sleeve while avoiding her gaze. He swallowed, his jaw clenching together, and then cleared his throat before giving her a sketch of a bow and leaving.

Sagging on the bench, Eloise held her head in her hand, wincing at what had passed. Perhaps she did need a lie-down, for she could not stomach the thought of facing the family yet.

As she was plotting her escape, Mr. Godwin cleared his throat again.

Leaning upright, Eloise stared at him. He'd turned back to face her, but his eyes were focused on the ground.

"Miss Andrews..." His voice broke, and he cleared his throat once more. "Might you need more time to make a definitive decision? Or is there no hope at all?" Eloise opened her mouth to answer, but Mr. Godwin rushed ahead to add, "I do not mean to pester you, but I find myself quite confused."

He paused. "I... you..." Another pause before he rushed through saying, "You've shown a marked interest of late, and I had thought it a sign that you would welcome my declaration. Did I do something to change your mind?"

Her hands shook, and Eloise clenched them in her skirts to calm them, but there was no containing the tremors taking over her. Her heart sank to her toes, and Eloise was grateful she was already sitting as her last bit of strength seeped from her.

"I never meant to show more than I felt, Mr. Godwin," she said, her own words now hitching. "I do apologize if I raised your hopes, but it was unintentional, and I am truly sorry for causing you any pain. However, I am quite decided."

With a final nod, Mr. Godwin turned away and strode into the house.

Collapsing forward, Eloise hid her face and wished she could disappear. Simply vanish. Escape this tangled mess that was her life. The look on Mr. Godwin's face plagued her. Though she did not care for the gentleman as a wife ought to, he did not deserve to have his heart broken, and unintentional or not, it was she who had shattered it.

The garden door opened, and she braced herself.

"Eloise, what is going on?" asked Mother. "Mr. Godwin left with hardly a word and looked quite unhappy. Please do not say you rejected him."

Hunched over, Eloise kept her face pointed to the ground as she sighed. "Of course I rejected him. He was your choice. Not mine."

A hand patted the back of her head, and Lily murmured, "Don't be sad, Eloise."

Sitting up, she gave her cousin a sorry attempt at a smile and found Mother standing before her, spine as straight and unyielding as iron.

"I thought you cared for him," said Father, standing off to the side.

"As a friend, perhaps, but not a husband," said Eloise.

"Why is Eloise sad?" asked Oliver, tugging on his father's jacket, but Aunt Mina hushed the lad.

"How could you raise his hopes like that?" asked Mother, her brows drawing together. "You've been practically hanging on him of late. Everyone expects you to announce your engagement any day now."

"I did not hang on him." Even if she was unsure of the accuracy of her words, the whole affair was none of her mother's concern. "You were the one who encouraged the match from the beginning. You were the one who led him to believe I welcomed his attentions. And I do not care what everyone expects! I am not going to marry Mr. Godwin or anyone else for that matter!"

Mother's expression tightened. "Ridiculous. You do not want to be a spinster."

Shooting to her feet, Eloise glared at her mother. "Do not tell me what I want."

Aunt Mina cleared her throat, drawing the fierce gazes of both mother and daughter. "Eloise, might I ask what has brought on this sudden change of heart? Last we spoke, you seemed keen on the idea."

Mother's lips pinched. "She is my daughter, not yours, Mina, and you have no part in this conversation."

Uncle Simon scowled, stepping towards his sister, but Eloise interrupted before he could speak.

"How dare you speak to her like that!" She fairly shook as she stomped her foot. "I wish Aunt Mina were my mother, for she has been more of a mother to me than you!"

Thick silence followed that pronouncement as Mother's

mouth slackened into a large, unseemly gape. But Eloise was finished. Stepping around the others, she fled the garden.

"Eloise." Her father tried to stop her, but she evaded him, hurrying through the house and up to her bedchamber.

Barring the door behind her, Eloise tried to sit, but the events of the past hour were too much for her to hold still. This was all her mother's fault. That determined lady did not care two jots about what anyone else wanted. She forged ahead as though no one's opinion mattered.

Pacing the room, Eloise tried to sort through the issues plaguing her life, but the only thing she knew for certain was that her mother would never stop until she was married off. There was no reasoning with her. The lady was intractable, and Eloise could not stand suffering through Season after Season while Mother tossed eligible bachelors at her.

And that was when Kitty's words came into her mind. They had been hovering in the back of her thoughts ever since the young lady had spoken them. They had seemed too drastic, too audacious, but now, they seemed to be her only hope.

"...you have a reputation to protect, and I have none. There is no point in my mother going to such lengths when it will do no good."

Though Kitty had said these words in passing, Eloise suspected they may be her salvation.

...

Guilt twisted Norman's heart as he watched Emmeline's mouth slacken into an ungainly gape, her eyes widening as Eloise's words dug deeper into his wife's heart. Though he did not wish for Emmeline to receive such a hearty blow, he was grateful to see any emotion written on her face. It was a rare enough sight that even this heartbreaking moment was welcome. There was even a tremble of her chin, and that blasted mask of hers cracked and crumbled before their eyes.

Mina stepped forward and touched Emmeline's shoulder, but his wife jerked away as tears trailed down her cheeks. Simon stepped forward, but Mina stopped him and herded her family away, giving Norman a farewell nod as they left.

Lowering herself onto the bench, Emmeline gathered herself enough to properly mask the pain once more, but there was no life in her eyes as she stared into the distance.

"Emmeline?" But he received no response.

The slam of a bedchamber door echoed through the townhouse, and Norman held in a sigh. Something needed to be done, though he had not a thought about what that was. Deciding it best to face Eloise first, Norman slipped out of the garden and went in search of his daughter.

Chapter 20

"Leave me be!" was the answer he received when he knocked on her bedchamber door.

"Eloise, please let me in," he said.

"If you are here to force me to marry Mr. Godwin, I shan't do it!"

Leaning his head forward, Norman sagged against the door and wished he knew how to handle such scenes. There was a time when Emmeline had had quite a temper, but he'd never succeeded in calming it. The best he could do was offer simple nods at appropriate intervals while she vented her spleen about whatever troubled her. Perhaps that was all he needed to do now. Once he got past the door.

"I would never force you to marry anyone," he said. "Please, let me in."

The door flew open, startling him, and he saw Eloise storming back to the center of the bedchamber to continue her furious pacing.

"And I will not apologize." Eloise did not pause in her march. Jabbing a finger in the general direction of the garden, she said, "She is forever browbeating me, and I have every right to be upset."

Coming over to her bed, Norman took a seat, stretching out his legs and crossing his ankles and arms. Silently, he watched his daughter. Her movements and tone were so like those of Emmeline in a high temper that it struck Norman as quite funny, though he hid his amusement; such a display would not be welcomed.

"She deserved it," said Eloise, stopping at the window to scowl at the world.

Those words struck Norman.

Though he was not blind to the strained nature of their relationship, he hadn't thought Emmeline and Eloise were at such odds. Frowning, Norman thought back on his own behavior and wondered if he should have done more to intervene.

Eloise continued to make indictments against Emmeline, and Norman merely nodded as he mulled over that question. He would never have allowed the children to be neglected, but there was much more to this moment than a mere argument. Eloise vibrated with resentment, and Norman wondered if he'd neglected his own duties by not stepping between his mother and his wife long ago. The manner in which "Mother" Andrews had poisoned Emmeline was having more far-reaching effects than he'd ever expected.

"I do not wish to marry Mr. Godwin," said Eloise.

"Then you shan't," he replied.

Eloise paused and turned to look at her father. "Pardon?"

"My greatest desire is for my children to be happily settled. Forcing you into a marriage you do not desire runs rather contrary to that, don't you think?"

Coming to stand before him, Eloise asked in a quiet voice, "And if I shouldn't like to marry at all? Would you help me get settled in a house of my own?"

Norman raised his eyebrows. "Running away from your troubles is not going to make you happy."

Eloise straightened with a scowl. "That is not running away."

Sighing, Norman dropped his gaze to the floor. Yet another

example of just how alike she was to her mother. Norman wondered how the pair didn't see it. Emmeline's stubborn streak was still alive and well, and of all the wonderful traits Eloise could've inherited from her mother, being blindly bullheaded was not what Norman would've wished for his daughter.

At that exact moment, an epiphany made itself known, and Norman was startled to realize his daughter had a dash of himself, too, and not a part he wished to pass on. After all, he was living in a mess that was due in part to his tendency to avoid rather than confront.

Which was not a pleasant revelation to receive.

Taking a breath, Norman decided that perhaps he needed to be a bit more direct. "I suspect it has more to do with your desire to avoid Patrick than a desire to remain unmarried."

Her cheeks pinked, but Eloise shook her head, turning away so she could not look at him directly. Shoulders slumping, Norman watched his daughter as she stuttered her way through a litany of false excuses. He'd never seen it as clearly as he did now, and he could not deny that his little Eloise had inherited his most despised quality.

"Mother is determined to see me married," said Eloise. "If I do not put distance between us, she will harp at me until I surrender."

Norman had serious doubts about that, for he was quite certain Eloise was every bit as intractable as Emmeline, but that was best left unsaid at this juncture. "Why are you so decidedly against marriage?"

Turning to face him again, Eloise held his gaze for a brief moment, her hand fiddling with her necklace. Then she looked away, moving towards the window. "I don't understand why any lady would wish to marry."

Coming to his feet, Norman moved to Eloise's side and put an arm around her shoulders. He had no thought as to what he should say, but he stood there as his daughter leaned against him, gazing out at the row of houses.

"Why do men do it?" she asked, her words broken by a hitch

in her voice. "How can they declare their undying devotion to their wives and then keep company with other women?"

Norman stiffened and looked down at Eloise. "What do you mean?"

Pulling away, Eloise wiped at her eyes and said, "Lucinda and Mother told me about 'the club.'"

Norman scratched at his chin, casting through his thoughts for understanding, but when he found none, he asked, "The club?"

Eloise whirled around to face him, her chin quivering. "Gentlemen say they are at their club, but in truth, they're visiting their mistresses."

It took a moment or two before Norman comprehended his daughter's accusation, then another two to fully believe it. Held in place, he stared at Eloise, blinking, for that was the only thing he could manage at the moment.

"Your mother and sister told you that?" It was not the most pressing question, but the only one Norman could form at present.

Chin trembling, Eloise nodded before going into a halting explanation of what she had witnessed and her trip to her sister's home. Throughout her tear-filled explanation, Norman's heart constricted. His breaths came out quick and short as he listened to his daughter recount the allegations his wife had laid against him. Norman had never been good with words, but all fled from his mind as his character was thoroughly impugned.

When Eloise finished speaking, there were several silent moments while Norman forced his thoughts to gather. Stepping around to face his daughter, he took her by the shoulders and held her gaze.

"I never thought I'd need to defend my honor from such slander—especially in my own home and from my own family— but I need you to know the absolute truth: I have not now, nor have I ever, broken my wedding vows," he said, his heart in his eyes. "Your mother and sister are wrong. Though there are gentlemen who see no harm in such behavior, there are plenty who never betray their wives or their honor in such a manner."

Eloise's expression pinched, her chin trembling all the more as tears filled her eyes. "Patrick did."

"Patrick made a mistake. One he truly regrets," said Norman. At Eloise's puzzled expression, he added, "Do you think I would allow a gentleman to pursue you without having a word with him?" And doing a thorough investigation into his background and behavior, though Norman wasn't about to admit that.

"You spoke with Patrick about... that?" asked Eloise.

"Absolutely. He did not wait for me to confront him about the rumors I'd heard. Though not proud of his behavior, he did not hide from it. It was quite admirable."

"Then you think I should pursue a courtship with him?"

Norman wished he could give his daughter an easy solution for her questions. "That is for you to decide. I am merely saying that I feel he is truly repentant, and it is unkind to hold mistakes against a person when he is trying his best to make it right."

"But how can I trust him?" Eloise whispered with an expression so pitiful that Norman's heart broke at the sight of it.

"I have no answers, Eloise. You must figure out for yourself if you feel Patrick is worth the risk," said Norman. "But forgiving is a good place to start, for we are all flawed creatures."

Leaning forward, Eloise wrapped her arms around her father and held him tight.

...

Motionless, Emmeline sat on the stone bench, her eyes staring at nothing. There was an emptiness in her heart, and only the weight of the world pressing on her chest testified that it was still there. It was as though she was disconnected from everything around her. The sun shone above, the breezes caught the foliage, but Emmeline felt none of it.

Eloise despised her. There was no pretending it untrue, for

Emmeline had seen the look on her daughter's face and heard the vehemence of her words.

Emmeline could not reconcile the life she had with the one she'd wanted. She had given her family everything they needed. Sacrificed her very self for their well-being. Yet they were not happy. What more could she do? What more could she give? Was Eloise correct in thinking her life would be better with another mother?

Thoughts of her own childhood resurfaced, breaking through the numb haze that surrounded her. Memories best left buried came to mind, and a shudder passed through Emmeline at the thought of Eloise suffering such treatment. Her daughter may hate her, but she had never been propositioned. Had never struggled through a dance while fending off the wandering hands of her partner. Had never been made to feel undeserving of the dignity afforded other ladies. That was enough for Emmeline.

It had to be, for she could not give up protecting Eloise.

The door to the garden opened, but Emmeline did not glance towards the intruder until her husband stormed into view.

"Did you tell Eloise I had a mistress?" It was more accusation than question, and Emmeline cocked her head to stare at his dark expression.

"She caught James—"

"I know what happened, Emmeline," he said with a scowl. "I want to know why you felt it necessary to tell her that *all* gentlemen—including myself—behave in such a manner. That is a blatant lie! How could you accuse me of such a thing? And to my daughter, of all people? She is having a difficult enough time without you filling her head with such rubbish."

Norman was not one to shout. Emmeline could not think of a time when he had raised his voice to her, but at that declaration, his volume raised enough that she found herself quite startled.

"She wanted to know the truth—" she began.

Coming to stand right before her, Norman glared down at her. "I have never strayed! Such a thing has never crossed my mind."

Blinking up at her husband, Emmeline struggled to stay afloat in such a shift, but her mind was still too befuddled to mount much of a defense. "But you haven't visited my bedchamber in years, so you must be seeking your pleasures somewhere."

"Do you have a paramour?" asked Norman.

Leaning away, Emmeline gaped at him. "Of course not."

"But you have not visited my bedchamber, either, Emmeline. If you doubt my loyalty because of that, there is no reason I shouldn't doubt the same."

"You are a man."

Huffing, Norman shook his head, looking up into the sky and turning away from her. His head dropped again as he stared at his feet for several long moments. "I see. Since I am a man, I am little more than a rutting beast."

Standing thusly for several more moments, Norman finally turned to meet her eyes. "It was you who left our bedchamber. It was you who withdrew your affections. It was you who imposed all these rules and strictures on our relationship. You pushed me away and then expected me to welcome you with open arms whenever you deemed it appropriate."

"I did what needed to be done for the good of our children," said Emmeline. "The way we were behaving was ruining our family's reputation. Mother Andrews was quite adamant about it."

Crossing his arms, Norman dug the heel of his boot into the moss filling the gaps between the flagstones. "I see we have now circled round to that old argument."

With another shake of his head, he strode away, leaving Emmeline alone again.

Chapter 21

Emmeline
Age Twenty

Smoothing out the wrinkles in her gloves, Emmeline swayed with the coach. Her shoulder bumped against her aunt as Emmeline tried to keep herself in place. Papa sat opposite, the shadows obscuring his face, though she knew he paid her no heed. If only Aunt Vivian would do the same.

"I wish you'd agree to Mr. Dice's suit, Emmeline. Young ladies nowadays have the strangest notions about courtship and marriage."

"Wishing to choose my own husband is not strange, Aunt Vivian," replied Emmeline with a sigh while watching the passing streetlamps.

"Modern claptrap. You'd best leave such important matters to those who know better." In the dark recesses of the coach, Emmeline could hardly make out her aunt's expression, but she felt the accompanying scowl. "You of all people should know the dangers of following your heart."

"Vivian." Papa fairly growled the name, but Aunt Vivian would not be deterred.

"You know it to be true, John. You married as your heart

dictated, and that harlot has made you miserable."

Emmeline stifled a huff of laughter. It was not as though Aunt Vivian's own arranged marriage were any better; Uncle Edgar had not been in the same county as his wife in a decade.

"Leave it be," said Papa. "Suffering through yet another insufferable evening is agony enough without your harping."

Crossing her arms, Aunt Vivian turned her gaze from her brother to stare out the window. "If we are not on our guard she will end up making a horrid match."

Unable to stop herself from twitting her chaperone and father, Emmeline smiled to herself and said, "Perhaps I do not mean to make a match at all."

"No match?" Aunt Vivian fairly gasped at the words.

"And why not? I do not lack fortune, and I have no interest in marrying for marrying's sake."

"Ridiculous," said Aunt Vivian, gaping like a cod. "Every young lady must marry—"

"Calm yourself, Vivian," said Papa. "She is goading you. Like her mother, Emmeline takes perverse enjoyment in tormenting those around her. However, unlike Amelia, Emmeline understands her duty and will do it. A woman's only use in this world is bedding and breeding."

Emmeline's lip curled at her father's revolting words, but she remained silent as it did no good to confront him. Papa was as changeable as a rock. Less so, for a bolder must bend to the wind and water that slowly shape it over the years. Emmeline was certain that given a millennia, her father would still spout the same nonsense, convinced his opinion was eternal, unshakeable truth.

Across from them, Aunt Vivian quieted, her eyes fixed on the window. Though she couldn't see the coloring in her aunt's cheeks, Emmeline felt the embarrassment radiating from the childless lady. She placed a hand on Aunt Vivian's knee, gently squeezing it, but the lady gave no acknowledgment of the kindness.

The coach rolled to a stop, and Papa emerged before handing down the ladies. Though decorum forced Emmeline to take his arm, she dropped it the moment they stepped into the Grovers' ballroom.

It was one of the finest in the area, yet Emmeline had no eyes for the ornate ceiling, myriad of candles, or finely carved colonnades that lined the dance floor. Her attention was drawn to the people watching her entrance. Though she'd never thought herself vain, Emmeline was astonished at how much she reveled in the gentlemen's admiring gazes and the jealousy it inspired in the ladies.

It was all a bit of foolishness. Emmeline had never wished to be the focus of such attention, but having gained it, she found it quite beguiling. Intoxicating. Standing here, she was not merely the unfortunate daughter of unfortunate parents. She was society's darling. One of them.

All it took was the first gentleman to approach before the rest flocked to her, and with hardly a moment to breathe, she was swept from set to set, her partners all charms and polite flirtation.

"Would you care for a stroll about the gardens?" Mr. Carson asked. "You look a little flushed."

Pressing a hand to her glowing cheek, Emmeline nodded. "It is quite warm tonight, and I could use a moment to catch my breath."

Mr. Carson led her through the crowd and onto the veranda with Aunt Vivian following at a discreet distance. Glancing at the sky, Emmeline wished she could see the stars, but the lights of the city dulled their shine. Taking the steps down, the couple followed the gravel pathway into the center of the courtyard. The lamps along the edge cast a warm glow on the area, giving her enough light to identify the plants filling the beds, and Emmeline was pleased to find so many of her favorites.

"You adore flowers?" asked Mr. Carson.

Emmeline gave a start and looked at her companion. "Am I that obvious?"

Mr. Carson smiled down at her. "You are delightfully easy to read, Miss Kingsley. Your eyes betray you every time."

Blushing, Emmeline glanced down, but Mr. Carson nudged her chin upwards again.

"You needn't hide from me," he whispered.

The warmth in his gaze wove its way through Emmeline. In truth, she hadn't considered Mr. Carson a serious suitor before tonight, but his expression was so enticing. It was as though he truly saw her. Not merely the gowns and decorations she used to attract the attention of the masses, but the heart beating beneath it. And for one so often overlooked, Emmeline had no ability to fight the magnetic pull of it. His fingers brushed her cheek, and Emmeline leaned into the contact, her eyes sliding closed.

"Emmeline," he breathed, his lips drawing closer to hers.

The shock of hearing her Christian name broke the spell, allowing her to lean away from him. "Mr. Carson, I am pleased to have earned your affection, but I am not ready to return it."

The gentleman sighed, his breath tickling her cheek. "I know I am not the obvious candidate for your heart, but I am the most devoted of your conquests. You will never find a gentleman more enraptured by your beauty nor more desperate to seek your approval."

"Mr. Carson..." Emmeline's voice faltered as she had no response for such a declaration.

"Please tell me I have a chance of winning you." Taking her hand, Mr. Carson held it to his chest. "My heart beats for you alone."

Emmeline's hand trembled, a fluttery energy taking hold of her, and she wondered if the weakness and warmth she felt was love. It was not at all what she thought love would feel like, but having little experience with it, she was at a loss to identify the emotions filling her.

"Mr. Carson, I do admire you," she whispered. "But I am not ready to accept your proposal."

"I will give you anything your heart desires," he said as his arms enfolded her. Though she knew she should step away, the feel of his embrace set her heart thumping in her chest, and she found herself leaning into his touch. She couldn't remember the last time someone had held her, and she reveled in it. "Trips abroad, if you wish. More jewelry and gowns than you could ever wear in a lifetime. A house of your own and a massive garden filled with flowers."

His lips brushed her cheek, and Emmeline closed her eyes for a brief moment before his words registered.

"A house of my own?" Her eyes flew open, and she leaned back to stare at him. "Why would I need a house for myself?"

Mr. Carson chuckled. "For you and the children, of course…"

Blinking, she struggled to form coherent thoughts. "You are not proposing marriage?"

Brows knit together, Mr. Carson released Emmeline and stared at her. "Why would you assume I am speaking of marriage?"

"Because I am a lady and not a light-skirt," she said, stepping away and wrapping her arms around her middle.

"I mean no disrespect, Miss Kingsley, but you cannot expect a gentleman of good fortune and breeding, such as myself, to marry someone from a questionable family. But that does not mean we cannot enjoy an… acquaintance," he said, his finger brushing the edge of her décolletage.

Emmeline slapped his hand away. "Yes, it does, sir."

"Then someone else holds your heart." Mr. Carson's expression fell, and she gaped at him.

"That has nothing to do with it, sirrah. I am not that sort of woman and do not welcome such advances." Emmeline stepped around him, but Mr. Carson grabbed her by the hand.

"Do you honestly hold out hope of an honorable offer?" The gentleman's expression was so thoroughly confused that Emmeline longed to slap him, but with Aunt Vivian watching in the distance, she refused to cause a scene. The last thing she needed was an audience to such a humiliating moment.

"And why should I not, Mr. Carson?" she demanded. "Though you have a low opinion of me, there are plenty of other gentlemen with honorable intentions."

Mr. Carson gave a faltering chuckle, his head cocking to the side as he stared at her. "You think the gentlemen rush to your side because they wish to marry into a scandalous family and taint their name and bloodline with such a connection? You cannot be serious. Your dowry and beauty are not large enough to balance that sacrifice."

Wrenching her hand from his grasp again, Emmeline took several steps away, her chin quivering at the implications. Not caring two whits about ruining her silk gloves, she dabbed at her eyes, wishing she had the composure to hide the heartbreak.

Mr. Carson's expression fell, his brow furrowing. "Miss Kingsley, are you well? I did not mean to upset you—"

He reached for her again, but Emmeline shook her head and fled. Though Aunt Vivian hurried after her, the lady was too far to intercept her before Emmeline hurried from the garden.

Taking a trembling breath, she fought to keep the tears at bay, but there was no way to stem the sorrow filling her heart. Disappearing into a quiet corner until the ball ended was the best course of action. Stealing along the edges of the crowd, Emmeline slipped into a sitting room and collapsed onto a window seat tucked off to one side.

Curling inward, Emmeline let loose a torrent of tears.

Nothing had changed. The gentlemen had grown more subtle in their propositions, but they were no less filthy. She'd given Mr. Carson no reason to believe she'd accept such a demeaning arrangement, yet he thought her eager for it. He'd known her for some months now and still thought her that sort of woman. Not good enough to wed, but good enough to bed.

"Miss Kingsley."

The voice was little more than a whisper, yet it startled her, making Emmeline jump from her seat. Turning away from the intruder, she wiped her face.

"I do apologize," said the gentleman, his voice faltering. "I didn't mean to frighten you."

Emmeline tried to respond but could not form the words. And then a handkerchief appeared before her. Stepping away from the offering, she straightened her spine. "I do not wish to be bothered. Please leave me be."

There was a hesitant chuckle. "I hate to contradict a lady, but it is you who intruded on my solitude."

Casting a cautious glance at the stranger, Emmeline asked, "Pardon?"

The gentleman's cheeks reddened, and he cleared his throat. "I was hiding here when you burst in, so it was you who bothered me. Not the other way around."

Emmeline blinked, startled that she hadn't noticed him before. He gave her a hint of a smile, his eyes softening as he offered up his handkerchief once more. Her eyes darted between the gentleman and the linen in his hand.

"I mean you no harm," he said. "Truly."

Her mind warned her not to forget the duplicity of men, but her heart warmed to this gentleman who had little polish and an air of utter earnestness. Though his hair must have been combed at some point, it now stuck up in the most amusing manner. His clothes were of the finest quality, but they hung askew. Clearly, someone had attempted to refine his sensibilities, but the gentleman had not the interest in maintaining the polished facade.

Even as she watched him, his dark brown eyes darted away from her, his cheeks reddening as he rubbed his right shoe against the back of his left leg, which made the stocking sag.

Inching her hand forward, Emmeline snatched the handkerchief from him and dabbed her cheeks.

"My thanks," she said.

"And my pleasure," he replied.

Emmeline moved to the far side of the sitting room, and the mysterious gentleman moved in the opposite direction, giving her the space she craved. Prudence told her to leave. She should not remain in such a compromising situation, but the thought of facing the masses was enough to bring on more tears. Emmeline saw a similar war between propriety and discomfort reflected in the gentleman's gaze.

"Is there anything I might do?" he asked. "I could fetch someone for you."

Emmeline shook her head, dabbing as more tears trickled down her cheeks. The pair stood there awkwardly with only the sounds of her sniffles breaking the silence. The gentleman's eyes darted between her and the floor, but he seemed no more inclined to speak than she.

Giving in to her shaking legs, she returned to the window seat. "I apologize for intruding on your solitude, Mr...."

"Andrews," he said, his voice catching, which made his cheeks burn brighter. "Mr. Norman Andrews, Miss Kingsley."

Emmeline's eyebrows rose. "Have we been introduced before?"

Mr. Andrews shook his head. "I've long wished to make your acquaintance, but I could never make it past your throng of admirers."

Spine straightening, Emmeline fought back the sudden rush of embarrassment and anger. For all his benign appearance, Mr. Andrews was nothing but another gentleman seeking a bit of easy affection.

Getting to her feet, Emmeline strode to the entrance. "I am sorry to inform you my favors are not forthcoming, no matter what the others believe."

Mr. Andrews grabbed her hand to stop her, but he released it almost as quickly, that ever-present blush deepening. "I would never presume, Miss Kingsley, nor do I have any interest in sullying your virtue so."

"It appears I have no virtue to sully." Frustration pulled the words from her mouth before she thought better of it, and then it was her turn to blush.

"That is as untrue a statement as any I've heard," he said, while once again rubbing his shoe against the back of his other leg so that both of his stockings sagged.

Emmeline huffed. "You may be the only person to believe that."

"Then they are all fools," blurted the gentleman with a scowl. His cheeks blazed red, his eyes darting away from her, but he squared his shoulders as though daring her to disagree.

"And what would you know about it? You speak in such firm terms, yet this is the first time we have met."

Mr. Andrews gave a self-deprecating laugh. "This is the first time you've noticed me, but it is not the first time I've noticed you. I am used to being overlooked. It gives me the chance to observe, and from what I've seen, you are a lady of the highest quality."

"Perfect for a paramour, perhaps." Yet again, the bitter words crept up on Emmeline, bringing a new sheen of tears. The embarrassment was too much for her to bear, and she moved to the exit.

"Never," said Mr. Andrews, the force of his word drawing Emmeline to a halt. His lips pinched, his expression strained. "A man would be blessed with you for a wife, and if anyone tells you differently, they are not worthy of your time."

Emmeline's chin trembled, her fingers twisting the gentleman's handkerchief. "How can you believe that?"

"How can I not?" Mr. Andrews' speech was slow and stuttering, as though each word took great effort. "Anyone with eyes can see you are kindhearted and comport yourself with honesty and dignity, though your upbringing likely taught you the opposite. You have every reason to follow your parents' example, yet you choose a better path. That is a rare and admirable quality."

He stood apart from her, not using any of the flirtatious nonsense other gentlemen employed. Mr. Andrews simply spoke the truth as he saw it, and each unpolished word sank into Emmeline's heart, inspiring a new sheen of tears. It was perhaps the greatest compliment she had ever received, and Emmeline could not think of another person who thought so highly of her.

"Mr. Andrews—"

The door to the sitting room shot open, and Aunt Vivian came flying in. "There you are, girl! Why did you disappear so suddenly? You should know better than to go wandering off—"

But Aunt Vivian's tirade halted as she saw Mr. Andrews.

"What have you been up to, Emmeline?" she demanded, coming over and taking her niece by the arm.

"I assure you it was harmless," said Mr. Andrews. "Miss Kingsley was distressed, and I was offering my assistance."

Aunt Vivian's disapproving frown did not ease as her gaze traveled Mr. Andrews, catching each imperfection. Emmeline's own eyes narrowed at the judgment showing in Aunt Vivian's expression. Rumpled or not, Mr. Andrews did not deserve such harsh assessment.

"Come, dear," said Aunt Vivian, pulling Emmeline towards the exit. "Mr. Bentley hopes to claim you for the next set."

Emmeline's stomach twisted and wrenched at the thought of leaving her sanctuary and facing the polished pretenders in the ballroom. But duty called, and Emmeline had no choice in the matter. Not with Aunt Vivian tugging on her so.

"Thank you, Mr. Andrews," said Aunt Vivian with a dismissive wave, but Emmeline could not leave things as they were.

"Would you care to join us for tea tomorrow?" she asked.

Mr. Andrews blinked at her, his eyelids fluttering in rapid succession. "Me?"

"Of course," said Emmeline.

"It would be my honor," he replied with a low bow.

But Emmeline was certain it was hers. Having met a wealth of gentlemen, she was intrigued by this odd specimen. He had none of the usual airs and graces, but that only enhanced his charm. As Emmeline had discovered, earnestness was far more important than eloquence, and Mr. Andrews had that superior quality in abundance.

Chapter 22

Clutching her reticule, Eloise stood outside the servants' entrance and took a breath of the afternoon air. The scent of the city was unpleasant, but the feel was invigorating—though more so because of what she was about to do.

Eloise studied the stairs leading up to the street and braced herself for the larger step she was taking. To walk unaccompanied through London would not go unnoticed, and there would be consequences, but they were the unavoidable toll for liberating herself from Mother's control. Surely, Maria and Susie would not snub her. Would they? Shaking her head at herself, Eloise clung to the knowledge that Kitty would not abandon her once her reputation was well and truly tattered.

Though she'd planned a more regal ascent into freedom, the sounds of servants behind her forced Eloise to move with more economy than grace. Hurrying up the stairs, she scurried down the street and did not halt until there was some distance between herself and the townhouse.

With light footsteps and head held high, Eloise meandered along the pavement. A barouche drove towards her, and she was especially pleased to see the hood fully down, allowing the occupants to witness her scandalous behavior unobstructed.

"Good afternoon, Mrs. Collicott," said Eloise with a nod as the lady and her companion passed. The biddy looked fairly agog at the sight of the young lady parading around alone, which set Eloise giggling.

Was it possible that the sunshine was brighter and the air more fragrant? There was little birdsong to be had in the city, but Eloise heard it all the same; those happy melodies swirling around her.

And so Eloise strode through the streets, calling greetings to all who crossed her path. Though the majority of the fashionable people were still at home, Eloise was pleased with all the work she'd done. Years of Mother's harping undone in a quarter of an hour. It was positively marvelous.

However, there was still more to do.

Eloise hailed a coach and imagined the tabbies tittering over tea about the scandalous Miss Andrews hiring a hackney. Gasp! For shame.

The driver stood in his box at the back of the vehicle, watching her as she approached the hackney's steps, but the fellow did not alight and assist her. Eloise waited on the pavement, watching him as he stared right back.

"Are you getting in or not?" he barked.

Giving a faltering smile, Eloise stepped forward and fumbled with the door latch. With a few silent grumbles, she managed to climb in and situate herself.

"Where to?"

And that was the question. Eloise had thought to visit the Park, but as this was one of the rare moments in her life where she could do as she pleased, it was wiser to go somewhere Mother would never allow. A particularly intriguing place.

"Burwell Terrace on Farthington Road. It is five houses down from the apothecary's on the corner of Havering Street," she said with a smile.

...

"My, but you are a pretty little thing, aren't you," said Grandmother Kingsley as they stood in her parlor. She grabbed Eloise by the chin, turning her face this way and that in a manner that made her feel like a horse being inspected by a buyer. "Yes, quite lovely."

Eloise smiled and pulled back, freeing herself of the lady's hold. "And it is good to finally meet you, Grandmother Kingsley."

The lady's expression pinched, her lips puckering into a sneer. "Oh, my dear, please do not call me that, for it makes me sound so old. I prefer Amelia. Please, sit."

A woman of middling years sat in a corner of the parlor, her knitting needles flying through her work.

"Do not mind Mrs. Bell. She keeps me company since my children refuse to visit me," said Amelia with a wave. But Eloise found it difficult to dismiss the woman as the click-clacking of her needles served as a constant reminder of her presence.

"I apologize for dropping by unannounced," said Eloise.

"Nonsense. It is a pleasure to see you, though I cannot imagine your mother will be pleased to discover that you are missing." At that, the lady smiled, her wrinkled face beaming, though there was something in her eyes that made the back of Eloise's neck prickle.

The door opened, and a maid carried in a tea tray.

"Over here," said Amelia, pointing beside her. But when the woman set it as directed, Amelia waved it away. "Not there." She pointed in a different place than before. "Here."

The maid laid out the array of tea and sweets and disappeared with a curtsy.

"It's a tad embarrassing to admit I had to sneak away," said Eloise, taking the refreshments Amelia offered. "I am a grown woman, after all, and should not be forced to such clandestine methods to visit family."

Amelia shook her head and gave an airy wave of her hands. "It's good to see an Andrews with backbone. I had all but despaired for your branch of the family, as my daughter has far too much starch for her good."

Eloise chuckled into her tea. "That is a perfect description of Mother."

Sharing a grin with her granddaughter, Amelia took a bite of cake. "Heaven knows where she got it. I taught her better than to live such a confined life. I wanted her to embrace the world, and instead, she became a dried-up prune."

Amelia followed that with a puckering expression that looked so like Mother that Eloise laughed and promptly choked on her tea. Dabbing at her lips with a napkin, Eloise felt lighter than she had in days. Coming here had been exactly what she needed, and her heart warmed at the thought of becoming acquainted with this lovely lady and her wicked sense of humor.

"It's a shame we shan't see her when she discovers I am gone," said Eloise, echoing Amelia's impersonation but twisting it even further, causing Amelia to laugh heartily.

"My dear," she said, wiping at her eyes, "I can see we are kindred spirits, you and I. It is such a shame she denied us the opportunity to know each other sooner."

Setting aside her dish, Eloise sighed. "Unfortunately, my mother is determined to control my every movement and has a keen dislike of you for some odd reason."

Amelia rolled her eyes. "It is not odd at all. She is a cold-hearted wretch of a woman who cannot stand to see others enjoying their lives as they ought. I spent years trying to breathe life into her, but she grew spiteful of my *joie de vivre* and hasn't spoken to me in almost fifteen years."

That deflated some of Eloise's newfound joy, for it was clear at a glance that the lady was in need of support. Her house was of decent quality in a moderate neighborhood, but it was a far cry from what it ought to have been. Amelia's furnishings were worn from age, though clean and cared for, and the lady herself was dressed in fashions that were several years old. Though Amelia's life was comfortable, it broke Eloise's heart to see the lady with less than was her due as the matron of the Kingsley family.

She wondered why Uncle Simon allowed his mother to live like this, and she vowed to speak to him directly after this visit. Feeling quite pleased with that decision, Eloise took up her tea again and bit into a bland slice of cake.

"I am pleased to see you have not been tainted by her sour view of life. I love a girl with spirit, and it is clear you have that in spades," said Amelia, raising her teacup to her lips with shaking hands.

Eloise wrinkled her nose and smiled. "I certainly hope so, for it will take spirit to stand firm against my mother. She is determined to marry me off and refuses to listen to anything I have to say on the matter."

Setting down her dish with a clatter, Amelia leaned forward. "Oh, you must hold strong, girl. You must. Marriage is a prison, and I would hate to see you shackled."

Unbidden, Patrick crept into her mind, and Eloise could not understand why she still yearned for him after all that had passed. Yet even as she tried to dismiss all thoughts of matrimony and love, she could not forget his arms encircling her as they danced or the way her heart stuttered when he smiled. Or that she missed him at the oddest times. Or how much she longed for his advice and clarity.

"I am not set on marriage," said Eloise, but she felt the need to be honest. "However, I am not set against it, either. I merely wish to be free to make the choice as I see fit."

Amelia inched forward on the sofa, holding Eloise's eyes with a fiery gaze. "Marriage will ruin your life. My husband was the source of every pain and heartache in my life, and the happiest moment during our years together was the day I received word of his death. Do not repeat my mistake and trap yourself in matrimony."

Though Eloise could not pinpoint the precise cause of her unease, the tickle at the back of her neck grew as Amelia spoke. Eloise felt Mrs. Bell watching her, the noise of her knitting needles not stopping as Amelia expounded on all the hardships her husband had heaped upon her. The lady required nothing more than an occasional smile and nod, for she hardly paused to draw breath before launching into more of his shortcomings and vices. The gentleman sounded like a veritable monster.

After a good long while, the lady slowed enough for Eloise to ask, "But do you wish for companionship?"

Amelia barked out a laugh and then smirked. "Though my health is restricting me as of late, I never wanted for companionship except when my husband forced me to return home to him. Then I was subjected to weeks or months of loneliness in the country with limited society and no one of note."

Eloise bit her lips as she tried to think of what to say next. Why she felt the need to defend the merits of matrimony were beyond her, but the question came to her lips. "But surely, children are a happy result of marriage. Though not reason enough to marry where one will be unhappy, it is an enticement."

Eyes wide, Amelia stared at Eloise for a heartbeat before breaking into great peals of laughter. Holding her stomach, the lady chortled and guffawed until tears filled her eyes.

"Oh, my sweet, naive girl," said Amelia when she was finally able to speak once again. "Children are the results of the bedchamber—whether or not marriage vows have been spoken."

Perhaps if Amelia had made such a suggestive comment at another time, Eloise would have gasped or blushed or reacted in the proper fashion, but there had been too many shocking revelations in the past few days for her to take much notice.

"And children are not a happy thing. Many a lady has cried her heart out at the thought of being weighed down by another squalling brat," continued Amelia. "Most children are a disappointment. Mine certainly were. Only my poor Priscilla was worth the bother, and her child killed her. Emmeline was a constant pest. Always demanding my attention and never giving me a moment's peace when I was at home. And Simon turned out to be just like his father—dictatorial and uncompromising."

Shock jolted Eloise, forcing her to speak. "Uncle Simon is hardly dictatorial. He is very kind."

Amelia waved that away. "You wouldn't say that if you'd

seen him in a temper. He is a cruel and heartless man who has treated me poorly. Though I do think most of the blame can be laid at his wife's door. He was a decent son until she turned him against me."

Eloise gaped at that, unable to picture her dear, sweet Aunt Mina forcing a wedge between mother and son. The people Amelia described were nothing like the uncle and aunt she adored.

"I understand you might have hard feelings toward them." Though Eloise could not understand it at all, it seemed like the right thing to say. "However, I believe them to be good people, and I do not like hearing them spoken of in such a harsh manner."

Amelia arched an incredulous brow at Eloise. "Are you honestly defending that horrid creature? My son's wife is pathetic. She was only able to find herself a husband by latching on to a poor, heartsick man who married her out of desperation. That hideous pig—"

Shooting to her feet, Eloise scowled at her grandmother. "I adore Aunt Mina, and I shan't listen to you speak of her in such a manner."

The click of Mrs. Bell's knitting needles halted as Amelia's eyes narrowed. "Then you are like the rest of them. So quick to turn on me."

"I am not turning on you, and I have no wish to speak so bluntly, Amelia. However, I cannot remain silent when you are saying such unkind things about a person I hold dear."

But Amelia turned her face away, waving a dismissive hand. "I will not be judged by small-minded people. Especially not in my own home."

This turn came so quickly that Eloise was still in shock when she was led by Mrs. Bell to the front door and summarily dumped onto the doorstep. Staring at the street, Eloise felt something she'd never thought to feel—sympathy for her mother. Only a few minutes in Amelia Kingsley's company had been taxing for Eloise. No wonder Mother was so dour. Eloise's own mood had soured quickly around that vitriol.

Forcing herself to clear her mind, Eloise scoured the street for a hackney, but there was not an available one in sight. Turning right and left, she tried to decide which direction to go, but neither provided any clues, so she chose at random and wandered down the street; she was bound to see a hack sooner or later.

A glance at the sky told her the sun would soon set, and Eloise was startled to realize how much time she'd spent with Amelia. Apparently, the lady's complaints had been more effusive than Eloise realized. At this late hour, she would not have time to reach the Park, but hopefully she had done enough damage for the day.

Turning a corner, Eloise found another identical street. Everything looked so similar and none of it was familiar. She wondered if she was headed in the right direction—though she supposed it did not matter, for once she found a coach she would be home in a trice.

Chapter 23

Emmeline
Age Twenty-four

Beaming at the mirror, Emmeline turned this way and that to examine her coiffure. Her lady's maid had fingers of gold, for they manipulated her stubborn locks into the most handsome of styles. Understated yet elegant, and utter perfection.

"Splendid, Marybeth. As always," she said, smiling at her abigail. "You are a master."

Marybeth's cheeks pinked, and she bobbed a curtsy before going to the bureau to rearrange the gowns that had been dislodged during their search for the perfect outfit.

Twisting a ringlet around her finger, Emmeline gazed at her reflection until her eyes caught sight of her husband standing in the doorway. Though dressed in his finest, Norman still looked slightly rumpled, as though his cravat were not entirely starched and his clothes improperly ironed, though she knew it was untrue on both accounts. And heaven help her, Emmeline thought it adorable.

Her husband.

Those two little words made her heart sigh with satisfaction.

Though it had been four years since their marriage, Emmeline was still awed that she had captured the heart of such a gentleman. Mr. Carson may have been a vile and vulgar fellow, but Emmeline would be forever grateful for his crude proposition at that fateful ball all those years ago; otherwise, she might never have met her beloved Mr. Andrews.

Striding over, Norman pulled her to her feet and brought his lips to hers. Four years since their first kiss and Emmeline still felt giddy in his embrace. Her pulse quickened at his touch, the scent of his cologne enveloping her, and she returned his affection with interest.

He released her several long minutes later, but Emmeline wanted nothing more than to pull him close again.

"I'm afraid you ruined Marybeth's handiwork," she murmured as a lock of her hair tumbled free of her hairpins. She did not know when his hands had traveled there, but the evidence was clear enough.

"Then you should not look at me so, dear wife of mine," he murmured back. "How is a man to control himself when given such a look?"

"And what look is that?" she asked with a coy smile.

Norman's right eyebrow rose, his fingers brushing her cheek. "You know full well."

And then his lips feathered her jaw, and Emmeline was lost once more.

"Your mother is expecting us," she whispered, and Norman froze.

With a sigh, he straightened, though he did not release her from his hold. "That is one way to bring a man back to himself in a hurry."

Emmeline chuckled. "She lectured me for a full hour about the importance of punctuality. She will not forgive us if we are late to Vera's ball."

"It is not as though my mother or sister would even notice

if we were in attendance," grumbled Norman.

"Your mother would notice. She always notices," said Emmeline with a sigh. "If only Deirdre were here."

Norman laughed, his hands resting on her hips. "I doubt my sister would appreciate the trouble the two of you would stir up.

Emmeline fiddled with his cravat, her eyes affixed to the layers of intricately folded linen. "True, but I wish she were here. It would be nice to have a friend among the throng."

"You have me," he whispered, and Emmeline's gaze drew to his, and she reveled in its warmth.

"I know, but I feel so out of sorts among the ladies of Town."

"Do you regret coming?" asked Norman, his brow furrowing.

Emmeline bit the side of her lip but shook her head. "No. Vera's introduction into society is important, and we must support the family, but your mother frightens me."

Norman laughed once more and stepped away. "You and everyone else. My mother has the personality of a block of ice." Raising Emmeline's hand to his lips, he pressed a kiss to her knuckles. "You are an incredible woman, my love, and have no reason to feel intimidated by the likes of her."

Emmeline touched her lips to his cheek and whispered, "I love you, Norman."

"I never tire of hearing you say that," he replied.

The mantle clock chimed the hour, shocking Emmeline into action. "Oh, dear! We must leave. Marybeth!"

The maid was at her side in a trice, working in steady movements to repair the damage her husband's affections had done. Minutes later, they were striding arm-in-arm out their bedchamber door and towards the townhome's entrance.

"Mama! Papa!"

Little voices rang in the hallway and tiny footsteps followed. Then arms wrapped around Emmeline's and Norman's legs.

"My little monsters," said Norman with a smile that belied

the declaration. Reaching down, he scooped up the child clinging to him as Emmeline did the same.

"Madam, your dress..." said Nurse Grove.

But Emmeline waved her off and held her dear girl tight.
"Now go straight to bed, my sweets."

"But why can't we go with you?" asked Joanna, clinging to
Norman's neck.

"You would be bored to tears," said Emmeline, nibbling on
Lucinda's soft cheek.

"We would far rather stay here with you," said Norman.

Joanna wrinkled her nose and stuck out a sad lip. "But we
want to go."

"Go!" cried Lucinda, clapping her hands.

Bouncing her babe in her arms, Emmeline cast a mischievous look at Norman.

"You know, perhaps we might allow it," he conceded, and
the pair clapped and squealed. "But if you do, you'll be too tired
tomorrow for the special treat your mother and I have
planned."

Joanna gaped at her father, and with wide eyes she asked,
"What is it?"

"An exhibit of exotic animals and a picnic in the park," said
Emmeline. "But if you'd rather go to a boring ball—"

"Do they have monkeys?" asked Joanna.

Norman nodded, and before he could say another word, the
girls pushed out of their parents' arms and sprinted towards the
nursery with their nursemaid trailing behind them. Emmeline
laughed, tucked her arm through Norman's, and the couple
went on their way.

...

Clinging to her husband, Emmeline attempted a look of
casual ease, but the ball was already a crush, and not a single
pair of eyes tracking their entrance were friendly. Norman

tensed with each step farther into the crowd, and Emmeline rubbed his forearm, leaning in close to whisper.

"Breathe, dearest," she teased.

"How can I be comfortable around these vultures?"

"That is rather harsh, Norman."

He gave Mrs. Peabody a pointed look. The lady had terrible posture and was often found with her head hung low. On top of which, she had the unfortunate tendency to wear layers of lace around the edge of her neckline, which accentuated her hunched shoulders. Add to that her propensity towards scavenging for the juiciest pieces of gossip, and she had both a physical and metaphorical resemblance to a vulture.

Emmeline's hand flew to her mouth to cover a bubble of laughter, but Mrs. Peabody's gaze snapped to them, her beady eyes narrowing at the pair before she moved on.

"Behave," said Emmeline.

"Why would I do that? Misbehaving with you is the only way I tolerate such occasions."

Emmeline blushed at the wicked tone he infused in his words, and she fought back a giggle.

"You are terrible!" she hissed.

"But you love me all the better for it."

Breaking into a broad grin, Emmeline gave him a saucy wink just as someone nearby cleared her throat.

"Mother," said Norman with a bow. "You look lovely. Where is Vera?"

Mother Andrews stood with her hands clasped before her in what Emmeline had come to think of as the lady's "perfect hostess" position. Though petite, Mother Andrews had a presence about her that belied her diminutive stature. Not a hair was out of place. Not even a stitch on her dress was anything less than perfection. She gave an approximation of a smile to her son, though it was more akin to a mild twitch of her lips than a true expression of joy.

"She and your father are sharing the first set of the evening," she said. "You are late."

"My valet was all thumbs tonight and took forever to get my cravat right," said Norman, covering for Emmeline with ease.

Mother Andrews' expressionless eyes fell to his neck and the messy cravat. "I understand you intend to throw her a dinner party."

Norman beamed at his wife. "It was Emmeline's idea. We thought it would be grand to throw her a more intimate celebration."

"If that pleases you," added Emmeline. Her mother-in-law's eyes turned to her, and she felt trapped in their dark depths. They gave no hint of her thoughts as she stared long and hard at Emmeline.

"That is acceptable," said Mother Andrews with a stiff nod. "Though I would like to discuss a few details with your wife, if I might borrow her for a moment."

Norman looked about as pleased with the separation as Emmeline, but as there was no way to refuse her steely look (which commanded more than asked) they were forced to listen. Giving Emmeline a kiss on her hand, Norman moved away in search of a quiet corner in which to hide. Tracking his retreat, Emmeline wished to join him.

"I am curious as to your guest list for the evening," said Mother Andrews.

"Guest list?" Emmeline watched Norman weave through the crowd, unable to fight the smile on her lips.

"For the dinner party," the lady prompted. "Who is to be invited to this 'intimate' affair?"

"I have not had a moment to think about it," said Emmeline, turning her attention to her mother-in-law. "We have a fortnight to sort that out."

"A fortnight?" Mother Andrews would never go so far as to look discomposed, but there was a flash of stern disapproval in her eyes that spoke volumes. "But the invitations should've already been sent. How are you to throw a successful dinner party if all your guests are already occupied?"

"We had planned on a simple celebration with family and

close friends. That is all."

"My dear, do you not understand how important it is?" asked Mother Andrews. "Do you truly not understand how much Vera is being scrutinized? I know you did not have a conventional upbringing, but do you not see that these short months we have to launch her into society will dictate much of her future social standing? It may be only a small, intimate dinner, but it could do damage if not done properly."

Emmeline smiled at that. "You make it sound as though all is lost if the place cards have a single misspelling."

She'd meant it to be a joke, but Mother Andrews looked positively affronted at the thought.

"Reputation is everything, Emmeline. And I need to be assured that you will not damage Vera's, even with something you believe to be innocuous. Which brings me to another important topic—your behavior with my son."

"Pardon?" Emmeline straightened and stared at her mother-in-law.

"I've held my tongue for some time, but I cannot remain silent any longer," said Mother Andrews, casting a furtive glance at the guests, and then motioning for Emmeline to move further into a quiet corner. "You must learn to control yourself in public. The way you and my son comport yourself is shameful."

"Shameful?" Emmeline could think of no other thing to say, as the whole conversation was beyond her comprehension.

"It is bad enough you and your children cavort about the city as though you were nothing better than street urchins, but the wanton way in which you and Norman behave towards each other is ruinous," she said. Though her voice never deviated from its perfectly moderate tone, that cold steel filled her gaze, slicing at Emmeline.

"Are you accusing me of being wanton?"

"A poor choice of words, but I am quite flustered," said Mother Andrews with a sigh. "When you go out in public, you ignore everyone else, choosing to seclude yourself in your own conversation rather than socialize as you ought. And then, you hang on each other, displaying flagrant affection that is entirely inappropriate for polite society."

"He is my husband, and I love him. I see nothing wrong in showing it."

"In the country, people are more forgiving—though I have heard talk of your behavior bandied about even in those quieter circles. Here in Town, such behavior is boorish. That gossip reflects poorly on you and the rest of the family."

"You cannot be serious," said Emmeline, blinking at her mother-in-law.

If possible, Mother Andrews grew even stiffer and more rigid, and though the room was warm from the throng of people and burning candles overhead, the temperature cooled by several degrees. "I am always serious when it comes to my children's futures. Surely, you understand how much damage a mother's behavior can do to her child. I would hate to see such things happen to your dear girls."

Emmeline stepped away, but Mother Andrews snatched her wrist, holding her in place.

"I do not say this to be cruel, Emmeline. I only wish to protect my children. Though men like to believe they hold the reins, it is often the women who set the tone for the...physical side of marriage. Please, show restraint in public, and protect what little reputation you have left."

With that, Emmeline pulled free and hurried away, searching for the one person in the house whom she loved and loved her in return. Her gaze scanned the rooms as she passed through them, hunting for Norman, but he'd disappeared. Slipping out of the ballroom, she went straight for his favorite place and found him in the library, relaxing in an armchair by the fire.

Norman sighed and smiled at the sight of her, standing to pull Emmeline into his arms. Clinging to him, she buried her face in his neck and breathed in the citrus scent of his cologne.

"Dearest, what is the matter?" asked Norman.

With a few words, Emmeline recounted the exchange, and

Norman listened with that calm, reassuring air of his.

"She is wrong," said Norman.

As much as Emmeline wished to reject her mother-in-law's words off-handedly, she could not bring herself to be as cavalier as her husband. "Perhaps she has a point."

"We are nothing like your parents, and anyone with sense would see a world of difference between us and them. Not that it matters what they think."

It was impossible to argue with him when wrapped in his arms; Emmeline adored his touch too much to keep him at a distance as decorum dictated. But a wriggling worm of a thought burrowed into her mind, leaving her to wonder if Mother Andrews was correct. Norman was blind to the judgmental stares they elicited in public, but she had always attributed them to her own history. And that tiny worry whispered that her parents' reputation wasn't the problem in this instance.

But that was silly. Emmeline shoved away that depressing thought and brought her lips to his.

Chapter 24

Patrick's sweaty palms made it decidedly difficult to keep a proper grip on the reins, and it was foolhardy to drive while his thoughts were so thoroughly preoccupied with Eloise, but Patrick could not bring himself to turn the reins over to another nor could he forgo this errand. Rumors were well and good, but he could not rest until he knew the truth.

So, there was nothing to be done about it.

Had Eloise truly refused Mr. Godwin? She'd seemed keen on the fellow, but whispers abounded that she refused his offer of marriage. Though his own courtship was as fragile as spun sugar, Patrick could not help but hope that her turning away such a fine gentleman meant that her heart was already engaged. However minutely.

Regardless, Patrick needed to see her. There was still so much to say, and they were never allowed time enough for it. If he could just get her alone without the busybodies hovering nearby to snatch whatever titillating crumbs they could, Patrick might have a chance to fully explain himself. Eloise's heart was in turmoil, but he sensed some part of it still belonged to him. If he could simply get enough time to woo her properly, he would be able to rebuild what he had ruined.

Pulling into the Andrews' stable, Patrick hopped down and handed the reins to a groom. He brushed himself off, righted his hat, and then took the path around to the front of the house.

"They're not at home to visitors," said the footman before Patrick offered up his calling card.

"I understand that they might not be to others, but I am an old family friend," said Patrick.

The footman shook his head. "Mrs. Andrews is not to be disturbed."

"I am here to see Miss Andrews."

The lad's expression froze, though his cheek twitched. Glancing behind him and then back at Patrick, the footman opened the door just enough to allow Patrick into the foyer.

"Stay here," he ordered, snatching the calling card.

The parlor was the first room on the right, but the footman ignored it and continued down the hallway and into the library. He opened the door and stepped through, closing it behind him, but the footman wasn't quick enough to hide the sounds of crying coming from within. Before he knew it, his feet carried him after the footman, and Patrick pushed his way into the room, but it wasn't Eloise. Mrs. Andrews sat, slumped over in an armchair with great tears wetting her cheeks. She shot to her feet and turned away, dabbing at her face, but it was too late to hide.

"I asked to be left alone," she said through halting breaths.

Ordering the footman to leave them, Patrick came to her side, taking her by the arm to sit her back down. "What is the matter?"

Mrs. Andrews made a most peculiar sound that was part sob and part laugh with a heaping portion of hysteria.

"What is not the matter?" she asked, twisting her handkerchief in her hands. Pausing, she stared at it and then at Patrick, who squatted beside her chair. His heart squeezed at the sight of her naked pain, for he knew that the lady must be in utter distress to allow anyone to see her in such a state.

"I am making a fool of myself," she said with a trembling chin. "I apologize, but I cannot seem to help myself. So many awful things have happened today, and my nerves are a wreck."

"Shedding a few tears is hardly making a fool of yourself. You've seen me at my worst, so it would take something greater than that to embarrass either one of us," said Patrick with a comforting smile.

"You must help us. She doesn't understand how dangerous the city can be," said Mrs. Andrews, grabbing his arm. "London is so big, and there are so few of us to search for her."

Patrick blinked at her, thinking through the words to see if he could decipher her meaning. "Is someone missing?"

Mrs. Andrews nodded, her fingers digging into his sleeve. "We had an awful row, and Eloise snuck away. No one knows where she went or how she got there. She simply vanished without a word, and we only just discovered it."

Straightening, Patrick looked down at the lady. "She went alone onto the streets?"

"I don't know what she was thinking, but she could get lost or hurt..." Mrs. Andrews' voice trailed off, and Patrick's heart seized at the implications the lady could not say aloud: there were far worse things that could happen to her in London.

"We sent most of the footmen to look for her, and Mr. Andrews left on horseback a few minutes ago," said Mrs. Andrews. "The grooms are readying the coach for me, but the city is so large, and we need assistance."

"Of course. I would do anything for your family."

The footman reentered with a bow. "The carriage is ready, ma'am."

Mrs. Andrews wobbled as she rose to her feet, and Patrick steadied her. Looking at him with eyes so like Eloise's and filled with such anguish, Patrick could not restrain the impulse to hug the poor lady. Though a wholly improper thing to do, he'd known Mrs. Andrews for too long to be confined by such things—especially when he sensed how desperately she needed it. She stiffened for a moment before wrapping her arms around him.

"We will find her," said Patrick. "You know Eloise is so

headstrong. She likely went to her aunt's and is sitting in the Kingsley's parlor with a pot of tea, oblivious to the uproar she has caused."

Mrs. Andrews pulled away and nodded, wiping at her cheeks. Taking a breath, she closed her eyes and straightened, though there was a frantic energy lying just under the composed surface she gathered about her. With another nod that was far calmer than anything Patrick could manage, the pair strode from the library and hurried to their carriages.

...

The Kingsley townhouse held too many memories for Emmeline to feel comfortable there, and that unease only grew when she thought of those she would find inside Trafford Place. In her present state, Emmeline could not think of a place she desired less to visit than her brother's home, but it was also the most likely place in which Eloise would seek asylum.

The footman took her card, and Emmeline waited as he went in search of his mistress. Since Simon spent so little time in London, Emmeline had avoided stepping through these doors for many years. Though the Kingsleys' country seat held more memories, the ghosts haunting these halls were far fresher and had fewer pleasant reminiscences to counteract that taint.

Emmeline's eyes were drawn to the main staircase, as the architect had meant them to be, but instead of the fine woodwork and marble accents, she saw the shadows of her past. It was there that she'd await the evening's entertainment with all the hope her young heart could muster. Magic always seemed possible in that moment, promising her that night would be perfect. But that joy never lasted.

Some nights her parents kept up the civil appearances long enough for the last guest to return home, only to devolve into verbal brawls that shook the rafters. Other times, they would not bother with pretense, and she and Aunt Vivian would be left to see to their guests as dear Mama and Papa lost themselves in some dark nook with their paramours *du jour* in a constant effort to strike a blow against their spouse.

At their worst, they did both, and Emmeline was subjected to the subtle mockery of the guests asking after their "missing" hosts and then lulled to sleep by the sounds of shouts and breaking things. Regardless of how the party went, Emmeline was always certain of one thing: her mother would vanish the next day, leaving her father with no other target for his vitriol than his eldest daughter.

A sickening shiver ran down her spine, and Emmeline took in a breath to steel herself against the memories. Such things had no hold on her. Not any longer. She had found a proper home. A proper family. Mother Andrews was more of a mother than Amelia Kingsley had ever been, and Emmeline's children were blessed with a kind and loving father in Norman.

Her children.

Those two little words had such a profound effect on her that Emmeline struggled to keep herself from devolving into that horrid, sobbing mess Patrick had stumbled upon.

"Do control yourself, Emmeline. You are a lady and above such common behavior," came Mother Andrews' voice.

The words were faint, but Emmeline pictured Mother Andrew's face and that hint of a smile she gave when she was especially pleased. Though heaven knows Emmeline did not deserve such a happy look after her behavior the past few days.

Her foot tapped against the floor as she awaited the footman; Mina's servants were shockingly slow if it took such a long time to deliver a simple calling card. To be left standing in the foyer like some common visitor was beyond the pale. Emmeline had lived at Trafford Place longer than Mina Kingsley had been its mistress.

The footman returned and ushered her into the parlor, and Emmeline forced her fears and worries away. Whatever else happened today, she would not allow any more slips in decorum. There was no better tribute to Mother Andrews' memory than to hold firm to the lessons that good lady had taught her.

Mina Kingsley stood to greet Emmeline, and at least her sister-in-law had the decency to curtsy rather than forcing some sentimental display they both knew to be hollow. Even if Emmeline would condescend to welcome guests with a buss on the cheek or some other crude act, she had no desire to greet Mina in such a fashion.

When they were seated, Mina asked all the polite questions about her health and if she wished for refreshment, but Emmeline was in no mood to prattle.

"I am here to fetch my daughter," she said.

Mina's brows creased. "Why do you think Eloise is here?"

The lady continued to speak, but Emmeline only heard the pounding of her heart. The time required to travel to the Kingsleys' home had allowed her to calm herself, and with that had come a certainty that Eloise would be here. Even without the confirmation Eloise had given her just hours before, Emmeline had long known her daughter adored Mina. Worshipped her, even. If Eloise was distraught, she would cry on her aunt's shoulder.

"Emmeline, are you unwell?" asked Mina, leaning forward with a concerned look. "You look quite distraught. What is the matter?"

Shaking her head, Emmeline stood and moved as though to leave, but Mina came to her feet and grabbed her sister-in-law by the arm.

"Is it Eloise? Has something happened?"

Emmeline jerked her arm away. "She disappeared. Snuck away and ran off."

Mina's eyes widened, her hands coming to her mouth as she cast a glance at the window and the dimming light outside. "Let me fetch Simon. We can help—"

"I do not need your assistance," said Emmeline, stepping towards the door once more, but Mina grabbed her yet again.

"But we must find her before it gets dark—"

Wrenching her arm from Mina's hold, Emmeline whirled on her. Any thought of decorum fled her mind as she stared into Mina's watery eyes. Her expression was so pained and so innocent that Emmeline felt a surge of pure venom shoot through her, breaking through her fragile control.

"Yes, of course. Perfect Mina Kingsley will come to the rescue."

Mina flinched at Emmeline's tone, leaning back with wide eyes as her hands clenched the sides of her skirts. "Why do you hate me so?"

The breath in Emmeline's lungs froze, her expression hardening. Some small, niggling impulse warned her to remain calm, but she was beyond reasoning. Her heart was strung too tightly, her nerves too frayed, and the perfect target for Emmeline's anger stood before her.

"Everything I do is scrutinized," said Emmeline, her voice low and rough as she glowered at Mina. "Society judged Emmeline Kingsley the moment she was born, and it is not enough for me to be good. I must be perfect. Every misstep I make overshadows any good I do, so I can never step out of bounds. And you wonder why I hate you?"

Mina blinked at her. "I have never said a word about you—"

"You swan about, flouting the rules, and people ignore it or laugh and say, 'Oh, that's our Mina!'" Emmeline's chest squeezed, her chin trembling as her muscles quivered. Her vision blurred, but she could not move to wipe away the tears. Standing there, she glowered, pouring all those hidden feelings she had harbored for so long into her gaze. "You do as you please when it suits you, and yet no one ever speaks ill of you."

"No one speaks of me at all," said Mina, gaping. "I am below anyone's notice and certainly not worthy of jealousy."

An incredulous sneer twisted Emmeline's expression. "Do you have any idea what I would give to be able to live below Society's notice? To be free of my family's reputation?"

"But Simon and Priscilla—"

Emmeline gave a cruel huff. "You mean my dear siblings? Priscilla decided to stop fighting the reputation and embraced it, becoming a copy of our mother. And Simon simply didn't notice the stares and whispers. I had to sacrifice everything to make certain my children would not be faced with such unabashed condemnation. I did what I had to..."

Her words trailed off as reason took hold once more. Straightening, Emmeline realized the words she had spoken and the scene she'd caused, and her cheeks blazed bright red. Struggling to control herself, she drew on the memory of Mother Andrews to help, but her heart did not wish to return to its staid existence.

"Forgive my outburst."

"Emmeline, please do not—" began Mina, but Emmeline could not stand to be there a moment longer. Rushing past her sister-in-law, she escaped and hurried back into her coach.

Chapter 25

Emmeline
Age Twenty-four

Lucinda clapped as the coach bobbed along the street, and Emmeline leaned forward to nibble at her daughter's sweet neck, eliciting a squeal from the child as she wriggled on her mama's lap. Joanna was perched on Norman's knee, and her papa struggled to keep her upright: the girl was practically hopping while she recounted their grand adventures.

"I loved the rhinoceros!" said Joanna. "I touched it. Did you see it?"

"Yes, my darling," said Emmeline, but Joanna was not pacified until both her parents affirmed this repeatedly while Lucinda clapped her hands and repeated, "Monkeys!"

"Then you enjoyed the menagerie?" asked Emmeline.

Joanna's head bobbed up and down with vigor, but she stopped with a furrowed brow. "But the monkeys weren't nice. Why were they so mean? It's not nice to throw things. You and Father say so when I throw things at Lucinda. Nurse Groves doesn't like it, either."

Norman caught Emmeline's eye, and the pair shared a silent laugh at the memory.

"Too right," said Norman.

Scrunching her face, Joanna pondered that for a moment before concluding, "The monkeys' mama and papa should have stopped it."

The logic was flawless, with the exception that Emmeline was certain the monkeys' parents had been equal participants.

Lucinda rocked forward, letting out a fierce growl, and Emmeline asked her, "Did you like the lions and tigers?"

That was met by more clapping and another roar.

The carriage slowed, and Emmeline glanced out the window to see a green haven among the cityscape. Norman alighted, helping Joanna down before retrieving a picnic basket from the coach floor. With a smile, he assisted Emmeline's and Lucinda's descent and pressed a quick kiss on his wife's hand before releasing it. Together, the family strolled down the gravel path in search of the perfect picnic spot.

It was a beautiful afternoon. Though it had rained for days before, the skies had cleared to a crystalline blue and the spring chill had evaporated, as though the weather knew of their picnic plans. Out in the air with the sun beaming down on her, Emmeline felt as though she could finally breathe. Though there was pleasure to be had in the city, she found herself missing their quiet country life.

"Ducklings!" squealed Joanna as they drew up to a pond, and Lucinda began wriggling in Emmeline's arms, begging to be put down so she might join her sister.

Norman quickly deposited the picnic basket and followed the children to the water's edge. Holding her hand, he escorted his daughter along the pond, and Lucinda finally got free of her mother's hold and toddled after them.

The scene before Emmeline was not unique. These felicitous moments had become a constant companion after she had met Norman, and they continued to multiply with the additions of their daughters. Not to say her life was perfect, but it was such a far cry from those lonely years of her childhood that the trials of daily life faded into nothing.

At the oddest moments, the difference between her present and her past struck her with such resounding force that her heart could hardly contain it. It was both ridiculous and perfectly natural for tears to gather in her eyes, for though it was an ordinary scene on an ordinary day, Emmeline marveled at the splendor of her life.

Her family.

Norman had the girls in hand, so Emmeline used the opportunity to spread a blanket on the grass. Not that it would do any good to keep the girls' clothes clean (as they already had mud caking their hems), but a picnic seemed incomplete without it. She spread out the collection of pies and treats Cook had provided while the girls laughed and threw pebbles into the water.

Retrieving an obliging piece of bread, Emmeline joined her family and gave the girls a few crumbs to throw to the ducks; with all the hubbub her children had caused, the least they could do was feed the waterfowl in recompense. The girls squealed with delight as the birds drew closer, some getting so bold as to snatch a bit from their hands.

Before long, Emmeline noticed another girl about Joanna's age watching them with naked longing. Emmeline smiled at her and offered her some bread, and the lass was swept into the fun.

"Harriet!"

A harried nursemaid called out, the tone speaking of the poor woman's fear at having lost her charge, and the young girl gave Emmeline an apologetic smile.

"Here, Nurse Smith!" called Harriet in reply, handing back her bit of bread with slumped shoulders and an expression so devastated that even the hardest of hearts would break at the sight of it.

Moving over to the nursemaid, Emmeline intercepted her. "Nurse Smith, might we borrow Harriet for a bit? We were feeding the ducks, and the children are having such a fun time together."

Nurse Smith looked at Harriet, who had taken the opportunity to return to the frivolities. "I don't know, ma'am. My mistress is quite particular about the schedule."

Glancing over her shoulder, the nursemaid motioned to a lady who was occupied in conversation; though Emmeline did not know most of the party, she recognized Nurse Smith's mistress.

"Allow me to speak with Mrs. Devereux," said Emmeline, and though Nurse Smith twisted her hands in front of her, she stayed put and allowed Harriet to play while Emmeline crossed the lawn to the trio.

"Mrs. Devereux, how lovely to see you this afternoon," said Emmeline with a curtsy.

"Mrs. Andrews," she said in return. Upon hearing the name, one of the other ladies' eyes widened a fraction before she schooled her expression.

"It is good to see you again," said Emmeline. "I was wondering if we might borrow your sweet Harriet for a bit. She and my girls are having such fun, and it would be a shame to ruin it."

Mrs. Devereux stiffened, casting a quick glance at her mysterious companions. "I am afraid we must return home shortly."

Stifling a sigh, Emmeline nodded. "I understand. But perhaps we might schedule another time when they can play together. So many families leave their children in the country, and my girls miss their playmates. Perhaps we might have your entire family over for luncheon and some games. Are you available Thursday next?"

Stiffening even further, Mrs. Devereux turned to her companions, asking for a moment alone. The others moved away, giving them space before Mrs. Devereux finally spoke. "I appreciate your invitation, but we must decline."

"Then another day?"

"No, Mrs. Andrews. I do not think it wise for my Harriet to mix with your daughters."

The statement was so shocking that Emmeline stood there silently blinking at Mrs. Devereux for several seconds before speaking. "Pardon?"

"I was attempting to be politic, but as you are pushing the subject, I am forced to speak plainly. Your daughters are not suitable company for my Harriet." The lady spoke as though the situation ought to be clear to anyone listening, but Emmeline was at a loss to comprehend her meaning.

"I beg your pardon, but that is nonsense," said Emmeline, though at that moment, she caught sight of Lucinda stuffing a handful of pebbles in her mouth while Joanna laughed; Norman swooped in to keep the babe from swallowing them, but the pair certainly looked like wild creatures. There was a stark difference between them and Harriet, whose clothes were still pristine; even the bow in her hair was perfectly straight.

"I have seen the way you carry on. Mr. Andrews was a decent, upstanding gentleman before your unfortunate alliance," said Mrs. Devereux with a haughty sniff. "It is bad enough being forced into your company at parties and balls, but I will not allow my daughter to be corrupted by your inappropriate behavior like your husband has been. And I doubt there's a mother in the city who would disagree with me."

"How dare you, madam," said Emmeline, fighting to keep her voice low. "They are children, and it is unkind and unfair of you to judge them—"

But Mrs. Devereux would have none of it. With a frigid look, the lady turned away, called to her nursemaid and daughter, and bundled them off.

In a heartbeat, all of Mother Andrews' warnings came back to her in a flood of pain. Emmeline could hardly believe it to be true, but there was no mistaking Mrs. Devereux's meaning. Despite all the changes in her life, Emmeline was still nothing more than Amelia Kingsley's tainted daughter.

Chapter 26

Standing beneath the gas lamps lighting the street corner, Eloise stared down the crossroads, struggling to discern which way to go. With the last rays of sunlight dipping beneath the horizon, there was nothing but the streetlamps to light the way, and there were few of those in this section of the city. The houses and shops along the street had few windows and even fewer candles burning inside. Only the orb of burning gas above her head gave any illumination, and Eloise was reticent to step outside its dim glow.

Twisting the drawstrings of her reticule between her fingers, Eloise prayed for help. The few hacks she'd seen were occupied, and it had been some time since she'd spied even those. If she could only find a thoroughfare or major crossroad, perhaps she might get her bearings, but every step only led her deeper into the twisting turns of London.

Raucous laughter erupted behind her, and Eloise jumped, glancing at the sound. They were nothing but grey figures stumbling in the dark, but she felt their eyes on her. Straightening, she tried to swallow the lump forming in her throat, but her mouth was too dry. Now was not the time to stand about dissembling, so she pointed herself in the opposite direction of the strangers and walked. Surely, she would run into something familiar soon.

Running her hands over her forearms, she tried to warm herself, but the temperature was falling with each minute. Her spencer had been plenty warm for the daytime, but the cool night air seeped through the thin layers of fabric.

A bottle crashed to the cobblestones, and Eloise jumped once more. The sound had come from somewhere to the left, but she could not make out from where precisely. When the last of the glass stopped skittering, silence fell. She had never heard the streets so quiet, yet there was not a whisper of sound.

And then a few footsteps echoed behind her, followed by a low chuckle.

Prickles ran down her spine, and Eloise resumed walking, though she moved at a brisker pace. Her own footsteps drowned out the ones behind her, and she glanced around to see if anyone was still there—only to find three or four figures following.

With a hop in her step, she moved faster. At the next corner, Eloise searched either direction and saw another crossroads to the right that had a fair bit of traffic. Turning that direction, she hoped it would be her salvation.

And the other footsteps quickened.

Eloise was nearly running down the street. She cast a glance over her shoulder here and there, but she could see little of what was happening, though the footsteps told her they still followed. Her pulse quickened, and the sound of her heart filled her ears until it surrounded her.

The crossroads drew closer, and Eloise's pulse calmed when she stepped onto the roadway. She still did not recognize the street, but there were more lamps and the houses were better lit, adding to the weak gaslights' illumination. Eloise searched the street she'd left, but with the lights at her back, it was swallowed up in darkness, and the clatter of carriages hid the noises that had spurred her on.

Looking up and down the busy street, she searched for a

hackney, but there was not an empty one in sight.

A hand grabbed her arm, and Eloise jumped, pulling free with a shriek. Whirling, she saw a man; his face and hair were coated in grime, his mouth cracked and craggy. He stepped forward, grabbing at her reticule, and she scrambled backward. A horse whinnied, and Eloise spun around again and nearly collided with the passing carriages; the horse shied away, and the driver shouted profanities at her as he calmed the beast and continued on his way.

Eloise grabbed her skirts in one hand and ran with no thought of where she was going. A curricle pulled to a stop ahead of her, and the driver stepped down, but just as she was about to pass, he stretched out a hand and grabbed her, yanking her to a stop. She screamed, but he did not let go.

"Eloise!"

She paused, finally looking at her captor's face. With a happier cry, Eloise threw her arms around Patrick and clung to him with a string of grateful babbling. But he forced her away, standing her before him with a dark scowl.

"What were you thinking?"

Patrick felt liable to shake apart as he glowered at her, his heart pounding against his ribs at the thought of what would've happened had he not stumbled across her. Anyone with sense would not stop in this section of Town, and Eloise had been strolling right through the middle of it. Even now, the shadows watched the pair of them with piqued interest.

"I am so happy to see you—" she began.

"What were you thinking wandering the city by yourself?" he asked, his words growing more heated with each syllable. "Have you any idea how dangerous that is? What could have happened to you? People are robbed, beaten, and worse every hour, and you willingly wandered out into it unprotected?"

Those figures in the dark moved closer, and Patrick knew

now was not the time to dither. Turning her towards the curricle, he fairly shoved her into it. Another time, he might have worried about Eloise's hurt and frustration at his cold treatment, but his attention was trained on the growing danger.

Climbing in next to her, Patrick flicked the reins and set the horses at a steady trot while keeping a watchful eye on the vermin retreating into the shadows. That had been too close, and his heart would not stop pounding that hard, rapid beat. It felt like it was trying to break free of his chest. He let out a long, shaky breath through his nose and tried to take control of the fear coursing through his veins.

And then he heard her sniffle.

"Eloise?"

Her breath hitched. "It has been a wretched day."

Hours of worrying had culminated in the triumph of finding her, quickly tempered by the discovery of how precarious her position was, which left Patrick in perfect agreement with Eloise's assessment. Wretched indeed. Not only due to what had happened, but what could have been. Even now, he felt so tightly wound he was liable to snap, though having Eloise safe and at his side was helping to calm his anxious heart.

"I got in a terrible argument with Mother."

"And wanted to spite her, no doubt," he mumbled.

The shadows hid most of her face, but there was enough for him to see the scowl she pointed at him. But it softened into chagrin, which she attempted to hide. "Please do not bring up that argument again. I cannot stand the thought of fighting about her. Not now."

With their complicated history, it was not surprising that her mother was a tender subject, but the hardness in her tone set the back of Patrick's neck prickling.

"I hadn't meant to wander so far, but I got lost," she said.

Though Patrick knew she was skipping over other details, they were not pertinent at present, and he decided to keep his own counsel.

"You came looking for me?" Her question was quiet, but

Patrick clung to every word, not letting one slip by him.

"Of course."

Eloise rested her head on his shoulder and whispered, "Thank you."

Patrick hated that his hands and arms were occupied with the ribbons, but as much as he wanted to pull her closer, he would not risk Eloise's safety for such a thing. So, he contented himself by leaning his cheek on her head; the night was thick enough that no passing person could identify them.

Eloise smelled of flowers, something beautiful and delicate. And intoxicating.

"I am still mad at you," Eloise added with a huff that held more humor than malice.

"Can you even remember the reason?"

A pause. "There are too many to point to a single one. You can be very vexing at times."

"Which is good, as you are quite adorable when you are in a huff," said Patrick.

Several silent moments passed before Eloise spoke again.

"I feel lost, Patrick. At odds with everything and everyone. And I don't know how to right myself."

Patrick's heart fell at the sight of Caswell House. Though it was best for her to return home immediately (for her parents' sake, if nothing else), they had finally found a bit of calm, and he worried it would be some time before they were granted another such moment.

"I am always at your disposal should you need to talk," said Patrick, steering the horses to stop before the townhouse.

Lifting her head, Eloise stared at him through the darkness. Patrick felt her eyes tracking his features, studying him before she replied, "You are at the heart of the problem, Patrick."

With the curricle paused, he released the reins. A footman hurried from the front door to take hold of the horses.

Turning to her, Patrick clasped her hands, his thumbs running over her gloves. How he wished to pull them off and feel the real Eloise. They had held hands many a time in their youth, and it had been too long since he'd felt the touch of her skin.

"When I said I would leave you be if you should desire it, I meant it. Do you wish me gone?" Though he hated to ask the question, he knew he must.

Eloise's expression shifted, the muscles moving between all her emotions, but there was not enough light for Patrick to see each tiny aspect of her heart playing out on her face. He felt as though he was back on that street corner, nervous energy racing through his veins as he awaited her answer.

"No," she said.

It was no declaration of love and was spoken with such hesitation that Patrick knew he was still far from securing her heart, but it was enough. Raising her hand to his lips, he pressed a kiss to her knuckles, and he heard her breath quicken.

Stepping out, Patrick helped Eloise down, and the lights from the house illuminated her face. Her eyes were wide and so uncertain, but there was a smile. Small and uncertain, but it was there. Tucking her hand in his arm, Patrick led her up the front steps.

"Eloise!" Mrs. Andrews stood in the foyer, looking so faint that Patrick was about to come to her side, but she hurried over to her daughter, arms outstretched.

"I am tired. I need to lie down," said Eloise, avoiding her mother's touch. Pulling away from Patrick, she escaped up the steps to the bedchambers.

Mrs. Andrews dropped her arms, her eyes dimming as she stared at the place where her daughter had been. The lady stood there for several quiet moments, and Patrick wondered what he should say to her.

"She had a bit of a shock," said Patrick. "She was quite overwrought when I found her."

Straightening, Mrs. Andrews turned away. "That had nothing to do with a shock, Patrick. She detests me."

"It's been a trying time for her—"

But Mrs. Andrews shook her head. Her expression veered between stoic and anguished, as though she were fighting with herself to gain control but without the strength to maintain that tight hold.

"I fear I have lost my daughter," she murmured.

Staring at the lady's sagging posture, Patrick had no idea how he might comfort her. Searching his thoughts, he tried to cobble something together, but nothing felt right. His words were not enough, but a few of hers came to mind.

"In one of my darkest moments, a wise woman told me that all is not lost until you choose to surrender."

Mrs. Andrews looked over her shoulder at Patrick, her expression pinched as though she were too afraid to even hope it was possible. "I fear I was too optimistic when I said that. Some causes are hopelessly lost."

"You did not allow me to say such things back then, and I will not allow you to say them now," said Patrick. "Without you and my mother, I would not have made it."

Mrs. Andrews moved to the stairs, gripping the banister for support with a defeated sigh. Her gaze grew vacant as she stared off at nothing. "So many things are not going as they ought, and I have no idea how to right them. I can barely keep myself in check. Even now, I hear Mother Andrews' voice cautioning me to be more circumspect in what I am saying, but I am just so worn through that I cannot muster the energy to do so."

Reaching for the pearls at her neck, Mrs. Andrews twisted them around her finger. "I wish she were here. I miss her so. Mother Andrews was always so much better at solving problems, and I am lost without her."

Clasping his hands behind him, Patrick wondered what he should say or if he should speak at all. The lady seemed to be speaking to herself, but curiosity got the better of him, and he could not hold his tongue.

"You are capable in your own right, Mrs. Andrews, and that was not your mother-in-law's doing."

The lady's eyes rose to meet Patrick's, but they were as sad as the smile that pulled at her lips. "Perhaps, but she was such a wonderful confidant and always knew the right thing to say.

She was so kind and loving. Better to me than my own mother."

Patrick's eyebrows rose at that. "I am not certain we are speaking of the same lady. The Mother Andrews I knew was a cold and judgmental creature. I cannot recall her ever saying something genuinely kind."

Shaking her head, Mrs. Andrews replied, "You sound like Mr. Andrews, but I knew her better than most. Though she had high standards, she could be very warm and complimentary when one met those expectations. She helped me become the woman I am."

Tapping his fingers, Patrick thought through possible responses, but the pure fiction Mrs. Andrews believed was difficult to contend with. "I do hope you'll forgive me for being so bold, but my memories do not reflect well on the lady. The only kindnesses I saw her bestow were upon those who behaved as she wanted them to, but that is not true kindness."

Patrick paused, choosing his words carefully. Though he would rather not invite trouble by stepping into such a quagmire, he was not about to abandon his duty, and Mrs. Andrews needed a bit of blunt truth.

"I fear you've imagined more affection than Mother Andrews truly felt, for I am not certain she was capable of loving anyone but herself. And you are a far better woman on your own than when you are parroting Mother Andrews."

Mrs. Andrews stared silently at him as he spoke, sparks of pain flashing in her gaze, though Patrick hoped he had not hurt her too much. With a nod, she straightened and climbed the stairs without another word, leaving Patrick to hope he'd said the right thing.

Chapter 27

Emmeline
Age Twenty-four

Staring at the piles of papers around her, Emmeline sorted through seating charts, menus, and invitations. For every decision made, there were two more awaiting her, and she felt ready to surrender and succumb to the sea of details.

"It is a simple dinner party, my love. There is no reason to fret," said Norman, taking the pages from her hands. Standing her up, he wrapped her in his arms, and Emmeline sighed, sinking into his hold.

"I thought so, too," she replied, her voice muffled by his shoulder. "But it is our chance to prove we are good, upstanding people."

"Mrs. Devereux is a shrew," he replied.

Emmeline gave a huffy chuckle and then lifted her head to meet his eyes. "Perhaps, but what if she is right? My parents' reputation ruined mine. What if we are doing the same to our children? I could not live with myself if it were true."

Norman's expression darkened, his brows knitting together. "That is decidedly untrue, Emmeline. Our little girls are blessed to have you as their mother."

Her heart melted, and Emmeline burrowed into his hold, reveling in the comfort found there. "You are too good to me, Norman Andrews."

"Never," he murmured, pressing a kiss to her head. "Now, are you going to drop all this nonsense and plan the simple dinner party we intended?"

The suggestion was so enticing that Emmeline wished dearly to accept. Her lips yearned to form the words, but there was still too much fear in her heart to be cast aside. "But what if throwing the proper party shows those busybodies I am not like *her*?"

Norman had no need to ask for clarification, for there was only one person Emmeline ever meant when she spoke of "her."

"Might I point out that she knows how to throw proper parties?"

"Mama never did a proper thing in her life," said Emmeline, meeting his eye once more. "But if it could help even a little, don't you agree it would be well worth the effort? For our daughters' sakes?"

With a sigh, Norman replied, "It sounds as though you've decided the matter, and I must submit to being tortured by endless discussions about table linens and place cards."

His look of resignation was too comical for Emmeline not to laugh. Leaning close enough that her lips brushed against his, she murmured, "What if I promise to make it diverting?"

A smile grew on his face and a wicked gleam sparked in his eye, but before he could speak, another voice chimed in.

"Really, you two," said Mother Andrews. "You have been married for several years, and you still behave like a couple of cow-eyed fools. Such displays are common."

"You walked into our home unannounced, Mother, so you cannot be appalled at having witnessed a private moment," said Norman, refusing to release his wife.

Mother Andrews moved to the sofa and sat down without invitation.

Leaning into Norman's ear, Emmeline whispered, "I shall

keep her occupied. Make your escape."

With a peck on her cheek, Norman whispered back, "You are the best of wives," and with a few polite words, he hurried from the room.

"With the way you two carry on, it's a wonder you get anything done," said Mother Andrews.

"Might I offer you some tea or refreshment?" asked Emmeline, choosing to ignore her mother-in-law's words.

In short order, the accepted offer was carried out and the ladies were plied with tea and cakes. When the last of the servants closed the door and left the pair alone, Mother Andrews spoke.

"How are preparations for the dinner party?" she asked between demure sips of tea.

"All is in hand." It was far from the truth, but her mother-in-law did not need to know the full extent of Emmeline's ineptitude. But the severe look she received in return made it clear she'd fooled no one.

Putting down her cup, Mother Andrews frowned. "Don't be coy. Every young lady needs assistance with their first social functions."

Emmeline's foot tapped the floor beneath her skirts as her eyes darted away from her mother-in-law's hard gaze. "I appreciate your offer, but I have everything in hand."

Mother Andrews' eyes narrowed, and Emmeline nearly quailed under the sternness. "I know we do not always agree, but I had thought you respected me enough to be honest."

"It is not disrespect that holds my tongue, madam. It is fear." The confession was not spurred by bravery or frustration, but rather, desperation and a fair dose of exhaustion. Too many restless nights followed by too many anxious days had addled Emmeline's wits.

Rather than looking affronted or shocked at the declaration, Mother Andrews simply nodded. "That is how people often view me, but that is neither here nor there, and dwelling on the obvious is hardly constructive."

When Emmeline did not reply, Mother Andrews' lips pinched. "I see I must reassure you further."

Though the lady would never be so gauche as to show her frustration with a put-upon sigh, Emmeline felt the undercurrent of one as her mother-in-law paused before continuing. "I am here to assist, that is all. I wish for your party to be a success."

Again, boldness seized her tongue, and Emmeline replied, "But you do not care for me."

"You are not the lady I would have chosen as my son's bride, and I will not hide that fact. However, his choice is made and I see no need to cause contention by belaboring the point." Emmeline stared at the lady, but she had no chance to reply to that blunt statement, for her mother-in-law continued, "Though I do not show it as you and my son wish me to, I do care for my family and their success, and I have been anxious about your efforts. I thought it best that I offer my assistance."

Toes tapping, Emmeline struggled between the dual desires to accept and reject that aid. She was desperate for such an offer, yet to admit to this stern lady that she was hopeless at such a basic task felt like more than she could bear, especially in light of Mother Andrews' confessed disapproval. But prudence won out, and Emmeline handed over her notes. If Mother Andrews could help make the evening a success, it was worth the humiliation.

"And where is your plan for the table settings?" asked Mother Andrews.

Emmeline's head tipped to the side. "The footmen and butler oversee such things."

"They manage the place settings, but not how the food is displayed," said Mother Andrews, peering at Emmeline from over a page. "Table setting is an art, and you and your household will be judged on its presentation."

At that implication, Emmeline felt a flush of heat pass through her. One of her many governesses must have covered such a weighty topic, but any such lessons escaped her mind.

"Surely, it is not as serious as all that," said Emmeline.

Mother Andrews' eyes narrowed again, and she set the papers down on her lap, folding her hands in front of her. "Appearance is vitally important. For good or ill, it is one of the key aspects on which people judge you. Most never gain a close enough acquaintance to see beyond the surface, which makes it all the more important, for it may be the only thing people know about you."

The logic was sound, and Emmeline knew too well about the judgments of others. Seeing the party in a new light made her certain that she had made a monumental mistake in offering to organize it in the first place. She was better off in the country, where society was far less stringent in its strictures.

"This is worse than I feared," said Mother Andrews. "You are wholly unprepared."

"I was taught by my governesses," insisted Emmeline.

"Governesses, as in plural? How many were there?"

Given time, Emmeline could have counted them all, but the pause she gave as she thought it over answered the question well enough.

Mother Andrews' posture stiffened further, her jaw clenching. "Ridiculous! Such constant changes must have left you with gaping holes in your education."

Emmeline had nothing to say in reply to that, for the words made her feel so inferior and lacking that she doubted there was any point in attempting to fix the situation. Surely, it could not be done.

"Now, don't get weepy on me, Emmeline," said Mother Andrews with pinched lips. "Tears never solved a thing, and this situation is not beyond hope."

Gathering up Emmeline's notes, the lady moved to her daughter-in-law's side, taking a seat on the sofa beside her.

"This is not your fault, young lady," said Mother Andrews. Though her posture and expression remained as rigid as ever, there was a softening at the corners of her mouth and eyes that gave Emmeline a start. In the years she had known Mother Andrews, this was as close as Emmeline had ever come to seeing any sort of warmth from the lady.

Reaching over, she gave Emmeline a brisk pat on the knee. "It is a mother's responsibility to educate her daughters, and not just in the schoolroom but in practical settings as well. Now you are bearing the consequences of your mother's reckless disregard for her duty to her children. But do not fear. I shall set you straight."

Chapter 28

G lancing up, Eloise marveled at the Hartleys' ballroom ceiling. Perhaps that was a silly thing to stare at, but it was entrancing. Though others relied on ornate chandeliers to provide the ornamentation, the Hartleys had the most beautifully preserved frescoes. Eloise was by no means well-versed in art, but even she appreciated the vibrant motion the artist had captured in the figures, as though they were living, breathing creatures and not mere dabs of paint on plaster.

A tap on her wrist brought her attention down where it ought to be, and Eloise sighed at the reproving look her mother gave her. The ballroom was stuffed with people, yet she was sequestered with some group of insipid matrons Mother had deemed acceptable company. Gazing about, Eloise wondered if she might be able to sneak away, but Mother had been vigilant since "the incident."

And other than brief interludes, Eloise had not spoken to Patrick since his rescue last week. Perhaps it was for the best.

"I hear you had quite the excitement last week," said Mrs. Hugo.

Eloise stiffened, her heartbeat quickening. Perhaps rumors were finally circulating.

"I don't know what you mean," said Mother.

Mrs. Hugo gave the young Miss Andrews a pointed look, and Eloise fought to keep her smile at bay. It had worked. The gossip was spreading. Opening her fan, Eloise batted it, affecting an innocent air as the lady continued, "I heard from a reputable source that a certain young lady was wandering the streets alone."

But Eloise's triumph was short-lived when Mrs. Elkins chimed in with a vehement head shake, the plumes in her hair fluttering back and forth. "Oh, that is most wicked of you to imply any wrongdoing on our sweet Miss Andrews' part, for it was quite innocent. Even kindly."

Turning to Eloise, Mrs. Elkins patted the girl on the arm. "You are a dear to visit your grandmother. I hear she is doing poorly."

Mother could not hide the flash of surprise, her eyes widening as she turned to Eloise, but she quickly recovered, turning back to the ladies. Mother's expression shifted in a vague manner that gave the ladies free rein to believe Mrs. Elkins' story, and Eloise was astonished to see how much her mother could imply without speaking a dishonest word.

"I apologize for believing anything was amiss," said Mrs. Hugo, and Eloise struggled not to gape at that. This was all going so horribly wrong. "Though it did have all the appearance of being inappropriate, one could never suspect an Andrews girl of impropriety."

Eloise could not believe what she was hearing. All she had gone through that day had amounted to nothing.

"Oh, yes," said Mrs. Elkins, patting Mother on the arm. "Though there were times when I thought you quite wild in your younger years, the Andrews family has proven to be quite the making of you."

Mrs. Hugo gave an emphatic nod, though Mother said nothing. For her part, Eloise froze, her fan blocking out most of the shock she showed at that pronouncement.

"Most definitely," said Mrs. Hugo before turning to Eloise.

"And you must watch yourself around your grandmother. Though I applaud your Christian behavior towards her, I would caution you to keep your distance, my girl. I would hate to see the Andrews family tainted by Amelia Kingsley's influence. Follow your mother's sterling example instead."

Now it was Mrs. Elkins' turn to nod. "Oh, yes."

Turning her eyes back to Mother, the lady added with a smile, "You have done well for yourself, Mrs. Andrews."

Another horrid busybody caught the ladies' attention, and Mrs. Hugo and Mrs. Elkins bid them farewell, leaving Eloise and her mother alone.

Turning on Mother, Eloise stared at her. "How could you stand there silently as those ladies insulted you?"

Leveling a cold look at her daughter, Mother asked, "Because you are the only one allowed to speak to me in such a manner?"

Eloise paused, her mouth hanging open, though she had no thought as to what she should say. Before she could form a response, Mother left.

Try as she might, Eloise could not understand that woman.

Not that she wanted to.

But Eloise knew that wasn't the truth. Not a whole truth, at any rate.

Shaking her head, Eloise knew now was not the time for such thoughts. Now was the time to act. The previous attempt left much to be desired, but at its heart, her plan was sound. If nothing else, those ladies' judgmental words solidified her resolve. Being free of such ridiculous company was yet another reason why ruining her reputation was the only way forward; she could sort out the Patrick question later.

As she surveyed the ballroom, a perfectly simple idea came to mind. There were always tales of girls caught in a compromising embrace at balls. Mother had lectured about just such a thing many a time, and there was no manner in which an embrace could be misconstrued or overlooked. All she needed was a most unsuitable gentleman.

Standing along the outer rim of the gathering, Patrick tucked his hands behind him and surveyed the ballroom. Which Eloise would attend tonight? Would she be coy and flirtatious? Hard and unyielding? Joyful? Angry? She'd always been a temperamental soul—that had not changed in the ensuing years—but her behavior seemed extraordinarily erratic now. Something had changed in his Eloise, and a sliver of worry buried itself into his heart.

Patrick shook his head at his own misguided musings, for he knew the precise source of her upheaval. Any fool could see it. He had bungled his way back into her life, and that was reason enough for her distress. Once more, Patrick wished to turn back time and undo their disastrous reunion.

Staring at the strangers, gratitude swelled in his heart. That feeling struck at the oddest times and always left him marveling at the change that had been wrought in him. He'd spent years hiding from his pain, which only added to that great weight bearing down on him; Patrick hadn't realized just how heavy it was until his mother and Mrs. Andrews helped him to free himself of it. And now, he could breathe again.

But such thoughts were best left at home, for he did not need to become emotional in the middle of the Hartley's ball.

"Mr. Lennox."

He nearly missed the timid voice among the throng of people and music, but Patrick turned to see Miss Hennessey a few steps behind him.

"Good evening," he said with a bow and a grin. Noticing the manner in which she clung to the wall, Patrick asked, "Are you hiding?"

"Not hiding, per se," Miss Hennessey replied with a wrinkle of her nose. "Merely attempting to be inconspicuous. I feel a bit out of place in this gathering."

"Then you must keep me company, for you are the only person I recognize," he said.

"I fear I am not very good in these settings. I find it quite unnerving to attempt conversation with strangers." Miss Hennessey gripped her fan, twisting it in her fingers as she came to stand beside Patrick.

Nodding towards several of Eloise's usual set, Patrick asked, "Are you not acquainted with them?"

Miss Hennessey's lips scrunched to one side, her eyes drifting in the opposite direction. "Though they accept me when Miss Andrews is present, they are not quite as welcoming when she is absent."

Patrick began to respond, but Miss Hennessey held up a staying hand. "Not that I am complaining, mind you. I am quite blessed to have been invited at all. My parents and I were shocked when the invitation arrived at the last moment, though I am certain it has more to do with my association with Miss Andrews than my own merit. She has been so good to me."

Her praise warmed Patrick's heart as thoroughly as if Miss Hennessey had praised him directly.

"Miss Andrews has a great capacity for kindness," he said.

Miss Hennessey smiled, turning her gaze to his. "There are not many who would have taken me under their wing as she has. Few seem willing to risk the taint of association, and I have greatly missed having friends since..." Her cheeks pinked, and she let out an irritated huff. "I do apologize. I always seem to say more than I should and cannot keep hold of my tongue."

"Do not trouble yourself," said Patrick, turning his eyes to the dancers to give her some privacy to compose herself, should she wish it. "Your honesty is refreshing."

"Miss Andrews often says that."

Patrick nodded. "And in honor of your confession, I will add one of my own. I understand how difficult it can be to find yourself adrift in society."

Miss Hennessey turned her head just enough to examine him from the corner of her eye. "Then perhaps we are both lucky to have Miss Andrews help us find our way once more."

"Speaking of whom, do you know if the lady in question has arrived yet?" asked Patrick.

Nodding, Miss Hennessey stretched to see over the crowd. "I spied her an hour ago."

"And how did she seem to you?" Perhaps it was a silly question to ask, but his curiosity got the better of him.

Miss Hennessey set herself down on her heels again, her brow furrowed. "We have not spoken yet. I thought she was coming to join me, but she never appeared. She seemed rather preoccupied."

"And might I ask how she was when you spoke with her last?" asked Patrick. Yet another silly question, but he could not help himself. If such inquiries were a sign of his insecurity or weakness, so be it. Any insight Miss Hennessey could offer into Eloise's state of mind could prove useful.

But Miss Hennessey was no fool. Though he affected a casual air, one of her eyebrows rose as she examined him, a smile pulling at her lips. Shaking her head, she chuckled to herself. "Assuming I would break a confidence—"

"I am not asking that."

Miss Hennessey paused, the laughter in her expression fading as she examined him. "I fear I cannot tell you how Miss Andrews is, for I have not spoken with her since the Pooles' card party."

"But weren't you planning to visit the National Gallery yesterday?"

Nibbling on her lip, Miss Hennessey nodded. "We were, but Miss Andrews did not join me. It must have slipped her mind."

And now it was her turn to feign indifference, but Patrick saw the disappointment and hurt shining in her eyes.

"Miss Hennessey..." Patrick began, though he had not thought as to how to finish that sentence. He wanted to give her some reassurance that Eloise had not thrown her over, but something inside him tightened, as though unwilling to give that platitude.

In truth, Patrick wasn't certain how to interpret Eloise's behavior. Having seen the pair together, Patrick knew that Eloise cared for her new friend. Doted on her in many ways. However, there was a new shadow to Eloise's personality for which he could not account.

"Do not trouble yourself, Mr. Lennox," said Miss Hennessey, her smile brightening, though sadness lingered in her gaze. "I count myself blessed for having gained any bit of Miss Andrews' good opinion. However fleeting."

"You have certainly gained mine, Miss Hennessey, though it is not worth much to most people," said Patrick with a slight bow of his head.

Her cheeks blazed red and her gaze drifted out to the crowd, but it was accompanied by a pleased smile.

"Thank you, Mr. Lennox. You are most kind—" Her words halted, her flushed cheeks paling as Miss Hennessey stared with panicked eyes at the dancers.

Patrick's gaze followed hers, and it took a moment before he found the source of her agitation. Mr. Reginald Gouldsmith stood at the far end of the ballroom; his back was to them, but Patrick knew exactly who it was from just the occasional flash of his handsome profile. Though ladies swooned at the sight of his alluring smile, it had always raised Patrick's hackles. He had not needed to hear the plethora of rumors and whispers about his abhorrent behavior to know that Gouldsmith was a gentleman in name only.

Miss Hennessey's eyes flicked to the floor and back to Gouldsmith as though she wished to avoid seeing him yet did not want to lose sight of him. Judging by the way her hands trembled, Patrick guessed it was not for a pleasant reason. Even if he did not know Gouldsmith's reputation, he would have to be a fool not to connect the fellow to the villain of Miss Hennessey's past.

"I hadn't realized Mr. Gouldsmith was in London," she stammered. "My parents were told he was traveling abroad."

Patrick cleared his throat. "Miss Hennessey, I find it unbearably stuffy in here at present. Would you join me by the windows?"

He nodded towards the part of the ballroom that was as far

from the object of her distress as possible.

"Thank you, but I should return to my parents," Miss Hennessey said with a weak approximation of a smile, her eyes not meeting his. Touching her forehead, she said, "I feel very peaked, and I think it best that we leave."

Miss Hennessey flinched when he offered up his arm, so Patrick dropped it once more. Shifting their positions so he stood between her and the others, he helped navigate the crowd as Miss Hennessey fought for control.

Keeping an eye on the scoundrel, Patrick wondered what lady was fool enough to get herself trapped in Gouldsmith's company, for though he could not see the cad's companion, there was no doubt that it was a lady: Gouldsmith never wasted time with gentlemen when there was fairer prey to hunt.

The thought of him set Patrick's blood boiling. Gouldsmith was vile, and anyone with sense would avoid him as they would any other danger, but his continued presence in society was further proof of the power of noble ties—even if he was only the untitled grandson of a degenerate earl.

Navigating around a rather raucous group, Patrick spied Mr. and Mrs. Hennessey. Catching Mr. Hennessey's eye, he motioned for the pair to join them.

"I'm afraid Miss Hennessey is feeling unwell," said Patrick. Mrs. Hennessey touched a hand to her daughter's forehead and started fluttering about the girl. Holding Mr. Hennessey's gaze, Patrick silently gestured towards Gouldsmith. Her father's expression hardened, his hands clenching at his sides, and with a nod of thanks, Mr. Hennessey herded his family to the door.

But Miss Hennessey froze.

"What is she doing?" Miss Hennessey's voice was a tremulous whisper, her eyes widening as she stared at Gouldsmith's back. And that was when the fellow moved enough for Patrick to see his companion.

Eloise gazed up at the blackguard, a coy smile on her lips as she said something that made Gouldsmith laugh. Cold swept through his veins like a winter wind as Patrick watched her flirt.

Every inch of her conveyed unspoken invitations. Patrick quickly scoured the ball, wondering where Mrs. Andrews was and how Eloise had been introduced to that rake in the first place.

Miss Hennessey gasped, drawing Patrick's attention back to her, and then his eyes darted to Eloise, and they watched as Gouldsmith led her from the ballroom. Leaving Miss Hennessey to her parents' care, Patrick hurried after the pair.

Chapter 29

Absolute perfection. There were not many times in the past few weeks that qualified for such a description, but this moment certainly earned it. Glancing up through her eyelashes as she had seen many a lady do in such situations, Eloise smiled at Mr. Gouldsmith. His arrival was so felicitous that she wondered if fate was giving her a guiding hand.

Eloise had never thought brown eyes particularly handsome, for she preferred blue, but Mr. Gouldsmith's had a richness to their hue that was quite entrancing. His lips curled up, amusement sparkling in those dark depths.

"And what would the precious little Miss Andrews want with the nefarious Mr. Gouldsmith?" His voice was so low that Eloise had to lean in to catch the words.

"I have long wished to make your acquaintance," replied Eloise—and it wasn't entirely a lie. Though Mr. Gouldsmith had not seriously occupied her thoughts until this moment, Eloise was curious about the man who made matrons faint at the very mention of his name. Perhaps being seen in public with him would be enough to taint her, but Eloise was not willing to take another half-hearted step towards ruination.

"I can only imagine," he said, perusing her figure with half-lidded eyes.

Eloise blushed, and though the room was quite warm, a sudden chill had gooseflesh rising beneath her gloves. Mr. Gouldsmith chuckled, and it brought to mind a certain gentleman whose laughter also made her heart thump faster, though that sensation was far more pleasant.

Struggling to think of what to say or do next, Eloise wished she were more adept at flirting. Though she had witnessed that subtle play between the sexes, she had never truly participated in it herself; only one gentleman had inspired any such fluttery feelings in her, and he had never been fond of such games.

Giving herself a shake, Eloise forced herself to focus. Patrick had no place in her head at present.

"I would think a gentleman such as yourself would find a ball far too mundane," said Eloise, bringing her closed fan up to tap on her lips, as she had seen others do. Perhaps drawing attention there would put him in mind of kissing.

Though that sultry smirk of his did not leave his face, Eloise saw thoughts turning in his mind as he leaned in, capturing her in his gaze. Mr. Gouldsmith held her there for several seconds before a low chuckle sounded in his throat, growing as he drew scandalously close. Eloise's eyes darted to the side, for she was certain others were watching, but Mr. Gouldsmith was so close she could hardly see around him. Surely, such a display was enough to set the gossipmongers gabbing, but Eloise would not risk it. She needed more.

A kiss was a small price to pay for freedom.

A whisper of a thought warned her that this might not be the best course. Her heartbeat quickened, bringing to mind her perilous walk about Town, but that was nonsense. They were at a ball, and though Mr. Gouldsmith did not have a sterling reputation, he was a gentleman. She was safe.

As he leaned forward, his breath tickled her ear, sending another discomforting shudder down her spine.

"Perhaps you might serve as a pleasant diversion for the evening," said Mr. Gouldsmith, his tone eliciting a nervous twist of her stomach. But surely, it was just the thought of kissing this stranger that was so unsettling.

Taking her by the arm, Mr. Gouldsmith slipped them out of the ballroom and down a side corridor. Having never been in this part of the house, Eloise was uncertain as to where they were heading, but Mr. Gouldsmith didn't falter in his path as he pulled her into a room. The fire had been abandoned for the evening, but there were still a few flickering flames giving some light to the library. Though Eloise could hardly see the shelves, she was startled by how many volumes the Hartleys had in their collection; Eloise made note to ask if Mrs. Hartley would lend her a few.

Arms grabbed her, and Eloise squeaked as they pulled her flush to Mr. Gouldsmith's chest. His face drew close to hers, and she jerked back, fully forgetting that kissing was precisely what she wanted. The gentleman paused, and though she could barely hear it, Eloise felt his chest rumbling with a laugh.

"Such a shy little maiden," murmured Mr. Gouldsmith. "Trying to play the part of the seductress?"

His fingers moved to her hair, running through her thick tresses. Eloise winced as he pulled her hairpins free with sharp tugs of her scalp, but Mr. Gouldsmith only smiled and leaned in again.

And Eloise jerked back.

Mr. Gouldsmith's eyes sparked with something new that she did not fully comprehend; it was almost like glee but with a coldness that had Eloise looking towards the door. But Mr. Gouldsmith's hold was firm, and he walked her backward at a quick clip, her feet tripping over themselves. Eloise gasped when she collided with the wall, wincing as he pressed her against it.

The library door swung open, crashing against the wall, and Patrick rushed the room, lunging at them. Wrenching the man off of her, he dragged Mr. Gouldsmith away from Eloise, shoving him towards the exit.

"Get your hands off me, Lennox!" bellowed Mr. Gouldsmith as he steadied himself. "What is the meaning of this?"

"You know full well," said Patrick as he stood between the pair. His back was to her, so Eloise could not see his face, but his tone was angrier than she'd ever heard before. "Get out!"

With a few tugs, Mr. Gouldsmith straightened his clothes and hair, giving Eloise a slow perusal that had her covering her décolletage. Patrick stepped forward, blocking her, and Mr. Gouldsmith chuckled.

"Until next time, Miss Andrews," said Mr. Gouldsmith before taking his leave.

Her unease fled as Eloise realized she'd failed once again. "Why did you run him off like that?"

Patrick whirled on her, fury hardening his expression and crackling in his light eyes. "What were you thinking? What possessed you to go off with that cad?"

Straightening, Eloise opened her mouth to answer, but Patrick continued before she could speak. "Do you have any idea what he was going to do to you?"

Crossing her arms, Eloise shook her head, moving past him to give herself some room. "A few kisses are hardly worth getting all lathered up like a snarling dog, Patrick. It was none of your concern."

Patrick's tense posture relaxed, but his expression did not warm. He stared at her, gaping as though she were some oddity. "Are you truly that blind or merely that ignorant of Gouldsmith's reputation?"

Waving an airy hand, Eloise huffed. "I've heard the stories, which is precisely why I chose him. A scandalous embrace would ruin my reputation and release me from my mother's constant harping. I wish to be free like Kitty."

Blinking, Patrick watched her as though he could not form words. And in that silence, Eloise heard footsteps. A quick glance at the door showed that it was still open, and in a heartbeat, Eloise knew what was needed, even if her original partner was no longer available.

Just as the footsteps drew closer, Eloise lunged for Patrick, bringing her lips to his.

The world had shifted multiple times in the last quarter of an hour, and none so greatly as when Eloise kissed him. Wrapping her arms around him, Eloise pulled him to her, and even with anger burning in his veins, Patrick could not resist her. One touch of her lips, and all other thoughts fled his mind.

Patrick held her close, reveling in her embrace. They'd shared a few kisses before, but those had been little more than an innocent brush of skin. Now, Eloise clung to him, and Patrick deepened the kiss, his heart fueled by years of longing, and she returned every ounce of his passion.

There was nothing in the world but this moment. It was only them, and the love that made his heart swell until it was fit to burst. Patrick wished they could remain secluded here, free from all the headaches and drama that plagued them. This was where he belonged. With his Eloise.

As the kiss slowed, Patrick gazed at his beloved, whose eyes were unfocused and dazed; he was practically holding her upright as her lips pulled into a hesitant smile. Her hand moved up his shoulder to brush his cheek.

"Patrick..." Eloise murmured, her lips grazing his.

Gasps came from the doorway, and Patrick swung his head to see three ladies gathered in the hallway, watching with wide eyes. His gaze shot to Eloise, who blinked rapidly for several seconds before her confusion gave way to comprehension. Patrick's mind refused to clear; his thoughts moved sluggishly as they tried to decipher what was happening.

Eloise still stood on her toes, firmly wrapped in his arms, and her hair tumbled down her shoulders, making her look thoroughly rumpled.

"Fetch Mrs. Andrews," said one of the ladies, batting her fan as she stared at the couple.

Eloise gaped. She wanted to say something that would right the situation, but she remained mute as understanding dawned in Patrick's eyes. Her heart broke as his ardor faded to confusion before shifting into disappointment. Euphoria gave way to a lead weight that dropped into her stomach, and Eloise fought to think of a way that she could revive that light of love that had been burning in his expression, for she would give anything to return to that blissful moment they had shared.

"Patrick..." she began, but Eloise had nothing to follow it. The kiss had seemed like the right thing to do, but she'd intended it to be a means to an end, not something that upended her entire world.

His arms fell away, and Eloise dropped from her toes, stumbling at the sudden withdrawal. Patrick steadied her, and she hoped for some hint of warmth from him, but his eyes were averted and his hand retreated the moment it was no longer needed.

"Patrick, please..." Eloise murmured, reaching for him, but he pulled away, tucking his hands behind him.

"You got precisely what you wanted, Eloise," he whispered, his head turned away from her.

And he was right and wrong at the same time. Though Eloise had felt regrets before, never had she gone from desiring a thing to despairing over it in such a flash. Standing there, watching Patrick distance himself, Eloise struggled to understand how she'd believed that kiss was the right course of action. It had seemed so logical at the time.

The world around her continued to move, but Eloise was trapped. The torment in her heart and the pain in Patrick's expression consumed her. Mother appeared at some point, and Patrick gave a few short words before taking his leave. Others spoke, but Eloise simply stared at the empty space where Patrick had been.

What had she done?

...

The candles were melted to the barest nubs, their flickering flames casting wavering shadows around Patrick's bedchamber. The room had grown chill, but he remained in the armchair facing the dying fire. He hardly remembered the journey from the Hartleys' or coming to this very spot. He certainly could not recall how many minutes or hours he had sat here in the cold darkness.

Eloise had betrayed him.

No, it was more than that. If it were only a hurt that needed forgiving, Patrick could face that; he had done plenty of wrong in his life, and he could not withhold forgiveness when others were in need.

Eloise had changed.

Just thinking those three words made his stomach tighten. An itch traveled down his spine, and his throat burned, begging for relief. Getting to his feet, Patrick paced, as though he could outmaneuver the desire picking away at his resolve. But it haunted his every step, pleading for him to surrender. It was like a living thing, whispering in his ear, giving him every reason to do so.

It was only a little drink. A bit of numbing. An escape.

Though Patrick's mind recalled all the reasons why that was a terrible idea, his body craved a sip. That base need took control of him, forcing out everything but that powerful desire to drink. Sucking in several rapid breaths, Patrick shook out his hands, calling upon every ounce of resolve to shove the temptation aside. But it followed him like his own shadow.

In quick succession, Patrick thought through his options. There was not a drop of spirits in the house, but he knew there were public houses nearby in which he could find a bit of blessed relief from this all-consuming urge.

It had been months since he'd felt such a strong attack on his resolve, but tonight had left him raw and vulnerable. Closing his eyes, Patrick opened his heart, crying out for any divine intervention that might help ease this burden he could not bear alone.

Scrubbing at his face as though that might erase the craving consuming him, Patrick paused at the feel of the scars along his cheek. His fingers traced those angry ridges, following those familiar lines. And for a moment, the ground settled beneath him. With a deep breath, Patrick remembered the agony while the surgeon had worked on him. The sounds of his mother's tears. The sight of Mr. Dowding's pistol aimed at him. But more than all those harrowing memories, Patrick recalled the deep-seated disgust he'd felt when caught in Mrs. Dowding's embrace.

Patrick did not want to be that man, and he knew—fully and unequivocally—that if he gave in at this moment, he would return to that life, and salvation would not be so easily reclaimed.

His fingers followed the scars, bringing a dash of peace with each movement. It was tremulous and faint, but it came, and Patrick embraced it, focusing on that as the minutes and hours ticked away.

Chapter 30

Emmeline
Age Twenty-six

Fiddling with the glittering gems adorning her neck, Emmeline's eyes stared sightlessly at the wall as Marybeth added a few more pins to her coiffure. Flowers and food were all prepared and properly arrayed. The dance order finalized long ago. The invitations sent with time to spare. All was as it should be, yet Emmeline could not stop sifting through the details in search of anything she might have overlooked.

Marybeth bobbed and stepped away, but Emmeline did not move from her dressing table. Tonight had to be perfect. Not so much for herself or for the guests but for Mother Andrews. Emmeline could never express how grateful she was for the hours of effort her mother-in-law had put into training her, but showing her newly gained proficiency would be a start.

A kiss pressed to her neck, startling her, but Emmeline's eyes drew to Norman's, reflected in her looking glass.

"It's going to be a fine evening," said Norman.

Emmeline gave him a weak smile. "I wish I had your confidence, but I am certain to have forgotten something."

But Mother Andrews' voice echoed in her thoughts, chiding

her not to be so overwrought. A lady always maintains her composure.

"It will be a success," said Norman, rubbing her neck.

Taking a cleansing breath, Emmeline straightened her spine and nodded. Standing, she drew close to Norman, his arms coming around her.

"It will be a success," she echoed, reaching for his cravat to straighten the misaligned folds. "My first ball."

"Hardly your first," he said.

"The first I have organized on my own," she amended, her fingers tugging and smoothing the linen. The silly thing did not wish to lie properly.

"And it will be a success."

Emmeline nodded, leaning in to kiss his cheek. "Boyle should see to your cravat."

Glancing down at his neck, Norman shrugged. "It looks like it always does."

"No," she said with a shake of her head. "It looks a fright. You cannot go down with it like that."

Norman pulled such a grimace that one would think that she had asked him to leap out of the third story window.

"I know I am being a bit demanding, dearest," said Emmeline, drawing close to feather a kiss at the edge of his jaw. "I promise to be at ease once this is over."

Norman gave a low grunt, turning his mouth to capture her lips. Melting into his embrace, Emmeline allowed the euphoria of his touch to wash over her, giving her a sense of peace she had not felt in several days. Though she wished to throw away all caution and crush herself to him, there was not time enough to redo Marybeth's work, and Emmeline kept herself in check.

Breaking off the kiss, Norman whispered, "Perhaps we might spend a bit of the evening in our secret spot."

Emmeline sighed at the wonderful possibilities latent in his suggestion but drew herself back to reality. "A host cannot abandon his party."

"As if anyone would notice me gone," he said.

"I would miss you greatly."

"And that is why you should slip away with me." Norman gave her a warm smile, though they both knew it would not happen. His shoulders slumped as he released his wife. "I will be the dutiful host and greet all our guests, but promise me I shall be free to disappear to a quiet corner with Pottlesby once the ball is underway."

Emmeline rang for Norman's valet and then turned to the mirror for a final inspection of her outfit. "I will release you the moment it is acceptable if you please, but Mr. and Mrs. Pottlesby are not going to be here tonight, so you shall need to find another chum for the evening."

"I am surprised at that," said Norman, pulling his watch from his pocket to glance at the time. "Perhaps I should send a note around to ask after Mrs. Pottlesby."

"Whatever for?" Emmeline secured her earring as she turned to see every side of herself.

"Why else would they have thrown us over? I saw Pottlesby this afternoon, and he assured me he had no commitments this evening."

Emmeline paused and dropped her hands to face her husband with a furrowed brow. "They weren't invited, my dear. We spoke about this weeks ago. They do not rub along well with the Stricklands."

Norman sat on the bed with a frown.

"Now, don't be downcast, my darling," said Emmeline, coming to his side to hold his hand. "There will be plenty of others, and I am certain you shall find someone else to talk to."

Turning his gaze to hers, Norman looked no more appeased than she had expected him to be, but there was nothing to be done about it. The Pottlesbys were not the right sort of people to have at an event such as this, and for the sake of their family, everyone must make sacrifices.

"I promise it will be a wonderful evening," she said with a squeeze of his hand.

Though Norman did not voice the sentiment, Emmeline

saw the doubt stamped on his face, and she could not fault him for it. As much as she loved her dear husband, he had not the knack for socializing. But again, sacrifices must be made, and Emmeline gave him a tender kiss to ease his pain.

"Just give me your word that we will return home to the country as planned," said Norman.

"Of course. Why would you even ask?"

"You cannot be wholly surprised."

"I do not want to argue about this again, Norman," said Emmeline, stepping away to face the mirror once more. "Mother Andrews was right: the children are better off in the country. Yet, you act like I am an ogre for following her sound advice. And it's only a few weeks. Hardly any time at all."

Norman deflated, his eyes dimming as he gazed at his wife. "I miss our life, Emmeline."

"I know, darling, but we are doing this for our children—"

But Emmeline's words were cut short as a knock came at the door, and Boyle entered. Between his and Emmeline's instructions, the pair had Norman looking polished in minutes while Emmeline kept a firm eye on the time; they must be ready to receive their guests momentarily.

With a final inspection, Emmeline took her husband by the arm and led him downstairs.

...

"Mr. and Mrs. Drake, how kind of you to come," said Emmeline.

Mrs. Drake replied in kind, but Emmeline could hardly pay attention to her with the way Norman was behaving. He was not the type to fidget. With his quiet manner and unlimited patience, he was the epitome of an even temperament, but he was growing more fractious the longer they stood there.

With a few more pleasantries, the Drakes moved along, and the pair were afforded a brief respite. Luckily, the last few guests were arriving, and soon she could release her poor husband from the duty he despised so greatly.

"Only a little longer, dearest," said Emmeline, squeezing his arm. Impulse had her leaning into him, but she caught herself before she moved scandalously close to him. As much as she wanted to wrap her arms around her husband, Mother Andrews' voice came to mind, reminding her of just how terrible an idea that was.

Tension pulled at the corners of his lips while his gaze begged her to set him free. "Do you promise?"

"Emmeline, my dear girl, how good to see you!"

Every muscle in her body tightened at the sound of Mama's voice. Caught between panic and elation, Emmeline had not the clarity of thought to decide whether she was happy or angry about her mother's sudden appearance.

"Mama," Emmeline greeted as the lady leaned in to buss her cheek. "I heard you were traveling the continent."

"I was, but I had to return when I heard my dear Priscilla was to be married," said Mama, reaching over to take her youngest by the arm. "Your aunt would make a mess of the whole business, and I cannot allow that to happen."

Emmeline's eyes darted to Priscilla, her heart fracturing under the weight of a double betrayal. It was painful enough to know her sister had not bothered to tell her of the engagement, but it was unbearable to know that Mama would shoulder the effort of planning the occasion when she hadn't bothered to even attend Emmeline's wedding. Norman rested a hand at her back, his thumb brushing a gentle touch as Emmeline battled her gathering tears.

"Mrs. Kingsley," said Mother Andrews as she joined the group. Giving the others a slight curtsy, she lightly tapped Emmeline on the arm with her fan. It was just the reminder Emmeline needed to clear her mind. She could hear her mother-in-law's voice as though the lady had spoken the words aloud, censuring Emmeline about her lack of composure.

"It is a surprise to see you here tonight," said Mother Andrews, giving Mama's dress a hard look.

In the shock of the moment, Emmeline had not noticed her mother's garish gold gown. There was not a speck of mourning about it, though she was still far from the end of that solemn period. The tempestuous nature of their relationship was no secret, but this blatant affront to her husband's memory was beyond the pale.

"Why would I deny myself the opportunity for such entertainment?" asked Mama. "And I have not seen Emmeline in ages."

"We are pleased to have you both," said Norman, and Emmeline clutched her blessed husband's arm in relief, for he was able to find something to say when she was at a loss for words. "Emmeline has outdone herself tonight, and it is wonderful that you and Priscilla are here to celebrate her triumph."

Mama grinned, a cloying, coquettish thing, but her eyes were not directed at anyone in their party. Rather, her gaze lingered on a young gentleman standing at the edge of the ballroom.

Priscilla smiled, though hers was genuine in every aspect. "The decorations are quite lovely, Emmeline."

Their mother made a vague noise and waved her hand. "Rather ordinary, in fact. Nothing I haven't seen before, but not a terrible attempt. I am certain you will get better with time."

Though Emmeline thought herself a rational creature, those words stoked a fury in her heart that pointed itself inward. Her teeth nearly cracked beneath the clench of her jaw, and she swallowed down the seething rage, which burned in her stomach. Why must she be such a fool?

Emmeline knew precisely where she stood in her mother's estimation. Amelia Kingsley had made her feelings clear time and time again. Yet when her mother's apathy reared its ugly head, Emmeline's heart acted as though it was the first time. Through the self-loathing, her eyes prickled with unshed tears, which only made her anger grow, for she knew better than to hope for a morsel of affection from her mother.

Yet her traitorous heart longed for it.

Before anyone in the party could say another word, Mama took Priscilla by the arm, leading her into the crowd in search of finer companions.

"Do not listen to her, Emmeline," murmured Norman, wrapping his hand around hers.

Emmeline nodded, for she could not form a proper response. It was all well and good to say such things did not matter, but her heart refused to listen. Emmeline could not fathom how her mother still held such power over her. For goodness' sake, Emmeline had spent more time with most of the ladies in the ballroom than Amelia Kingsley. Why should Mama's opinion matter so?

"Norman, fetch your wife a drink," said Mother Andrews. "She looks peaked."

"But Mother—" he began, but the quelling look she gave him sent Norman scurrying towards the refreshment table.

"Compose yourself, Emmeline," said Mother Andrews, stiffening her posture and looking down her nose at Emmeline. "Such hysterics are hardly useful."

There were no tears or great gasping breaths, so Emmeline was far from hysterical, but she felt a tremble spreading through her as though the last of her strength had evaporated in the aftermath.

"Head up, child," said Mother Andrews, tapping Emmeline's chin with her fan. "Your mother is and always has been a fool of the highest order. Do not give her power by falling to pieces now. You have done an admirable job tonight."

"Truly?" Emmeline's voice warbled, the sad question wringing a tear from her eye.

"There are certain areas in which you can improve, but you have done fine work. Do not doubt that, and do not spend one more minute mourning Amelia Kingsley. She is not worthy of such efforts," said Mother Andrews. Though her rigid spine did not relax nor did the tightness in her expression soften, there was a warmth to her eyes that was all the more poignant for its rare appearance. "Now, compose yourself."

Emmeline nodded. With a slow breath, she straightened, forcing her nerves to settle as she erased any outward sign of her distress. Once she was calm, both inwards and out, she turned to face the next guests, who were fast approaching, and greeted them with a curtsy that was the picture of perfection. Just as Mother Andrews had taught her.

Chapter 31

Eloise sat like a statue, staring at the far wall of the parlor. Her eyelids felt like crudely spun wool as she blinked at the nothingness, her thoughts vacant. Having passed most of the morning thusly, Mother had given up coaxing her to speak, and the pair sat silent while the lady's gaze darted between her needlework and her daughter.

Would Patrick visit today? That question set her stomach churning, even though she hoped he would. How could one long to see someone yet dread their presence? It made no sense to Eloise, but the few sluggish thoughts she managed to formulate today were supremely unhelpful.

Of course, honor dictated that he call. Though few had witnessed the heated embrace, the ballroom buzzed with the rumor before the Andrews had taken their leave. If no announcement was made forthwith, Eloise would be ruined. And ruination was what she desired. Wasn't it?

Such thoughts were too big for her mind to contemplate at present, and they fled once more. However, Patrick's expression would not leave her be. In her spiteful moments, Eloise had wished to cause him the same pain he'd caused during his absence, but seeing it played out before her brought no peace or comfort. Rather than a tit for tat exchange, it left another bruise adjacent to those he'd inflicted.

The parlor door opened, and a footman entered, coming to Mother's side to offer up a silver tray with a calling card atop it, but Eloise needed no announcement to know who awaited them. Speaking a few words to the servant, Mother put aside her work, and moments later Patrick stood in the doorway.

Eloise went through the proper greetings, moving on instinct rather than conscious thought as she stared at him.

"Might I speak with your daughter alone?" asked Patrick while avoiding Eloise's gaze.

Mother looked between the pair and then left. Heat filled Eloise's cheeks as she took her seat again, her eyes dropping to the floor. Patrick strode to the fireplace, standing silently with his back to her.

"Eloise..." he began, but she could not allow him to continue.

"That is unnecessary. I know duty and honor require you to offer marriage, but my honor will not allow you to be forced into an engagement. We both know that was not my intention."

Patrick did not turn to look at her, but his head dropped. "No, but you intended to do as you pleased, regardless of the cost to anyone else."

Eloise stiffened at that accusation. "Perhaps I was being self-serving, but surely you understand my desperation. Being compromised was my only solution—"

Her words were cut short when Patrick let out a bitter laugh, turning to look at her with such disappointment and disbelief that tears gathered in Eloise's eyes. His head dropped again, and he stared at the rug, shaking his head.

"Are you that naive, Eloise? Or are you merely blind to the truth? You speak of being compromised as though it is a godsend."

"It is if it frees me of my mother's control."

Patrick's gaze shot up to meet hers, and she leaned away

from the intensity in his eyes. "Have you ever asked Miss Hennessey about her experience with it?"

Eloise frowned as she thought back to their conversations. They had spoken about so many things, but Eloise could not recall Kitty ever having broached the subject. In point of fact, Kitty rarely spoke of herself, and a spike of shame pierced Eloise's heart at the realization that she had never thought to ask many questions of her new friend.

"I heard she was caught in an embrace with a gentleman," said Eloise, her fingers tracing patterns in the sofa cushions. "Mr. Gouldsmith, in fact."

"An embrace?" asked Patrick with an arched eyebrow. Stepping closer, he glared down at her. When she did not meet his eyes, he let out a frustrated huff. "Mr. Gouldsmith is adept at preying on innocent young ladies, and though I do not know the whole of the story, it was no simple embrace. Have you never noticed how nervous she is around men?"

Of their own accord, Eloise's eyes snapped to his, and he held her gaze as he continued. "That monster delights in the struggle and forced himself upon her, Eloise. If others had not heard the commotion and caught him before the deed was done, he would have ravaged her."

Patrick's face blurred as tears filled her vision, trickling down her cheeks. Her chin trembled as she pictured her poor friend in such a wretched situation.

"I had no idea," she whispered.

"I know," said Patrick. "But what I am trying to decide is if you were always so blind and self-centered. Did I simply not see it?"

Shock held her tongue silent, and tears fell freely. Never had words hurt so much, and perhaps the most acute pain came from the prickle of conscience that told her Patrick was right to say such things.

"You have such capacity for kindness, Eloise, but I see so little of it at present. I have watched the way you treat people, and I cannot reconcile the girl I knew with the young lady sitting before me." Patrick pinched his nose. Turning away, he faced the fireplace once more, leaning against the mantle.

"I grant you I've been preoccupied of late, but you make it sound as though I am purposefully cruel."

Looking over his shoulder at her, Patrick gave her a sad smile. "Not purposefully, Eloise. It would have been easier to see the truth if it had been purposeful, but I have watched you abuse good people for your own gain."

Eloise gaped. "That is a terrible thing to say."

"But true," said Patrick. "Mr. Godwin, for one."

Gripping the edge of the sofa cushions, Eloise leaned forward. "I did not mean to break his heart, but he inferred a deeper attachment on my part."

Straightening, Patrick faced her, tucking his hands behind his back. "You cared little for him, yet you flirted and hung on his every word to make me jealous, and by doing so, you encouraged his feelings."

Opening her mouth, Eloise wished she had words to fill it, but there was no defense she could mount; she had only to recall the broken look on Mr. Godwin's face to confirm the accusation.

"And Miss Hennessey—"

But Eloise spoke over him. "Whatever else you may accuse me of, Patrick, you cannot fault me for her."

He gave her another sad look. "Can you honestly say your decision to befriend Miss Hennessey was not fueled by a desire to disobey your mother?"

Eloise paused, gnawing at the edge of her lip. "Perhaps a bit at first, but I do care for her."

"Yet you ignore her whenever it suits you," said Patrick.

She opened her mouth to defend herself, but he continued. "You should have heard Miss Hennessy. Even after you missed your outing and fairly ignored her last night, she still praised you, saying she was simply grateful you showed any kindness to her."

Chin trembling, Eloise fought to breathe. In truth, she had

not recognized those slights until Patrick mentioned them. Each was unintentional, but her conscience would not allow her to excuse them.

"You complain about your reputation," said Patrick, his voice quivering. He paused, cleared his throat, and began again. "You act as though you are jealous of Miss Hennessey's situation, but you have no comprehension of what a blessing it is to have a sterling reputation like yours. Miss Hennessey was ostracized by even her closest friends, yet with only a few words from you, that changed."

"But you have no idea how difficult it is to be controlled by it," said Eloise, throwing her arms wide.

"And that does not change regardless of how good or bad your reputation is. Unless you have a magic spell that can change human nature, people will always judge. It is inevitable and irrefutable, and reputation is a commodity of which you have an abundance. However, rather than doing something good with it—such as raise the standing of those who cannot do so on their own—you choose to toss it away."

Eloise's posture slumped, her voice warbling as she tried to speak. "I had not thought of it that way."

"Because you've never been treated like a pariah."

The silence stretched out, filling the parlor with an oppressive weight that felt liable to crush her. There was no containing the tears pouring down her cheeks or the tremors that had taken hold of her hands. Though she wished to refute Patrick's words, they held too much truth to be turned away.

"I wish I had some better justification for my behavior, but I am ashamed to admit I have none. I am sorry," she whispered, staring at her fingers as she picked at the sofa cushion seams. Glancing at Patrick, Eloise searched for any sign of his thoughts, but they were locked away beneath his stony facade. Please say you forgive me."

Patrick stood there, inscrutable, and Eloise's heartbeat ed as she stared up at him.

"You have asked for my forgiveness so many times, and I

have freely given it," she said, but then paused, her expression crumpling as her heart twisted. "Perhaps not as freely as I should have, but I have forgiven you. Can you not forgive me?"

Another long moment of silence before Patrick spoke. "I forgive you, Eloise. I understand weakness too well and would never resent you for yours."

Eloise broke into a watery smile and rose to her feet, but Patrick stepped away as she drew closer. She clasped her hands in front of her, wringing her fingers.

"I am leaving for Ireland," he said.

Eloise straightened, her hands falling to her sides. "Pardon?"

"I am to inherit my grandfather's property one day, and I need to study under him for some time," he said, his gaze falling away from Eloise. "I had planned on putting it off until later, but I feel it is best if I go now."

"Now?"

Patrick gave a stiff nod. Eloise stared at him, pleading for him to look at her, but he did not meet her gaze.

"But you said you forgive me," she whispered.

"Forgiveness is not the issue, Eloise." Patrick shifted from foot to foot, tucking his hands behind him. He did not continue his thought, but as she had not the words to prod him, Eloise merely stood there, staring at him.

"I feel that I may have been too hasty..." He halted, shifting once more before continuing. His eyes rose from the floor and met hers, tears shining in them. "You helped me through the darkest days, Eloise. Even when I was too lost to find my way back, you were that bright shining hope for me."

His words faltered, and Patrick paused, his gaze jerking away as he blinked back his tears. When he had control again, he met her eyes. "There are moments when I catch a glimpse of that sweet spirit that has entranced me for as long as I can remember, but I fear the girl I loved became someone I do not recognize."

The strength left her legs, and Eloise had to sit once more.

Patrick cleared his throat. "The darkness of my past still lives inside me, Eloise, waiting for a weak moment to seize control again. I had thought I was strong enough, but I am not able to hold firm while you play your games."

"There are no games—" she began, but an exasperated look from Patrick had her rethinking her words.

"You are never willing to set me free, yet you are unwilling to open your heart to me. I am a patient man, and I am willing to spend the time and effort to rebuild a future with the Eloise I love. However, I am not certain she still exists." He paused, his brow furrowing. "Or perhaps she was merely a construct my broken spirit pieced together to give me a light amidst the darkness."

Shaking his head, Patrick waved it away and continued, "Regardless, I don't have the strength to stay and sort it out. I must leave or risk losing myself once more. I thought I was strong enough, but I was wrong."

Clarity came too late for Eloise. Her doubts and fears had seemed so important and insurmountable, yet when faced with a life devoid of Patrick, Eloise's heart broke as thoroughly as anyone who had ever loved. Though his departure after Kelly's funeral had devastated her, there had always been a flickering hope that he would return. But she felt it flee under the finality of his tone: Patrick would not renew his addresses.

The parlor door opened, and Mother strode in. "Then you two are not to be reconciled?"

Eloise turned her tear-filled eyes to Patrick, but he did not meet her gaze. She could not speak the words, and apparently, neither could he.

Mother stood before the pair, her hands clasped in front of her as though she were inspecting the maid's work.

"I see," she said, and Eloise swore she saw a flash of sadness, but it vanished before Eloise could say for certain.

"Then I am afraid we have no other recourse than to bar you from our home, Patrick," said Mother with a pinched expression that Eloise could not decipher. "It is the only way to salvage Eloise's reputation with this scandal looming over the pair of you."

Patrick's eyebrows rose. "I am leaving for Ireland, so I shan't be a problem for long."

Mother took a hesitant step forward, reaching for him, but she caught herself, straightening once more. "I do apologize, but I must do what is best for my daughter. If you two aren't going to marry, then we must distance ourselves."

Patrick's gaze flicked between mother and daughter for a moment before he gave a curt bow. "Then I shan't sully your family with my presence any longer."

And with that parting blow, he left, taking Eloise's heart with him.

Chapter 32

Emmeline
Age Twenty-eight

With a sigh, Emmeline rubbed at a spot her babe delighted in kicking. Yet another month before the child would make its grand entrance into the world, and Emmeline wished it were sooner, for the babe liked to treat her like a dance floor. Shifting the cushion behind her, Emmeline tried to find a more comfortable position, but it was a fruitless endeavor.

Retrieving her needlework from the seat beside her, Emmeline placed another stitch along the petal's edge. In truth, it looked identical to a dozen other flowers she had stitched onto a dozen different linens. A never-ending parade of fabrics for her to embellish with the same flora and fauna. Still, she worked. If only she felt the same love for her stitched garden as she did for the real one.

But a genteel lady did not muck about in the dirt.

Her fingers paused in their work at the sound of laughter coming from the window. Abandoning her needlepoint, Emmeline crossed the sitting room and looked to see Norman chasing the children about the garden. Lunging for Joanna, he gave a mighty roar and the child shrieked, speeding around a planting bed with her father close at her heels. Lucinda and Kenneth chased after him and latched on to his legs, giggling as he continued to stomp around the garden with the pair riding his feet.

The gleeful scene moved Emmeline, lightening her heart and bringing a smile to her lips, and she yearned to join them among the flowers and sunshine, but it would not do. Even as she watched Kenneth clap, pointing up at the birds swooping through the sky, she knew the frivolity needed to be curtailed.

Mother Andrews was fond of saying, "How are they ever to learn to be proper adults if they go about like vagabonds?" And as much as it pained her, Emmeline knew her mother-in-law was right. The children's clothes were a mess, and the girls were behaving like savages. Emmeline had put off hiring a governess for Joanna, but she feared it was long past time for her eldest to be in the classroom.

"Mama!" shrieked Lucinda, running to the window. "Come and play!"

Emmeline shook her head. She had to be strong for their sakes. No matter how much she longed to join them, Emmeline knew she must maintain her composure and dignity. Even one misstep could undo all the goodwill she'd garnered over the past few years.

Norman paused at that and joined his daughter, beckoning Emmeline to come outside, but she shook her head once more. With a wave, she motioned for the pair to return to their play, and Emmeline returned to her work. Seeing her children's joy made it both easier and more difficult to continue her stitches, for it filled her with a renewed sense of purpose and longing. But she would remain strong. Firm. For their sakes, she would never give anyone reason to reproach her family again.

"Emmeline, stop hiding in here," said Norman, striding through the sitting room door.

"I have work to do," said Emmeline, keeping her eyes on her needlework.

"Nothing that cannot be put off," said Norman. He reached for her hand, but Emmeline shifted away without pausing in her stitches. Undeterred, he took the seat beside her on the sofa. "This is ridiculous. I cannot remember the last time you played with the children. They miss their mother. At least bring your needlework outside. We can have a chair brought round and placed in the shade so you are comfortable."

"It is not appropriate, Norman." Emmeline jabbed her needle through the linen, working with more determination than care. "I must be an example of proper decorum to them, and you would do well to remember that, yourself."

"Emmeline, it is just a bit of fun. You seem to forget what that is."

Leaning closer, Norman ran a hand along her arm, and she smiled at his touch. His hand wandered up to her neck, tickling the skin as he brushed the hollow of her throat. Emmeline turned her lips to meet his but caught sight of Nurse Grove gathering the children.

Straightening, Emmeline slid down the sofa. "Not in public, Norman."

He sighed and slouched in his seat. "We are not in public."

"The servants talk."

"And what would they say? That their master is in love with their mistress?"

Wrenching the needle and thread along the now misshapen petal, Emmeline scowled. "That their mistress is wanton."

"Emmeline..." Norman groaned.

"How are the children to behave properly when their parents do not lead by example?"

Norman frowned at that, his eyes turning away from his wife. He said nothing, though Emmeline felt all the frustration simmering beneath his quiet surface. Luckily, a knock sounded at the door, followed by the footman's appearance, which effectively severed the conversation.

"We have everything moved as you ordered, madam," said John with a bow.

"Wonderful," said Emmeline. "I will be by shortly to inspect the work."

Norman's eyes darted from John to Emmeline. Once the door closed, Norman spoke. "I hadn't realized Mother was leaving. She said not a word about it at breakfast."

Glancing over at Norman, Emmeline shook her head. "Why would Mother Andrews leave? She is so happily situated here at Pendleton Place. It is her home."

"Of course, my dear," said Norman, standing to look out the window at the children. "I simply didn't think she would wish to stay now that Father is gone. She is forever complaining that the children are too noisy. The cottage I prepared for her will provide her all the privacy she craves."

"But we cannot do without her," said Emmeline, pushing aside her needlepoint. Joining her husband at the window, she drew her arm through his. "I depend on her so, and she is so helpful."

"Perhaps a bit too helpful."

Coming around to stand before Norman, Emmeline took his hand in hers. "Please promise me you will not send her away. I know you and she do not always see eye to eye, but I cannot stand the thought of losing her now. What am I to do should she leave?"

"Emmeline, you are plenty capable of handling the estate and the family on your own," said Norman. "And you have Deirdre and me. Isn't that enough?"

"It may be silly, but I need her, and I believe she needs us, too. She may not show it, but I think it will hurt her to be sent away. This is her home."

"I do not believe anything can hurt my mother, Emmeline."

"Mother Andrews has a far bigger heart than you realize." And Emmeline thought of all the many little kindnesses that dear lady bestowed. Those faint smiles and the odd compliment warmed her through. A proper mother, though she doubted her husband would ever truly understand that.

Pulling his wife into his arms, Norman placed a kiss on her

temple. With a quick glance, Emmeline looked for Nurse Grove and saw that she and the children had moved away from the window and were nowhere in sight. Turning her face to his, Emmeline leaned in closer, her lips drawing near his.

But Norman paused, his brow furrowing as he looked at his wife. "If Mother isn't leaving, what was the staff moving?"

Bringing her hands around to his chest, Emmeline smoothed his waistcoat while staring at his buttons. She had wished for a better way to tell him the news, but there was no hiding the truth once the question had been asked.

"They were moving my things," she said, her fingers playing with his buttons. "I thought it best if I move into the adjacent bedchamber."

Norman's arms tightened around her, his body rigid as he held her there, but Emmeline could not meet his eyes. She did not wish to see the pain she knew would be there, for it was precisely what she felt.

"It isn't proper for a husband and wife to share a bedchamber," said Emmeline. "It is common and vulgar."

Still, Norman said nothing.

The silence stretched out, and Emmeline struggled to find something to say, but she had no more words to offer up. Carefully, her eyes moved to meet his, and she was greeted with all the heartache she had feared to find.

"You wish for separate bedchambers?" he asked.

"Of course not," said Emmeline with a frown. "But it is must be done."

"Why must it? You are my wife. There is nothing shameful in spending the night together."

Emmeline sighed. "You and I do not think it is shameful, but there are plenty of others who do. And their poor opinions are cast upon our entire family—including the children. I cannot allow my selfish desires to taint their standing among their peers."

"It is no one's business but our own."

"People make it their business, Norman."

His jaw clenched, his brown eyes boring into Emmeline's with an anger and hurt she had never seen reflected there before, and she hated herself for being the author of such darkness. His arms fell away, but Emmeline refused to distance herself.

"So the decision is made, no matter what I think. No discussion. You simply moved your things and tell me after the fact?" he asked.

Wrapping her arms around his neck, Emmeline ran her hands along the nape of his neck. "I know it is a shock, dearest, but I assure you this will change nothing. We will still have our special time together." Leaning in, she feathered kisses along his jaw. "We will simply sleep apart. That is all."

Norman pulled her hands from his neck and stepped away. His eyes were anchored to the floor as he gave her a sketch of a bow and strode from the room without another word.

Emmeline's chin trembled, her eyes pricking at the emptiness surrounding her. Her heart screamed for Norman, begging him to return, but she closed her eyes against the urge, forcing such reckless feelings away. Mother Andrews' disapproving voice echoed in her mind, demanding that Emmeline get control of herself, but it was impossible to silence the longing in her heart.

Casting her eyes about, Emmeline spied her writing desk on the side table. Going to it, she yanked out a piece of paper. Ink freckled the surface as Emmeline grabbed a quill and allowed her heart to have free rein of her hand. Her silent agonies spilled out, scratching across the page. It was not enough to satisfy the need burning in her heart, but it would have to be enough.

For her children's good, she must remain in control. For her own sanity, Emmeline must allow herself to be free in this hidden place; no one need know.

Chapter 33

H ad she done the right thing? The question plagued
Emmeline, but she could not think of another way to
salvage Eloise's future without cutting ties with Patrick.

The quill flew across the journal page, her hand struggling
to keep up with her stream of thoughts. Emmeline didn't know
when tears had formed, but they blurred the words and left
droplets across the page. Memories of Eloise, Patrick, Norman,
and Mother Andrews swarmed her like flies, picking at her well-
being until she had no reserve left to shoo them away.

Why had she neglected her duty last night? Emmeline
could only attribute it to the shock of discovering that Eloise
had visited her grandmother. Combined with having her past
dredged up by those shrews, and Emmeline had been thoroughly out of sorts. She should have watched Eloise closer.

Emmeline's pulse raced at the thought of what might've
happened had Patrick not rescued Eloise from Mr. Gouldsmith.
Though the memories did not plague her as they once had, Emmeline could not forget the hands that had gripped her. The
weight of a man pinning her to the floor. The lurid whispers in
her ears. Wet lips covering hers. For all that Emmeline had

done to protect her daughter from such things, Eloise had willingly put herself in the path of such danger.

But Eloise was safe. For the time being. Though her daughter had done her best to destroy everything Emmeline had worked so hard to build, there were other steps to further mitigate this disaster. Emmeline would not allow her daughter to be painted with the same brush she had been.

That would not happen. It could not.

The door to the library swung open, and Deirdre swept in, anger vibrating off her.

"How dare you, Emmeline!" she said, slamming the door behind her.

Dropping the quill on the desk, Emmeline abandoned her journal. There was no point in feigning ignorance. "I did what I must."

"How could you bar my son from your home?" she asked, tapping her breastbone with a jerky movement. "My son!"

"Deirdre, please, can we not speak peaceably?" Emmeline asked, motioning for Deirdre to sit on an armchair, but her friend pulled away.

"Peaceably?" Deirdre asked, her muscles quivering. "How can you expect me to be peaceable about this? Do you think I will allow you to treat my son in such a manner and say nothing?"

Clasping her hands in front of her, Emmeline took in a breath, but it did nothing to calm her fraying nerves. "I have to protect my daughter's reputation."

"What tripe! The majority of people have already dismissed the rumors, for no one can believe *your* daughter would behave in such a manner."

Emmeline sighed. "After all that has happened of late, I cannot be too careful. I did what needed to be done for my daughter—"

"Patrick is best for Eloise. They are clearly meant for each other."

Emmeline tried ushering her to sit again but surrendered

at the fierce look Deirdre gave her. "You know I adore Patrick, and I would love nothing more than to see them happily settled, but it was clear they were not going to reconcile."

Deirdre rolled her eyes, waving her hands at that nonsense. "Don't be a fool, Emmeline. Of course they will reconcile. They've had a rocky go of it, but this is not the end of their story unless you keep standing in their way."

Slumped in his armchair, Norman stared off at nothing. His eyes blurred the world as a jumble of thoughts cluttered his head. His chin rested heavily in his hand, keeping him upright when his body wanted to sag to the floor, and he longed for a bit of sanity. Peace and quiet. Happiness.

Someone had painted over his beautiful life, leaving it a muddy, grey mess. The change had crept up on him, sucking the brightness from his world in slow but steady ways until it was nothing but a dull approximation of what it had been. It was no longer a case of merely lacking happiness; Norman was miserable.

Rubbing a hand along his head, he could not think of how to fix this. Perhaps there was no solution.

A door slammed somewhere in the townhouse, and Norman sighed. He had hoped that Eloise's mood would improve, but it appeared it had not.

However, the raised voices that accompanied the slam weren't Eloise's.

To his shame, Norman's instinct was to pretend he hadn't heard Deirdre's shouts, but he had hidden from such things for far too long. Getting to his feet, he went in search of the trouble and found it in the library.

"I had to ensure Eloise did not become a byword—"

Norman pushed open the door, and Emmeline paused. Both ladies turned to see him enter, and Norman froze. But it was too late to retreat. Deirdre's gaze burned him, and though Emmeline stood poised and proper, there was a frenetic energy resting just below the surface, as though she were barely holding herself together.

"I heard raised voices," he said, holding his hands up in surrender.

Deirdre turned her fiery gaze from Norman to Emmeline. "If you bar my son from your home, you bar me."

Norman sucked in a quick breath, his eyes darting to his wife as his blood ran cold, while Emmeline's hands fell to her sides, her mouth gaping as tears filled her eyes.

"I have been your friend for a long time," said Deirdre. The lady's lips trembled, a sheen of tears filling her eyes. "I have stood by you through everything. I have overlooked so much because I hoped the Emmeline I knew and loved would return to me someday."

Emmeline opened her mouth but paused when Deirdre held up a staying hand.

"Though I am ashamed to admit it, I was relieved when Mother Andrews passed," said Deirdre with a shake of her head. "I thought you would finally be free of her influence, and there are times when I see your perfect facade cracking, but I cannot stand it anymore. Not if you are going to do this."

Emmeline blinked at Deirdre, and Norman saw his wife struggling for words; he prayed she would make the right decision.

"I cannot risk my daughter's future," said Emmeline.

Norman's heart constricted, shrinking into itself, his whole chest tightening.

The fight seeped from Deirdre. Her posture slackened, and she pressed a hand to her stomach, tears falling from her eyes. "I have always admired how willingly you sacrifice for your family. You may be the most giving person I have ever met, but the disheartening thing is that you are too bullheaded to realize when you are doing more harm than good."

With that, Deirdre turned to the door, pausing as she passed Norman. Their eyes connected, and he saw his own heartache and disappointment echoed there. Giving his fore-arm a brief squeeze, Deirdre left.

What had Emmeline done? But quick on the heels of that question came another. What had he done? This hollow life had not occurred in the blink of an eye or even in two blinks. It was a culmination of years sitting idly by, hoping things would work themselves out.

"I cannot believe it," whispered Emmeline, dropping onto the armchair.

"I can," said Norman, and Emmeline's eyes jerked to his.

"Pardon?"

Habit kept his mouth shut tight, but knowing his wife believed herself the victim of Deirdre's wrath (rather than the appropriate recipient of it), made him realize he could no longer remain silent.

"You have gone too far, Emmeline."

Getting to her feet, she straightened. "I did what was needed to protect my daughter. For her happiness."

That oft-repeated refrain struck Norman's ears, and fire blazed in his veins. The words were an old companion in their marriage, and he couldn't pinpoint the precise reason why this recitation elicited such a response, but that conflagration swallowed him whole.

"Do you truly believe your actions have made Eloise happy?" he asked, crossing his arms. "She is unbearably miserable because you insist on behaving like my frigid, lifeless mother."

Emmeline blinked away tears and stilled the trembling of her chin. "I did what I must—"

"Do not say those words to me again, Emmeline," said Norman with a scowl. "You have said them so many times I do not think you truly comprehend what they mean."

Stomping her foot, Emmeline glowered back at him. "People were gossiping about our children. They judged them for every misstep I took... we took," she amended, gesturing between them. "My parents' choices tainted my life. You cannot comprehend the pain it caused me, and I had to protect our children from suffering as I did."

"You think I didn't hear all those things? Do you know how many people warned me away from you before we got engaged? Or that some of my friends cut ties with me because I ignored their caustic advice? Do you think I was unaware that some viewed us as scandalous and that it affected their opinion of our children?"

Emmeline gaped at him. "And how can you know all those things and still say I am wrong?"

"Because the opinions of a few ridiculous people do not matter. We were happy!" he said, not caring that his voice rose, allowing the servants to hear every word. Let them listen in, for it did not matter to him now. "You say you only care about their happiness, but do you really think your behavior has made them happy?"

"Of course!" Her nostrils flared, and her face reddened. "They never knew what it felt like to be shunned or to have to bear the shame of their parents' sins."

"Instead, they had to suffer through *my* wretched upbringing with a lifeless mother and complacent father." It wasn't until the words were spoken that Norman understood the extent of his wrongdoings; though he had not been the driving force behind the fracturing of their family, he was equally complicit.

Norman sighed, his shoulders slumping. "I can no longer stand by and do nothing."

Emmeline leaned away, staring with wide eyes. "What do you mean?"

"Like Deirdre, I am tired of hoping you will come to your senses," said Norman. Putting his hands on his hips, he stared at the toes of his boots. "I have loved you deeply, Emmeline. I still do. But I will not allow our family to continue on as it has."

Bringing his head up, he met her eyes. "Eloise needs unfiltered love and guidance, so I am taking her to stay with your brother. Perhaps Mina and I can undo the damage before she ends up as miserable as you."

Emmeline clutched her stomach, dropping down onto the armchair, her hands trembling. "You are leaving me?"

Norman pinched his nose, breathing through the unwanted tears that pricked at his eyes. "I..." But his voice faltered. He cleared his throat. "You left a long time ago."

He could not meet her eyes, but he felt her heart breaking; it was the truth, and it needed to be said, but that did not stop his own heart from aching in response. Without another word, he walked out of the sitting room, leaving Emmeline alone.

Chapter 34

The view from her bedchamber window was unremarkable, and Eloise had never cared for it. She preferred a room overlooking the garden to the gritty, grimy streetscape. But standing there as Lucy packed up the last of her belongings, Eloise ached at the thought of leaving it. She crossed her arms, her eyes tracking each passing coach, the steady hoofbeats of the horse, the flick of the driver's reins.

For these past weeks, Eloise had been in such a state of heightened emotion that she was left unprepared for the weighty emptiness that now filled her. Her heart had been strung so tight for so long, and now it had snapped, leaving a void in its place.

"Do you have everything, miss?" asked Lucy with a bob. "The footmen are taking your baggage to the coach presently, and your father would like to leave immediately."

Giving an absent nod to the maid, Eloise wandered from her room. This was precisely what she had wanted. When her father had announced his plans, Eloise expected elation or victory to fill the hollowness in her chest, but the void only expanded.

Two steps past the library, Eloise paused and turned back

to it. With sluggish movements, she went to the armchair, digging out her latest novel from beneath the cushions. It was too big for her reticule, though Eloise tried stuffing it in nonetheless. Not that it mattered, for she need not hide it anymore: Mother would no longer curtail her novel reading. Eloise straightened, glancing over at her mother's writing box atop the side table, wondering why that realization didn't bring her more joy.

Her mother's lap desk had traveled with their family for years, but Eloise could not think of a time it had been open and unattended. Mother was known to spend her afternoons scribbling away at it, but the sloped top was always kept locked with her personal papers tucked inside whenever she was away. Yet there sat her quill, ink, and a book.

Years' worth of curiosity pulled at Eloise, bringing her to the desk. Staring down at the words, she expected to see the polite nothings that filled Mother's usual conversation but found tear stains and near indecipherable scribbles. The image the page presented was so diametrically opposed to the poised image her mother presented that Eloise could not turn away from it, even if she wished to.

Eloise had never seen tears in her mother's eyes, yet here was clear evidence that she felt any such emotion. That she felt anything at all. The scrawls were hasty, as though Mother's hand could not keep up with the stream of thoughts in her head.

Glancing to see that she was completely alone, Eloise looked closer. Her eyes jumped straight to her own name on the page.

What more can I do? What more can I give to secure Eloise's future happiness? There is nothing left of me to sacrifice, and I fear it is all for naught, for she is so determined to throw away everything I have given her. I love her with all my heart, yet she despises me, and when I attempt to show her how I feel, I hear Mother Andrews' voice warning against it. I am trapped behind invisible bars, beating against my cage and shouting for someone to hear me, but I am alone—

"Eloise?" called Father from the hallway.

Jumping from the desk, Eloise moved to the door but paused, glancing back at the book. The right and wrong of her impulse played through her mind in rapid succession, but the temptation was too great. Snatching the journal from the tabletop, she scurried to her father.

...

Silence descended on Caswell House as though it had a life of its own, creeping through the building until it filled each nook and cranny with its nothingness. Gripping the edge of the sofa, Emmeline sat as though catatonic, her eyes blind to the world around her. But her ears could not stop hearing the silence. It choked her, stealing her breath. Emmeline had thought to escape those solitary years, but they had only been biding their time. Now, they had returned to swallow her whole.

A quiver began in her stomach, traveling through her chest and limbs.

The parlor door opened, and the footman bowed, bringing over the silver tray with the Hennesseys' calling card atop it. Shifting away from him, Emmeline turned her face to the fireplace so he would not see the evidence of her distress, though she knew it pointless, for the entire staff were well aware of the turmoil in the Andrews household.

"We are not at home," she said with a dismissive wave.

"But Miss Andrews invited them for tea, ma'am."

"She is not here, and I am not receiving company." She clenched her hands and fought to keep them under control.

It wasn't until she heard the door shut once more that she was able to let out a shaky breath. Emmeline's muscles tightened, her body trembling as she tried to hold the fraying bits of herself together. Her breaths were broken, jerking her with each stuttering inhale. Crumpling forward, Emmeline covered her face as a sob broke free.

How had she come to this? Life had altered greatly since she had been that solitary child begging for her parents' attention, yet nothing had changed. All alone once more.

Emmeline tried to lay hold of some comfort, but there was none to be found. As much as she wished to lay the blame on Norman or Deirdre or any of the others who had abandoned her, a voice from within whispered that it belonged to her.

"Do pull yourself together, Emmeline." Mother Andrews' voice snapped at her, and Emmeline felt the phantom rap of the lady's fan against her wrist. But Emmeline did not wish to repress her feelings. Could she not be free to do as she pleased in private?

"Don't be so childish, young lady. Such displays are ill-mannered."

Pressure built in her head, begging her to let it loose, but Emmeline struggled against the urge. Mother Andrews' presence still lingered in the recesses of her thoughts and heart, looking down her nose in that disapproving manner of hers.

Emmeline had to behave. Be good. Proper. For her children's sakes, she had to stifle her true nature. But Norman's words came to mind, accusing her of destroying her children's happiness, and there was no defense to mount against that accusation. Her children weren't happy. And neither was Norman. She certainly wasn't.

Shooting to her feet, Emmeline lunged for a vase sitting on a pedestal by the window. With a scream, she launched it across the room, the porcelain shattering against the wood door. Dropping to her knees, she covered her face as she let the sobs take control of her.

...

Curling up on her bed, Eloise stared at the heavy brocade

draping from the canopy. No doubt Aunt Mina was wondering where she was, but Eloise was in no mood to socialize. The day had been too exhausting for her to face small talk, large talk, or anything between. Peace and quiet were what she needed, yet she could not seem to find the former.

Eloise's heart wrenched at the thought of what she had done to Patrick. Her mind replayed each of his words in a never-ending loop. Selfish. Naive. How she wished to refute those claims, but the more she thought on his accusations, the more she came to accept that they held an element of truth, though she did not understand how she had become such a person.

She had betrayed Patrick. Used him. Played with his heart for her own benefit. Though some of it was unintentional, obliviousness was a sorry excuse for poor behavior. Whatever his past sins against her, Eloise had treated him ill, and it shamed her.

And now, he was leaving.

Mother's journal lay beside her on the bed, and she ran her fingers over the leather binding. Yet another sin to add to her list, though Eloise could not muster any proper guilt for pilfering it. Propping the book against the pillow, she opened to the first entry.

I caught Eloise sneaking away from her governess today. It is the third time this week, and I am struggling to be as firm as I should be, for my heart sympathizes with her plight. I would much rather be out picking wildflowers with her than sitting through another round of tedious morning calls. How I wish I could strip off my shoes and run barefoot through the fields with her and spend a lazy afternoon lying in the grass. Mother Andrews fully despairs that Eloise will ever become a lady, but I cannot bring myself to curtail her joy...

She nearly laughed at that. The thought of her mother enjoying such larks was so foreign that Eloise could not conjure

the image. At best, her mother strolled dignified along cultivated paths, but that was the furthest her imagination could ex-
tend. Glancing at the date, Eloise was startled to find that the
entry was dated only a few years ago, not long before her seven-
teenth birthday.

Minutes ticked away as she immersed herself in her
mother's journal, pouring through each entry. The words
showed a side of her mother that Eloise struggled to believe existed, even though the words were written by her mother's own
hand. In these pages, Mother poured out her heart, sharing
every hope, joy, sorrow, and heartache that touched her life.

The woman on these pages was far from an unfeeling creature; her mother was so full of life and feeling that Eloise could
not comprehend how the lady was able to bottle it all away.

Some pages were filled with such happy musings that
Eloise laughed aloud. Others brought tears to her eyes. And
then she came across one short entry with only three words.

Joanna is dead.

Tears littered the page, soaking through to others, and
Eloise's heart broke at the sight of it. That terrible moment
they'd lost Joanna had caused their family immeasurable pain,
yet Eloise could not recall seeing her mother mourn her daughter.

Here among these few pages, her mother opened her heart,
and Eloise was desperate to know her better.

...

With a hasty rap, Emmeline knocked on the door. They had
not answered the bell, but she would not be turned away. This
visit was long past due, and it was time for her to free the words
she should have spoken years ago.

Hardly waiting for an answer, she struck the door once

more. Her fist was coming down yet again when the door opened, and a young maid-of-all-work poked her head out. Before the girl could ask any questions, Emmeline strode in.

"What do you think you are doing?" the girl asked.

"Tell your mistress I wish to see her—"

"Let her in, Louise," called a voice from the front parlor.

Not bothering to relieve herself of her bonnet or spencer, Emmeline strode towards the sound to find her quarry seated on the sofa.

"If it isn't the illustrious Mrs. Norman Andrews." Amelia Kingsley looked up at her daughter with a wrinkled smirk.

Emmeline paused, trying to cover the shock she felt.

Though it had been fifteen years since she had seen her mother, the lady looked as though it had been thirty. Her mother tried holding herself erect, but her spine was bowed. The gnarled hands clutching the shawl around her shoulders were shaking, as though straining under that meager effort. More than the surface signs, Mama looked like a dried leaf, as though any touch might cause her to crumble away.

"To think I have received visits from my family twice in a fortnight. What felicity." Her tone was as dry and brittle as she looked.

Emmeline sucked in a fierce breath, holding it for several moments in an effort to slow her speeding heart, but it did no good as she glared down at Mama. There were years' worth of words she wanted to speak. So many wrongs to bring to light that Emmeline's mind could not sort through them all.

"If you are merely going to glower at me, you might as well take a seat," said her mother, waving a shaking finger to the sofa opposite, but Emmeline could not bring herself to sit.

"How can you be so selfish?" Emmeline blurted.

Mama raised a grey eyebrow. "I offered you a seat. Are you demanding refreshment as well?"

Emmeline clenched her jaw until her teeth ached. "You know my meaning."

"Has my Day of Judgment finally arrived?" asked her

mother with a smirking huff. "Am I now to be castigated for all my supposed sins?"

Turning away, Emmeline crossed her arms with a shake of her head. "You needn't mock me, Mama."

"And you needn't be so dramatic, Daughter."

Looking at her mother over her shoulder, Emmeline's brows drew together. "Do you truly have no idea how much you hurt your children? Ruined our family? Even now, I am suffering because of your selfish decisions. Your actions have caused irreparable damage."

Mama scowled, stabbing a finger at her. "You and your brother always blamed me for everything! You have no idea how much I suffered. How cruelly your father treated me. He is the one who ruined everything! I tried my best to be a good mama to you children—"

"You were absent more than you were present!"

"I did what I needed to survive, Emmeline. I could not stay in that house and keep my sanity. Did you expect me to waste my life in such misery?" Mama pulled the shawl closer, turning her gaze away from her daughter. "It is your father who deserves the blame. I tried my best to be a good mother to you children, but your father made it impossible..."

Emmeline stood there, blinking, as the woman spun tale after tale, citing every hurt and injury she'd sustained during her time as John Kingsley's wife. A thought leapt into Emmeline's head, appearing from nowhere and striking with such force that she sunk onto the sofa. As she listened to her mother shift all the blame, Emmeline knew that she was doing the same.

Amelia Kingsley may have done harm to Emmeline as a child, but the harm that continued to spring from her broken childhood was the result of her own decisions. Emmeline's righteous anger sputtered, blinking out of existence as she watched her mama.

With that one insight, more came flooding into her mind. A chill ran along Emmeline's spine, and her head spun as though the air had grown thin. Bringing a hand to her mouth, she saw her own children's childhoods echoing the same terrible pattern that hers had. She may have been more present in their lives than Mama, but that was not enough. They had needed love, and she had lectured them on propriety.

Hindsight brought painful clarity, and Emmeline's heart wrenched and twisted at the price that blindness had cost. Though her heart could not be more different than her mother's, they had followed the same path to the same conclusion. Amelia may have a servant or two, but there was no one else at her side, and the empty silence at Burwell Terrace echoed that which was to be found at Emmeline's home.

"Are you unwell?" asked Mama with more sympathy than Emmeline had thought possible.

Turning red-rimmed eyes on her mother, Emmeline knew what must be done.

"I forgive you, Mama," said Emmeline.

The words were both minuscule and monumental. For though few in number, they heralded a mighty change within her, serving as the first steps she had to take on that path. They did not erase all the bitter feelings buried deep in her heart, for they were too ingrained to be so easily dislodged, but they perfectly represented Emmeline's resolve; the past would hold no more sway over her present.

"I need no forgiveness. It was your father who ruined all our lives—"

"And if he were alive, I would say the same, for he holds equal blame. Neither of you are victims of your marriage. You each did your part, and I forgive you both."

Amelia Kingsley sputtered at that, huffing with indignation, but there was nothing to be gained by speaking further. With a final glance at her mother, Emmeline strode away, feeling a touch lighter when she stepped into the afternoon air.

Chapter 35

A soft knock came at her bedchamber door, and Eloise shoved her mother's journal under her pillow. "Yes?" The door opened, and Aunt Mina poked her head inside. "I was wondering where you had disappeared to."

Eloise feigned a smile, but she did not sit up. "I am not up to visiting."

Aunt Mina nodded but did not back away from the doorway. "I understand you've had a trying time of late. I imagine this Season has not turned out as you anticipated."

Eloise snorted, and her hand shot to her mouth as though she could cover it up after the sound had been let loose. Aunt Mina shut the door and came over to stand beside the bed.

"One of the best comforts for a broken heart is a good chat," said Aunt Mina, nudging Eloise over so she could sit beside her niece.

Leaning into Aunt Mina, Eloise laid her head on the lady's shoulder. "And when have you ever had your heart broken?"

This time, it was Aunt Mina who scoffed. Lifting her arm, she brought it around Eloise's shoulders. "I've had my fair share, young lady, and sometimes one merely needs a listening ear."

Opening her mouth, Eloise was startled when a great, heaving sob emerged. Aunt Mina wrapped her arms around her, holding the girl as she cried. When words were finally possible, the whole story spilled out in a flood, and Aunt Mina quietly rocked her as Eloise released it all.

"Everything is ruined!" cried Eloise, the words broken between jerking breaths.

But Aunt Mina chuckled at that declaration.

Jerking out of her aunt's hold, Eloise glared at her. "My life has fallen to pieces, and you are laughing at me!"

"Dearheart, I apologize," she said with a spark of humor in her gaze. "I am not laughing at the pain you are suffering. My heart breaks for you, but even you have to admit you are being a tad melodramatic."

Eloise threw her arms wide. "But everything is ruined, and I cannot see how to fix it."

Aunt Mina reached forward and took Eloise's face in her hands, drawing the girl's attention to her. "Indecisiveness is at the heart of your troubles, and it is time for you to decide what you want. If you wish to repair things with your mother, then do so. If you wish to be with your Mr. Lennox, then act on it. Choose a path, and fight for it, dearheart."

"And how do I choose?" Eloise whispered, her chin trembling.

"Neither I nor anyone else can tell you that," said Aunt Mina, taking Eloise's hands in hers. "But give no heed to your sister's opinions about husbands and marriage. When people speak about life in such absolute terms, it says more about their experience than reality."

With a sigh, Aunt Mina shook her head, "Lucinda was never romantic, and she treated marriage like a business arrangement. Thus, her relationship with her husband is that of financial partners and has no sentiment behind it. I can attest that a husband's attentions are anything but a burden when there is a foundation of love and devotion."

Eloise's thoughts traveled back to the kiss she'd shared with

Patrick. Though it had started as a means to an end, it had grown into something far more, and her heart fluttered at the memory of his touch.

Aunt Mina smiled. "Lucinda's 'truths' about marriage are incompatible with my experience. From the moment my husband gave me his heart, he has been true to me in every sense of the word. Every day, Simon shows me in little ways how much he adores me still, and I know many others with similarly loving marriages. Happiness in marriage is not an anomaly."

The truth of her aunt's words burned in her heart, expanding until the heat consumed her. Eloise knew it was true, felt it with such clarity that she could not deny it. It left no room for doubt or fear. She could make her marriage as she wished, but it was for her to decide, and Eloise knew what she wanted. And with whom.

"But how do I fix it?" asked Eloise, her chin trembling anew as she thought of the sheer disappointment in Patrick's expression at their parting. "He is gone, and I shan't see him ever again."

"Melodrama," warned Aunt Mina with a smile, and Eloise tried to stem her tears.

"He was right about me. About everything," she said, sniffling. "I have berated my mother for being heartless, but it is I who has been unfeeling towards others."

"That's what comes from focusing solely on your own problems, dearheart." Aunt Mina's smile turned sad. "We all have a tendency towards self-absorption. It is part of human nature. But the first step to overcoming it is to recognize the issue."

Wiping at her eyes, Eloise asked, "And what is the next step?"

Aunt Mina patted Eloise's cheek, and her smile widened. "You are a bright girl, and I am sure you know what it is."

...

There was a lightness to Emmeline's step as she descended the coach and climbed her doorstep. Isaacs greeted her, taking her things in silence, which suited her as she had much on her mind. There was a warmth in her heart and looseness to her limbs as a thrum of bright energy filled her. With the weight of her childhood gone, Emmeline was astonished to realize that despite the other circumstances in her life, she felt unburdened. Peaceful. Hopeful, even.

Clutching the edges of her skirt, Emmeline crossed the entry to the stairs. A tinge of regret discolored the brightness of the sun coming in through the entry windows as she realized she had willingly carried those heartaches for so long.

"Madam," said Isaacs with a cough.

Emmeline stopped on the bottom stair and turned to the butler.

"I feel I should tell you that Mr. Andrews has returned. He is in his bedchamber—"

Snapping around, Emmeline hitched her skirts, hurrying up the stairs in a manner that would have made Mother Andrews faint. Ignoring the maid gaping as she sped by, Emmeline did not slow until she arrived at Norman's door. She touched the door handle and faltered. Instead, she drew her knuckles to the door but paused again. Gripping the knob once more, indecision caught her as she tried to think of how she should approach him.

"Is someone there?" he called.

Taking a steadying breath, Emmeline opened the door.

Norman stood at his armoire, pulling open the drawers. Sparing her no more than a passing glance, he said, "I forgot a few things."

Clasping her hands in front of her, Emmeline gnawed on her lip as she watched him. That same stubborn lock at the crown of his head stood up in an awkward fashion, and Emmeline smiled at it. Mother Andrews had despaired over its unruliness and insisted he keep his hair shorn, but Emmeline was glad to see it shaggy. It was adorable and so thoroughly appropriate for Norman; and even more so with the flecks of grey coloring his black locks.

"I am sorry, Norman," said Emmeline, feeling no need to prevaricate. "I've driven so many wedges between us, and I cannot think how to undo all the damage I've done."

He paused, turning away from his work to look at her. His dark eyes watched her, and her heart broke at the distrust she found there.

"You were right," she said, her voice hitching.

Emmeline stepped forward but stopped herself, as there was no welcome in his expression. Opening her mouth, she tried to explain it all, but there were so many thoughts clogging her thoughts that it was difficult to grasp a single one, let alone articulate it. Taking a deep breath, she let it out in a slow gust, dropping her gaze to the rug. Her eyes traced the gold vines and flourishes as she sorted through her words.

"Your mother poisoned me—" she said, cringing at the choice of words. With a sigh, she tried again. "Though she holds some of the blame, I cannot lay it all on her doorstep. I *allowed* her to poison me." Emmeline put emphasis on that culpable word, for she knew she could not hide from the consequences of her actions any longer.

"I remember visiting Simon just after he married Mina," said Emmeline, her hands clenching together. "No matter how many times she ignored me, I was still so desperate to ingratiate myself to my mother. I always knew she doted on Priscilla but foolishly thought if I spent enough time with her, she might love me as well."

Emmeline sighed, her hands now gripping the sides of her skirts. "There was that family Priscilla invited as well, and Mama positively doted on the wife. My own mother could hardly spare more than a passing glance in my direction, yet she immediately took a stranger under her wing. I realized Mama only cared for those who were like her. Priscilla had become what she needed to be to earn our mother's affection, but I refused to pay that price."

The world around her blurred, and a tear trickled down her cheek. "I didn't realize Mother Andrews did the same to me. I feel so blind for not seeing how she twisted my affection to make me into her mirror image. I thought I was doing what was best for my family, but I—" Her voice broke, and she swallowed back the tears. "I ruined it. I ruined us."

That was all she could get out before the tears overtook her, and Emmeline's head dropped lower, her shoulders heaving with her jagged breaths. Norman's arms came around her, and Emmeline clutched him, burrowing into his hold until he surrounded her. He murmured soft things, rubbing her back as they stood there, entwined together.

Lifting her head, Emmeline's watery eyes met his. "Can you ever forgive me, Norman?"

His heart had already melted at the sight of her standing so broken before him, but when his beloved's pained eyes pleaded with him, Norman knew it would take a heart of steel to refuse such an earnest petition. Bringing one hand up, Norman brushed back a lock of her hair, tucking it behind her ear, his fingers grazing her cheek.

"Emmeline, that is all I have ever wanted," he said, tears pricking at his eyes.

Her lips quivered, great teardrops hanging on her lashes as her eyes begged for his love and acceptance. For all her fifty years of age, she looked very much like the lost and heartbroken girl he had met in a darkened corner of a ball. Even with the troubles they'd suffered, her stumbling into his life was the greatest stroke of luck fate had ever dealt him.

Norman leaned in, his lips hovering above hers; the whisper of her skin brushed his, yet he did not move. He waited, watching to see if she would rise to meet him. There was the barest breath of a pause before Emmeline pressed her lips to his.

His heart pounded in his chest, and he felt the flutter of hers. The scent and feel of her in his arms took possession of him, filling every thought and feeling. This was what he wanted. His wife. His lovely, kind-hearted Emmeline. The relief it brought and the passion it stoked nearly brought him to his knees, but he forced his legs to keep them upright as years of emotional and physical solitude made themselves manifest in their embrace.

Then Emmeline shoved against him, sending him back a few steps as she wrenched herself out from his arms.

Norman's foggy thoughts took several moments before he noticed the maid standing in the doorway, holding an armful of linens; the girl's face blazed red, and she bobbed, disappearing with all haste. His breaths came in heavy pants as Norman stared at his wife's back. Emmeline patted at her hair and dress in that horrid fashion of hers, and the softness and warmth in his heart fled as quickly as she had.

Nothing had changed.

Turning on his heel, Norman stormed out of the bedchamber. Emmeline called after him, giving more empty apologies and promises, but she had shown her true colors. This was nothing more than another false hope. A brief, shining light snuffed out. Norman couldn't love on Emmeline's terms any longer.

Chapter 36

"**B**reathe, Eloise," said Aunt Mina, patting her niece's hand as the coach came to a stop before the townhouse.

Glancing out the window, Eloise wasn't certain she could. She clutched the hatbox in her lap, nibbling her lip. "But what if they close their door to me, too? It was difficult enough being denied by the Lennoxes. I cannot stand to have Kitty do the same. How am I ever to make things right if no one will give me the opportunity?"

"Be patient," said Aunt Mina before leaving the coach. When Eloise followed, her aunt took her by the arm and led her up the steps. "Mending broken trust can take time, but it does no good to surrender without trying. Though I do find that a peace offering helps."

With said peace offering in one hand, Eloise placed a steadying hand on her middle and nodded. Their calling cards were accepted, and the door was not slammed in their faces, which she thought must be a good sign. And that hope rose even further as they were welcomed into the sitting room. However, her heart dropped when she saw Kitty sitting on the sofa, avoiding Eloise's gaze.

Balancing a sketchbook on her lap, Kitty focused on the movements of her pencil as Eloise sat beside her, placing the hatbox on the floor.

"Mrs. Hennessey, it is a pleasure to meet you at last," said Aunt Mina. "Eloise has told me so much about your family, and I have been quite eager to make your acquaintance."

The lady's eyebrows rose, her gaze darting over to Eloise and back to Aunt Mina. "That is kind of you to say."

Turning to a grand bouquet on the far side of the room, Aunt Mina said, "How lovely. Did you do those yourself? I adore arranging flowers."

With a few prompts, Aunt Mina had Mrs. Hennessey maneuvered over to the vase, where they launched into a discussion of their mutual interest, leaving Eloise and Kitty with a relative amount of privacy.

"Kitty, I am so terribly sorry for the way I have behaved," said Eloise, her hands twisting in her lap.

"Nonsense, Miss Andrews. It is of no consequence," said Kitty. The formal address pricked at Eloise's heart, though she could not blame the girl for using it.

"I did not mean to be so callous towards you or your *situation*." The word stumbled and tripped its way past her tongue. It was far too light a description for what had happened to poor Kitty, but neither did Eloise feel it appropriate to address the young lady's past in too direct a manner.

Kitty's pencil paused, and her eyes swung up from her page to meet Eloise's.

"I've been an abominable friend," Eloise continued. "And I wish to beg your forgiveness."

"You were quite a good one at first," said Kitty.

But Eloise shook her head. "Even at my best, I was focused on myself. I am ashamed to realize how little I know about you, for I never took the time to ask. I simply rambled on about my own heartaches."

Kitty opened her mouth as though to disagree, but her eyes

drifted away, and she sat there mute for a moment before closing it again. With a shake of her head, she replied, "There is nothing to forgive, Miss Andrews. I am grateful for the kindness you've shown me the past few weeks. It is far more than I have received from anyone outside my family since... a while."

Her friend's cheeks burned, and her eyes dipped back to her drawing. Reaching forward, Eloise rested a hand on Kitty's forearm.

"But I have not treated you as I ought to," said Eloise. "You have such a kind heart and do not deserve a friend who tosses you aside. Please forgive me. It was quite unintentional, and I promise to be better in the future."

Kitty peeked at her from the corner of her eye, and Eloise hoped it was a good sign while she steeled herself for what needed to be said.

"Though I do not wish to dredge up that which is painful, I must expressly apologize for my behavior with Mr. Gouldsmith. I had no idea..." But Eloise paused and rethought that untrue statement, amending it. "I did not understand the situation nor how greatly I was betraying our friendship by even acknowledging that horrid man. I wish I could explain my logic for behaving as I did, but I have no excuse."

Kitty did not respond. She merely fiddled with her pencils, her eyes fixed on her fingers. Then she gave a small nod.

"And I shan't push you to confide in me, but should you wish to speak to me about anything, I am always here to listen," said Eloise, wishing she had said such words far sooner in their friendship.

Kitty turned watery eyes to her friend and gave Eloise a tremulous smile. "I do not wish to speak of it at present, but I am grateful for your offer. Most wish to ignore what happened or only ask because they want fodder for their gossip."

Eloise longed for something more to say. Surely, there was some comfort or advice she might offer to ease the strain of Kitty's past, but even as she wished it, Eloise knew there was nothing more she could do. Time and friendship were the only remedy, and she vowed to give Kitty a heaping portion of both.

"Oh, and I almost forgot," said Eloise, reaching for the hat-box and offering it up. "To prove I am not a wholly selfish and useless friend, I've brought you a present."

"You didn't need to do that," said Kitty, putting aside her drawing supplies to take the box.

"Yes, I did." Though Eloise was near certain she had purchased the right one, her breath seized as Kitty tugged at the ribbons and pulled open the box. At the millinery, Eloise had sworn it was the one Kitty admired, but at the moment, Eloise thoroughly doubted herself.

"The bonnet from Mrs. Valentines?" said Kitty with a wide grin. Lifting it up, she placed the plaited straw hat on her head, glancing around in search of a mirror. Though the bicorne style had never suited Eloise, it looked positively lovely on Kitty, and the deep green ribbons complemented her coloring to perfection.

"Perhaps you might wear it to the National Gallery?" asked Eloise, fiddling with her necklace. "As I was terribly rude to forget our previous outing, I had hoped we might go today."

Kitty straightened and beamed at Eloise. "You wish to go?"

"Of course I do," said Eloise, and Kitty swooped in to hug her.

"Thank you," they said in unison before Kitty leapt up to speak to their chaperones about their plans.

...

Deciding to return to Trafford Place had been easy, as it was the next stop in Emmeline's grand tour of atonement, but standing in her brother's entryway was far more daunting than it had been in the hypothetical. There was no avoiding it, so Emmeline put all those years of training Mother Andrews had given her to good use and locked her anxieties away.

Emmeline stood in the foyer and ran a hand along the banister as she awaited the footman's return. The dark wood gleamed in the afternoon light, and she admired the intricately carved spindles that had been fashioned to look like vines. She couldn't recall the bannister's original style, but Emmeline knew this was a new addition. Then her eyes moved to the walls. The gaudy red color her mother adored had been replaced with a warm cream, allowing the raised texture of the paper to provide an understated pattern.

Emmeline looked past the bones of the house and was surprised to recognize how different it was from the Trafford Place of her youth. The touches were simple yet refined, and Emmeline was surprised she hadn't noticed the stark difference when she'd stood in this very spot a sennight ago.

The footman gave a discreet cough, and Emmeline turned to find him watching her. With a bow, he motioned for her to follow, and she found herself deposited once more in the Kingsleys' sitting room, though this time Simon stood beside his wife, a wary glint to his eye as Emmeline was ushered to a seat.

"What a surprise to receive another visit from you so soon," said Mina. The manner in which she clenched her hands said the surprise was not a pleasant one.

"Norman is not at home," added Simon, his tone as cold as his expression.

Emmeline's hand rose to her throat, taking hold of the pendant on the chain and rubbing it between her fingers.

"You are displaying your nerves, young lady." Mother Andrews' voice snapped at her, and Emmeline dropped the necklace—and then scowled at herself for the impulse. Like a well-trained dog, she still jumped to follow the commands of her master. With each, it became clearer just how lost she had been, for her actions and words were not her own. Straightening, Emmeline reached again for her necklace and ignored the frisson of panic that accompanied such blatant disobedience.

"I did not come to speak to Norman," said Emmeline. No, those restrictive instincts had made certain that her husband would not welcome a visit from her at present. "I am here to see my daughter."

Taking a strengthening breath, Emmeline added, "And you."

Simon stiffened and tucked his wife's arm through his.

"I need to apologize." She paused. "To you both."

Emmeline was certain her necklace would come apart as she twisted it back and forth, but once her hands were allowed that freedom, they were unwilling to relinquish it, and her hand kept fiddling with the thing. Mina's eyes watched with obvious curiosity.

"I've been unkind," said Emmeline, but she paused again, knowing that was not the right word. Blinking in rapid succession, she forced her apology past the growing lump in her throat. "Cruel, in fact."

Simon shifted and opened his mouth as though to speak, but Mina hushed him.

"The past few weeks have shown me how wrong my behavior is," said Emmeline, her eyes drifting away from the pair and coming to rest on her lap. "But I am hoping..." All the words she'd rehearsed fled from her mind as a flush crept up her neck and filled her cheeks.

"I am hoping..." But her voice faltered once more.

With a blanket tucked across her lap, Eloise clutched her mother's journal. Though there was no rain, she felt the moisture in the air permeating every inch of the house, making the grey day all the more miserable. Her fingers brushed against the leather binding as her mind sifted through all the revelations contained within it. The world around her had altered, leaving it unrecognizable.

There was a distant shuffling downstairs, and Eloise wondered who had come to visit. Father had disappeared hours ago and had not returned, and Aunt Mina was not one for many visitors, yet the sound was unmistakable. Curiosity and a desire to escape her thoughts pushed Eloise to stand and make her way downstairs.

It wasn't until her foot hit the bottom step that Eloise recognized the broken voice coming from the sitting room, speaking words that were foreign yet familiar. Though Eloise had never heard her mother say such things aloud, it echoed the heart and soul permeating the journal Eloise held in her hand.

Coming to stand in the doorway, Eloise stared at her mother's crumpled expression and the tears in her eyes as she begged forgiveness from her brother and sister-in-law. Aunt Mina took Mother in her arms, giving her forgiveness freely (as she did when anyone truly sought it), and Eloise wondered at the sight of her mother sobbing through more apologies.

A creak of floorboards had Mother straightening, her startled eyes turning to meet her daughter's.

"Eloise," she said in a tone far warmer than any Eloise had ever heard from the lady.

Getting to her feet, Mother stepped closer, her hands wringing and gaze pleading, which made Eloise keenly aware of the fact that she held her mother's pilfered journal in her hands. But before she could think what to do with it, Mother's eyes fell to the book.

"You read it?" she whispered, her eyes blinking rapidly.

Though Eloise could not say she was sorry to have done so, guilt still burned in her heart as she nodded. Mother's cheeks reddened and she bit her lip, and the sight of such emotion on her mother's face wreaked havoc with Eloise's thoughts, halting them altogether and leaving her to stare mutely at her mother.

Taking a breath, her mother's shoulders relaxed, and she nodded. Reaching forward, she gripped Eloise's forearm with a smile.

"Good. They're words I should have spoken aloud."

Eloise's breath caught, her insides fluttering. Her trembling fingers tapped against the book's cover as a question played through her thoughts. It begged to be released, pleaded for her to speak the words, but cold fear tightened around her heart. Eloise dropped her gaze as she gnawed on her lip.

"Then..." Eloise's breath hitched, but she pressed forward. "Then you do love me?"

Her mother's arms were there, surrounding her and pulling her tight, sobs shaking them both. Eloise could hardly understand the words streaming from her mother, but the heartbroken pleas for forgiveness and loving declarations melted any lingering bitterness in Eloise's heart. Letting the journal fall, Eloise brought her arms up and clung to her mother.

There was much to say and much more to rebuild, but in that moment, Eloise was filled with warmth and light that belied the cold, miserable day outside. Whatever else may come, she had hope.

Chapter 37

Most called the Lennox's ballroom small, though those of a charitable mind said it was quaint. To Eloise's thinking, the size was of no consequence as the design and decorations compensated for any spatial deficiencies. The entry door fed into a domed alcove, which Mrs. Lennox had draped with gauzy fabric to obstruct the view of the room, and stepping through that silken barrier was like falling through a portal into a fairy story. Flowers and greenery were in abundance, twisting around the pillars lining the room and hanging like bunting across portions of the ceiling.

But there were more pressing matters than admiring Mrs. Lennox's handiwork.

Standing just beyond the draped entrance, Eloise hunted through the crowd, looking for that familiar head of reddish gold. She edged the room, moving towards the double doors that led to the dining room. They were thrown wide, and Eloise scoured the faces gathered there but found nothing. Surely, Patrick hadn't left for Ireland before his sister's engagement ball, so Eloise searched yet again. And again.

Though the room was plenty warm, a chill took hold of her: Patrick wasn't here. Swallowing to ease the tightness in her throat and blinking to clear the gathering tears, Eloise gave a vague, tremulous smile to cover her overwhelming despair.

She caught sight of her mother, and Eloise blinked at the wholly different look the lady had affected. Mother's smile was a tad strained, but it was wide and broad, there for all to see. And she stood with Mrs. Hennessey, of all people. Coming to her side, Eloise gave her mother's hand a squeeze, which brought a warmth to the lady's eyes and eased the tightness in her shoulders.

"I am so glad you are here," whispered Mother when Mrs. Hennessey turned to chat with another in the party. "I cannot remember the last time I was anxious at a social function, yet tonight I feel ready to fly apart."

Linking her arm with her mother's, Eloise whispered, "I hadn't thought you would be here, and I am glad you are."

And she was even gladder that the statement was true.

"I think I've mended things with Deirdre. Or have begun to..." said Mother, her words trailing off as she caught sight of her husband from across the room. Eloise glanced between the pair, nibbling on her lip as she watched her father's expression shutter and her mother's eyes grow misty. Eloise squeezed Mother's arm again, and the lady returned it with a soft smile before shooing her away to join Kitty.

The young lady lifted her fan and whispered to Eloise, "I am so glad you arrived. I have been fairly swarmed by people, and I'm at a loss to understand why. I am in desperate need of a friend to help me weather all the attention."

"It was only a matter of time before others realized what a gem you are," said Eloise with a beaming grin. Of course, she was not about to reveal that she and her mother had spent much of the past week making certain the right people knew of the remarkable Hennessey family. That was an unimportant detail.

"I have gentlemen clamoring to dance with me," said Kitty, her smile straining. "Mr. Whitlock begged me to reserve the first set for him."

Eloise smothered the triumphant smile that threatened to

break through her feigned innocence. "He is a fine gentleman. Kind, honorable, and a beautiful dancer. I think you will enjoy standing up with him."

Uncertainty pulled at Kitty's brows, and a prickle of worry ran down Eloise's spine, so she hurried to add, "But you needn't dance if you do not wish it."

The furrowed brow relaxed, and Kitty blushed. "I would love to dance, but it is a bit unnerving when I am not well-acquainted with the gentleman. One cannot always trust appearances."

"That is true, but I assure you Mr. Whitlock is exactly as he appears." Eloise would not have allowed her mother to nudge the gentleman into taking a particular interest in Kitty if he was anything less than stellar. Patting Kitty's hand, she smiled at her friend. "It is your decision, but either way, I promise to stay by your side if you wish."

...

Arms folded, Norman leaned against the wall, content with his usual place in a secluded corner of the room; if luck was with him tonight, he would not have to move from the spot until supper. So many others flitted from one conversation to another, but Norman thought his situation far more enjoyable. Joining the throng did not terrify him as it had in his youth, but it held no allure. There was so much to be gained from quiet observation, and he had no desire to surrender his position.

A flash of familiar brown hair drew his attention, and Norman shifted his stance for a better view. Her back was to him, but he knew that gown. Though some bemoaned the simplicity of its decoration, the expert drape and cut flattered its mistress to perfection. Norman's eyes rested on Emmeline's shoulders and the way her dark ringlets draped across them.

Moving without thought, he shifted from his corner and

moved along the edge of the ballroom until he saw her expression. Warmth spread through his heart, filling him, and his smile grew in response to seeing hers. Uncertainty tainted her eyes, but she held that grin in place, though hints of panic flitted across her features at various intervals as she fidgeted and laughed. Though the gawkers might not see the internal battle being waged, Norman knew his wife and saw how she struggled against the frosty nature his mother had cultivated in her.

And he loved her all the more for it.

"She is trying."

Norman nearly jumped at the voice and turned to see Deirdre beside him, her gaze tracking her friend's movements as eagerly as he.

"I hadn't expected her to attend," said Norman.

"Neither had I, but she made it impossible to deny her," said Deirdre, a smile quirking up one side of her mouth. Her expression softened, a hint of tears brightening her eyes. "I think our Emmeline has finally reemerged."

Norman's heart begged him to believe the words, but his bruised pride cautioned him. After so many years of dealing with the detestable Mother Andrews duplicate, Norman could not bear another rejection. The hope he had sheltered for so long had brought him pain again and again.

"I believe she is in earnest, and not just to please us," said Deirdre, turning her smile to Norman. "Emmeline wishes to be different, and though she is frightened and uncertain about how to begin again, she is determined to do so."

Deirdre paused, chuckling to herself. "When she arrived at my home to beg forgiveness, I refused to see her, and do you know what she did?"

Norman didn't bother answering the question, for he knew Deirdre wanted to tell him the answer as much as he wanted to hear it.

"She banged on my door for a full ten minutes, and when that did not work, she sat on my doorstep and would not move until I relented." Deirdre shook her head, glancing over at her friend again. "It was the Emmeline I knew sitting there. Though it embarrassed her to be seen by everyone passing—and it was at a time of day when there were many of her acquaintance out and about—she did not move until I opened the door."

Pursing his lips, Norman watched his wife, wondering at that behavior. In their last interlude, Emmeline had made it clear that she still clung to Mother Andrews' horrid example, reverting to that frigid lady between one heartbeat and the next.

"Please allow her another chance to make amends," said Deirdre. "Change does not happen overnight, and it will take time for her to fully shed Mother Andrews' control. Now, if you will excuse me, I need to talk some sense into my son as well."

The lady took her leave, and Norman was grateful for it, as it was clear from her insinuating tone that Deirdre knew about his failed kiss with Emmeline. Tugging at his cravat, Norman disheveled it even further. It should not have surprised him that she knew; if the pair were on speaking terms again, Emmeline would have told her closest friend all about that embarrassing interlude.

Turning his gaze to his wife once more, Norman could not deny that she was trying, however awkward and uncomfortable it made her. His heart thumped in his chest, begging him to forgive and forget. Emmeline was so alluring that Norman could hardly fight her pull. If not for the fear holding him in place, he would be at her side. But she was trying. The more Norman watched her, the more he knew it was true. Holding court among her throng, the true Emmeline was fighting to come out despite how much she wished to disappear.

The song came to an end, and the dancers rearranged themselves for the next. Before he could rethink such a fool-hardy action, Norman moved, wending his way towards his wife.

Emmeline saw him approach, her eyes catching his. In the last few steps, her tension eased. She nibbled at her lips, and Norman felt a genuine smile grow in response to her adorable show of uncertainty. As he stood before her, neither said a word. With a motion towards the dance floor, Norman sent her a silent request.

Her breath caught, her eyes darting between him and the other dancers. They both knew what he was asking, and it was no small thing. Mother Andrews' protégé would not participate in even a minor infraction of etiquette to dance with her own husband, but his Emmeline had often indulged in that harmlessly uncouth behavior.

Emmeline paused for only a moment before sliding her arm through his, and Norman led her to the dance floor as the musicians began the opening notes for a waltz. She looked up at him through her lashes, her cheeks flushing like a young debutante at her first ball. Reaching forward, he rested his hand at her back, and they turned into the flow of dancers.

Norman tripped over his feet for the first few steps, and Emmeline did so herself just as he recovered. Holding a hand to her mouth, she laughed.

"We are hopeless," she said with a shake of her head.

But Norman brought up a hand, nudging her chin up so she would look at him. "Are we?"

He hadn't intended to use such a serious tone, but the question meant too much to be taken so lightly. Emmeline's lips trembled, a hint of tears gathering in her eyes.

"No," she whispered.

Norman's fingers brushed along her jaw as he released her chin, and they took another faltering start. With a step or two, they fell in time with the rhythm. The steps were simple and repetitive, and they came easier as the pair rotated around the floor.

Neither spoke. There had been so many words flung about, and Norman felt no need to add to them at this moment—not when his wife was encircled in his arms, gazing into his eyes with such unrestrained love. His chest swelled until it felt as though his waistcoat was two sizes too small, and though layers of fabric separated them, Norman was keenly aware of the way her fingers brushed against his arm.

As this style of waltz had been scandalous through the early years of their marriage, Norman had no personal experience with the dance. But as it had grown acceptable in recent years, he'd observed it many a time. The steps remained the same, but the position of the dancers varied greatly, and Norman chose one that seemed particularly inviting. With a shift, he brought Emmeline's arms around to rest on his shoulders, until they were standing nearly flush to each other. Her eyes widened for a fraction, but Emmeline did not falter or push away. The blush in her cheeks grew, but the turn of her lips told him it was not shock that had her so flustered.

The look in her eyes invited Norman to lean closer, but as much as he longed to touch his lips to hers, he felt no need to push the boundaries of propriety that far. For now, it was enough to hold his wife in his arms as the music enveloped them.

His Emmeline.

Chapter 38

Leaning against the wall, Patrick hid in the shadowy corner and watched the guests. He plucked his watch from his pocket and calculated how much longer he needed to torture himself before he could make his escape. He had done his fraternal duty by attending the wretched event; Nora could not expect more of him.

Patrick glanced at his sister and her new fiancé, who stood arm-in-arm as they greeted the well-wishers. Though he did not resent the happy glow that filled the air around them, his heart could not take the bitter reminder of his lost love.

"It has been a busy week for the Andrews ladies."

Patrick jerked upright to find his mother hovering nearby. "I don't know what you mean."

Mother scowled at him, the expression so filled with frustration that he half expected her to take him by the ear, as she had done to him as a boy. "You've never been good at lying, Patrick."

With a sigh, he stopped pretending not to notice her and turned his gaze to Eloise. Patrick had not spoken to her in a sennight, yet she haunted him, an ever-present regret lingering in his mind. He could not get any relief from her, for even if he sought refuge in company, he could scarcely go an hour without someone telling him the latest gossip about the Andrews family. And there was plenty to say about them at present.

"I don't know if I can trust this change. It is too sudden," said Patrick as he watched Eloise, seeing the truth of the rumors as she moved about the room with purpose. A few kind words here and compliments there, and she had ensured the Hennesseys' new sterling reputation.

Yet it was more than that.

Eloise spent time among the awkward wallflowers, enticing young men to escort the young ladies onto the dance floor. Then she spent a few minutes speaking with a group of older matrons, even fetching them refreshment when needed. So busy was she that Eloise had yet to stand up with a gentleman of her own, though she seemed not to care, for her smile grew with every small kindness.

His heart hammered against his chest as he watched her. This was the Eloise he'd known and longed for, but a niggling fear forced him away.

"It's best if I keep my distance for now," he said.

Mother grumbled something under her breath that sounded suspiciously like a harsh epithet against men before saying, "That is ludicrous."

Patrick's shoulders drooped. "I cannot risk losing myself. Would you have me hurt Eloise like that again? Or you and the rest of the family? I do not trust myself."

Coming to stand before her son, his mother smiled and placed a hand at his cheek. "You underestimate your strength, Patrick. Standing here with your heart breaking for that sweet girl, are you tempted to take up any one of the many glasses of wine surrounding you?"

Casting his thoughts inward, Patrick scoured his mind and heart, and with a jolt of surprise, he found not a trace of longing there. Thinking back on the past week, Patrick realized that no such yearnings had made themselves known since that awful night.

"Darling, you will always need to stay vigilant against that temptation, though with time, it will get easier," said Mother. "Closing your heart off is not the solution. Marriage can be a strain, but a good one will make you stronger. That is what you will have with Eloise."

Patrick opened his mouth to respond, but his mother would not let him speak.

"You can be far too serious and gloomy at times, sweetheart," said his mother. "Like your dear brother, Eloise has such passion and enthusiasm that she lightens your dour tendencies. Even with these difficulties, you have smiled and laughed more in the last few weeks than you have in years."

Yet again, Patrick attempted to speak, but Mother was in no mood for conversation, for she continued on. "You need her spirit, and she needs someone to balance her flightiness. You need each other."

And with a pat of his cheek, she moved away, leaving Patrick far more confused than calmed.

...

Eloise clenched her hands and bit her lips to keep her giddy energy at bay. Turning her gaze from the group surrounding Kitty, she looked out at the ballroom, searching for anyone else to assist. Each kindness added to the lightness in her heart, pushing her to seek out more to do. She remembered this feeling and wondered at how she had allowed it to slip away from her of late.

"Miss Andrews."

Her breath caught at his voice, her spine straightening. A rapid fluttering took over her stomach and heart, filling her with a mixture of apprehension and anticipation. Taking a breath to calm her overwrought nerves, Eloise turned to face Patrick.

She preferred his everyday attire, but Patrick's finery

looked splendid. His tailcoat was a blue so deep that it neared black, the darkness offsetting his light hair while the hue enhanced the color of his eyes. Her gaze traveled to his hair and the sadly shorn locks. How she missed his curls.

His eyebrows rose, and Eloise flushed as she realized how long she'd been staring at him.

"Mr. Lennox, I did not know if you would be here tonight." Eloise paused, holding his gaze though she knew it exposed the longings of her heart. "When I did not see you, I feared you'd already left for Ireland."

There was a wisp of hair that curled at her temple, and Patrick's fingers itched to touch it. He had tugged that unruly little lock more times than he could remember, and seeing it resurrected so many memories of their childhood.

"I had planned to go, but my family would never forgive me," said Patrick. "I fear I am stuck in London until after the wedding."

Her eyes widened with such hope that Patrick's heart warmed in response.

"I am very glad to hear that." Giving a quick glance at the others, Eloise took a step closer and lowered her voice. "Patrick, I need to tell you how sorry I am—"

But her words were cut short when another young lady grabbed Eloise by the arm.

"My goodness, what a perfect evening!" the girl gushed. "Is it not divine? I am positively enthralled with the decorations, and the food is heavenly."

Patrick held in the frustrated sigh that threatened to erupt at the interruption. Eloise's smile stiffened, though she gave no other outward sign as she returned the lady's comments with gusto.

"Miss Andrews," said Patrick, "Might I speak with you—"

The young lady's eyes widened as they darted between the pair. "Did I interrupt something important?"

Patrick nearly growled in response, but Eloise patted the girl's arm and gave a polite refusal, though her tone hinted that she was as unhappy as he with this development.

"I was just about to ask Mrs. Lennox to dance—" The words were out of his mouth before Patrick had time to think them through, and both sets of eyes watching him grew wider, though it took him another few seconds before he realized why.

"Miss Andrews, I mean," said Patrick, his pale cheeks burning. His cravat felt ridiculously tight as he struggled to keep his face from bursting into flames.

With a few hurried words, Eloise accepted and took his arm, practically dragging him away from that embarrassing scene. Taking their places on the dance floor, Patrick had only a moment to realize that dancing was a wretched idea before they were swept into the fray. He was not familiar enough with each dance to know the name of this particular jig, but he despised its creator and the flurry of steps and turns that required all his concentration.

Patrick cursed his impetuousness. He should have learned his lesson and avoided confronting Eloise in a public place, but the deed was done, and he was forced to pay the price. Yet another disaster of his own making.

A reel was a joyful dance, and *Miss Maxwell's Reel* was a particular favorite of hers, but Eloise cursed the horrid thing. They had been on the cusp of an important discussion, and now, they were caught up in this ridiculous set. The steps pulled them apart and brought them together with infuriating regularity, as though the dance itself was mocking them, taunting them with the nearness before sending them away once more.

Unable to contain her words any further, Eloise blurted as he passed, "I am so very sorry for what I said and did."

Patrick's gaze jerked from his feet to her, but he was swept away in another turn as he and the lady opposite crossed to the other's place. Before she could say another word, the dance forced her to do the same, and she let out a frustrated sigh.

They were finally offered a moment's respite, and Eloise seized the moment.

"I know I've been selfish," she said, though her words were interrupted as a couple danced down the row, passing between her and him. Patrick stretched to look around the couple, his mouth opening to respond, but the dance continued on, sweeping them into another round.

And so the minutes passed as Eloise fought to get out a word while silently pleading with her eyes for him to listen.

A string of words that were best left unthought streamed through Patrick's mind as he railed against dancing, music, and everything else that stood between him and Eloise. Those feelings only grew worse the more flustered Eloise became. There were too many listening ears and too many interruptions. They needed a bit of privacy.

In addition to all those infuriating things, Patrick was stumbling and tripping over every ridiculous step. His thoughts were too occupied for him to familiarize himself with the dancers' movements, so he was left to flounder through each agonizing minute.

As she took his hand to move between the dancers, Eloise gazed up at him, her eyes bright with unshed tears. "Please, I cannot lose you again."

The desperation and pain laced in those words resonated through Patrick, his heart telling him that the same was true for him. But before he could echo her words, they were separated once more, leaving Patrick to watch from afar as the heartbreak shone in Eloise's eyes. Each anguished look she sent him pricked him, and only rational thought allowed him to remain in place instead of sweeping her right into his arms.

The last note of the music was hardly finished before Patrick seized Eloise's elbow and pulled her away from the crowds before anyone else could interfere. Slipping through the dining room, he led her into the hall. There were only a few scant candles lit in that portion of the house to discourage guests from wandering, but it suited his purposes.

Eloise glanced at Patrick, and when she tried to speak, he shook his head as he led her down the darkened hallway towards a partially hidden alcove.

"Patrick," she said, a tremble in her voice, but her words died in her throat when they stepped in to discover another couple locked in a passionate embrace.

"Mother?" Eloise squeaked, and the pair broke apart, though her father did not release his hold on his wife. Mother looked quite thoroughly rumpled, and her eyes were wide. She pressed a hand to her lips, her cheeks blazing crimson, but beneath the embarrassment there was a joyful twinkle in her mother's eyes that Eloise had never seen before.

Time ceased and the world froze around her as Eloise stared at them.

"Pardon us," said Patrick, pulling Eloise back into the hallway as her thoughts tried to comprehend what she'd just witnessed. Luckily, Patrick was leading her along, for she could hardly put one foot in front of the other as the shock faded and a twitter of delight coursed through her: her parents were on the mend.

Caught up in that happy realization, Eloise didn't notice that they had stepped into a room until the library door shut behind them. Her heartbeat slowed, thumping in her chest as though there were molasses in her veins. Prickles ran along her spine, spreading through her limbs, and she cast a glance over her shoulder at Patrick.

"I would think you'd avoid being alone with me in a library again," said Eloise. The jest was weak and her voice trembled, but those pathetic words were all that came to mind.

Patrick turned a key in the lock before facing her. "Perhaps we might have a bit of peace to speak as we ought to. It is long overdue."

Clenching her hands, Eloise fought to keep the tremors under control.

"I owe you so many apologies that I do not know where to begin." Her voice caught, and the trembling increased. Eloise knew what needed to be said, but the importance of this moment pressed down on her, setting her thoughts and emotions into an uproar.

"I have been cruel to you, Patrick. I was so hurt by everything that happened. In one fell swoop, I lost two of the people I love most in this world. One from an accident and one from his own choice. And then you simply reappeared one day..." Eloise shook her head, pressing a hand to her stomach. "That is not important. You were grieving your brother, and no matter what precipitated the past few weeks, there is no excuse for how I behaved."

Struggling against the tears threatening to burst forth, Eloise continued, "I am trying to do better. To *be* better. Is there any hope that you can forgive me? Please tell me I have not ruined it all."

Patrick's heart twisted at her confession, but he stood there, allowing her to say what she must until he could not stand it any longer. Coming to her, he scooped her into his arms, bringing his lips to hers. Eloise gave a startled squeak before wrapping her arms around his neck. There were so many words he wanted and needed to say, but Patrick hoped his touch conveyed the depth of his feelings.

The urgency faded, and Patrick reveled in the feel of her in his arms and her tender touch as she met each loving kiss, giving back her heart with equal measure. Relief and hope coursed through him, filling him and expanding his heart until it filled his entire chest.

The kiss ended, but Patrick could not move away, and he rested his forehead against hers.

"But do you truly wish to tie yourself to me?" He did not want to say the words and give her any reason to reject him, but Patrick knew they must be spoken. "I have overcome my past, but that does not mean that I am completely free of it. I am trying, but it is a continual fight, Eloise. What if I should fall again?"

The fear and pain in his words sent a shiver through her heart and brought a fresh sheen of tears to her eyes. How she wished she had the power to protect him from such things.

"Then I shall help you pick yourself back up again." Bringing a hand to his cheek, Eloise brushed a thumb along his scars, gazing into his eyes. "Together we can both be better, Patrick. I trust in that."

Closing his eyes, Patrick leaned into her, burying his head in her neck as his arms squeezed her tight against him. "I love you."

Eloise ran her finger through the hair at the back of his neck before nudging his head up to meet her eyes. Her lips were so close that they brushed his as she said, "And I love you, my dearest friend."

And with that, Eloise pressed her lips to his to seal that pledge with all the love she could bestow.

Epilogue

Holbrook, Norfolk
One Year Later

Clutching the letter in her hand, Emmeline leaned back to stare up at the afternoon sun. Insects buzzed through the air and the birds twittered their happy tunes while the gentle breezes made the foliage shiver with delight. The heavenly scent of the flowers filled her nose, and the sun above warmed her skin. It was as perfect a day as she could ask for.

Emmeline shifted on the garden bench and broke open the seal, unfolding Eloise's latest missive. Her eyes soaked up the words as her daughter laid out all the intricate details of her life. More and more often, Emmeline found herself wondering if it were possible for a heart to burst from joy, for she felt ready to expire from it.

"I hear you received a letter from Eloise." Norman's voice announced his arrival just moments before he appeared on the garden path, but when he saw her, he hurried to her side. "What is the matter?"

She began to reply, but only the barest squeak emerged. Shaking her head, Emmeline waved away the concern growing in Norman's eyes.

"All is well," she finally managed. Tears blurred her vision, her lips trembling. "She is just so happy."

Norman gave a relieved chuckle and pulled Emmeline into his arms. Resting her cheek against his shoulder, she sniffled.

"Are you?" he asked, his hand running along her arm. "Happy, I mean."

Lifting her head enough to meet his eye, Emmeline felt liable to burst into tears again. "More than I could ever deserve, my love."

Norman smiled, and the lightness of it wiped away the growing signs of age until he looked precisely like the young gentleman she had met all those years ago.

"Good," he murmured. Lowering her head again, Emmeline snuggled closer.

"She's asked us to come for the birth." The emotions swelling in her chest made it difficult to speak, but Emmeline managed it.

"I told you she would," said Norman, pressing a kiss to her head. "Now you can stop fretting about it."

"I'm afraid I shall never stop fretting," she grumbled. No matter how she tried, Emmeline could not stop herself from such futile feelings.

Norman's chest rumbled with another chuckle. "I know, but I love you anyway."

"I love you, too," she said, lifting her head to meet his eyes as she said the words. Though she said them frequently enough, Emmeline needed him to see how much she meant them, for those three little words had changed her life in so many ways. They had given her the greatest joys and agonies. They were a healing balm and a promise. And they filled her heart and soul.

...

Carramore, Galway
Ireland
Four Days Later

Though she ought to be working on her letter, Eloise could not stop gazing out the window. No matter how many months she had sat in just such a position, she was still awed at the verdant beauty of the Irish countryside. Having positioned a table in front of the sitting room window, Eloise had an unobstructed view of rolling hillside and the dark green hedges that lined the bright grassland.

Turning her attention to the writing desk, Eloise ran her hands over the polished wood. They had received a number of gifts upon their marriage, but none of them filled her with as much pleasure as this. That was not to say that Eloise did not treasure the others, such as the heirloom jewelry set her mother-in-law had bestowed on her, but having her mother's writing box was like having a part of her there. Lifting the lid, Eloise shuffled the rapidly growing stack of letters her mother had sent her to retrieve a fresh sheet.

But before she had time to grab the ink and quill, lips brushed her cheek, and Eloise reached up to run her fingers through her husband's curly hair.

"You are hard at work," Patrick murmured.

"I received a letter from Mother," said Eloise, stretching her back and making her spine groan.

Patrick snatched a pillow from an obliging armchair and slid it behind the small of her back. With a few movements, he had her settled again, and he dropped a kiss on her forehead as his hand rested atop the swell that held their precious child. Laying her hand atop his, Eloise sighed in utter contentment.

"What news from home?" he asked as he stepped away to drop onto the armchair beside her.

"Noah is still struggling to decide his future. Last month, it was the army, and now, the law has caught his fancy," said Eloise, glancing over the lines. "And Baby Hudson is doing well, though Mother despairs that she is not able to see him as often as she would like; it sounds as though there is still much for her to repair with Angela and Kenneth, but she's hopeful that their moving home to Norfolk might help."

Lifting her quill, Eloise tapped the end against her cheek as she thought through her reply, but her mind drifted far from the missive when her husband leaned forward to place a whisper of a kiss on her free hand. His eyes lingered on her, and a flush of warmth spread from that lingering touch until she could stand it no longer and pressed her lips to his.

The letter could wait.

Exclusive Offer

Join the M.A. Nichols VIP Reader Club at

www.ma-nichols.com

to receive up-to-date information about upcoming books, freebies, and VIP content!

About the Author

Born and raised in Anchorage, M.A. Nichols is a lifelong Alaskan with a love of the outdoors. As a child she despised reading but through the love and persistence of her mother was taught the error of her ways and has had a deep, abiding relationship with it ever since.

She graduated with a bachelor's degree in landscape management from Brigham Young University and a master's in landscape architecture from Utah State University, neither of which has anything to do with why she became a writer, but is a fun little tidbit none-the-less. And no, she doesn't have any idea what type of plant you should put in that shady spot out by your deck. She's not that kind of landscape architect. Stop asking.

Website   Facebook   Instagram   BookBub

Printed in Great Britain
by Amazon